Amaranth

of the

Wild Things

Brieanna Robertson

Whimsical Publications, LLC

Florida

To purchase the authorized electronic edition of *Amaranth of the Wild Things*, visit www.whimsicalpublications.com

Cover art by Traci Markou
Editing by Janet Durbin

ISBN-13: 978-0-9787738-7-8

Published by
Whimsical Publications, LLC
Florida

With a sigh, Amara let the hot water relax her and she tried to banish the troublesome thoughts from her mind. Fretting about what could happen would do absolutely no good, and she knew firsthand that usually what a person thought was going to happen ended up being the complete opposite of everything one expected.

She soaked a little longer, then stepped out of the tub and dried off with a yawn. A cool summer night's breeze blew in from the window and touched her skin, raising goosebumps all along her arms. She shivered and frowned. It wasn't really cold. The evening was warm, in fact, but something in the breeze chilled her right to the bone. She pulled on her night dress and combed out her long blonde hair, plaiting it into a braid. An owl hooted outside, it's call low and mournful. For some reason, that made her shiver also.

She frowned, wondering where her jitters were coming from. She hadn't been scared of the dark since she'd been five, and she usually found the sounds of the night calming and peaceful. She shook her head. She was probably just on edge because of her worrisome thoughts. It would do her well to get a good night's rest.

Turning away from her vanity mirror, she moved toward her bed, but stopped with a gasp when she saw a shadow pass across her window. Her heart stuttered in her chest then thumped hard against her rib cage. She blinked and kept her eyes on the window for several seconds. No other movement came. She debated on her course of action and knew she should leave her room and go find a servant or a guard, but she was no cowering child. Besides, she didn't even know if she had actually seen anything at all. She was exhausted and there was a very good possibility that that, coupled with all the worrying she had been doing all day, had made her eyes play tricks on her.

Taking a quick glance around her room, she snatched up a heavy silver candlestick. It wasn't the best weapon, but it was better than nothing. Clutching it tightly in her hand, she approached her window, which lead out onto a balcony. Tentatively, she poked her head out and scanned the area.

Nothing...

She breathed a sigh of relief and stepped out onto the

balcony, letting her eyes gaze across the moonlit gardens of the castle.

Catlaan was a beautiful country, full of rolling hills and dense forest. Their kingdom was worth fighting for, and her father was a wonderful king. Benevolent and just, her father had ruled the lands with peace since before she had been born. She couldn't bear the thought of someone wanting to do him harm now.

She sighed, smiled sadly, and turned to go back inside, but instead of finding the open window granting her access into her chambers, she bumped into a solid object that caused her to gasp and stagger backwards.

She grasped the candlestick tight and raised it, ready to swing away, but her hand stopped in mid-air as her eyes fell upon the face of the stranger before her. He was very tall and dressed all in black, almost as if the night itself was cloaking him, and his face...it was wicked. Demonic almost in its darkness with green eyes that seared her...like jade fire. His black hair framed a face harshly and cruelly beautiful, and shivers broke out all over her body. Shivers of fear. The menace that radiated off of him was almost nauseating in its intensity, and her shock abated into horror. Something clicked back into place in her mind and she swung her arm at him in an attempt to hit him with her weapon.

He shackled her wrist easily with his own large, gloved hand and he squeezed until she was forced to drop the candlestick. It fell to the ground with an echoing thump. His burning eyes never left her face and her heart hammered in fear as his sculpted lips broke into a malevolent sneer. He stepped up close to her, trapping her with his presence alone, and she felt a scream boil up her throat. She opened her mouth to release it, but no sound emerged. He grasped the back of her head and pressed a cloth to her nose and mouth, restricting her air supply and replacing it with something noxious, something that made her stomach turn and her vision go blurry. She squeezed her eyes shut and was vaguely aware of the fact that she was fighting against him, not that it did any amount of good. The stranger was as solid and unmovable as an oak tree. Slowly, her consciousness slipped into dim confusion. Then...darkness...

Amaranth

Baptised with a perfect name
The doubting one by heart
Alone without himself

War between him and the day
Need someone to blame
In the end, little he can do alone

You believe but what you see
You receive but what you give

Caress the one, the Never-Fading
Rain in your heart - the tears of snow-white sorrow
Caress the one, the hiding amaranth
In a land of the daybreak

Apart from the wandering pack
In this brief flight of time we reach
For the ones, whoever dare

You believe but what you see
You receive but what you give

Caress the one, the Never-Fading
Rain in your heart - the tears of snow-white sorrow
Caress the one, the hiding amaranth
In a land of the daybreak

Reaching, searching for something untouched
Hearing voices of the Never-Fading calling

Caress the one, the Never-Fading
Rain in your heart - the tears of snow-white sorrow
Caress the one, the hiding amaranth
In a land of the daybreak

-Lyrics by Tuomas Holopainen of *Nightwish*
(Lyrics published with permission from the author,
Tuomas)

To one man—
The one with the music that stirs the depths of my
soul.

And to another—
The one whose inner self will always be the most beau-
tiful thing I've ever seen.

And to one more—
Who endured my endless brainstorming until I got it
right.

Also by
Brieanna Robertson

Serendipity Series

Stand Alone Books

Preface

Him and What He Allows To Be Seen
A Metaphor
Written by Shawn Skelton
Adapted by Brieanna Robertson

Inside he, there is a soft, velvet blackness. To find yourself there, you would think you were alone. So thick is the cushiony darkness, and so complete is the absence of color, one has no concept of time or space. There is neither up nor down, left nor right. The blackness is absolute.

The average traveler is lost there for all eternity, fully believing that this is all there is. This nothingness. A more perceptive person might discern that there is more than meets the eye, but never find out what. An extremely intelligent individual will know that there is something behind the veil, but they, even in their "great" wisdom, will not be able, without his permission, to penetrate the veil and get inside the trueness of his persona.

To better describe the layers past the black of the veil, I will start back to the beginning of my own journey...

I float in a sea of flowing blackness which is all at once mesmerizing and terrifying. Time passes. I cannot tell how long, for time has no meaning here. I feel alone and hollow. There is nothing, and yet, straining my senses, I can almost detect that something exists...

Time passes. I still find myself in the dark nebulae of swirling nothing, but as I look around, I can perceive the faint light of emotion. His emotion. I am not alone, after all.

This realization gives me no joy, however. For though I can see the streak of fiery temper, the cloudy, yellow stain of fear, the lightning flashes of pain, and the deep blue rain of despair, I still know next to nothing.

Time passes. More colors appear. The pattern and shades of the existing change as they mature. I start to see such things as the sticky, sick green of jealousy, the sky-blue maze lines of wonder and appreciation, the silvery gleam of justice, the stark gray blocks of shame and self-loathing, and the deep green crystals of a resoluteness to push past the experiences of a former time.

Time passes. The lightning flashes of physical pain are all but ignored while the destructive typhoons of emotional and mental pain seem to dominate the landscape. The orange glow of anger melts and forms a seething stream of molten, white-hot rage.

Time passes. A chrysalis forms within, and from it a cloud issues forth. It is everything and nothing, a sea of whirling black and purple plasma. There are occasional flares of intense emotion, but the overall shape and mass of his dark psyche is ever-changing. One more thing floats tentatively out of the fading, withered husk of the chrysalis. A small, nigh-impenetrable iron sphere. It swims through the nebulae of his psyche, seeking refuge in the darkness of the cloud. It does not open even though it can.

Time passes. The cloud grows heavy and it is difficult for him to support alone. The nebulae is a dark and dangerous place. It is lonely. He is lonely. He is dying of loneliness, feeling that he is lost completely within the confines of his own psyche.

Time passes. There is someone new, different than all the others. A she. A she who cares. She walks boldly the paths of the nebulae and almost seems as if she is ready and willing to support the entire cloud with her own two hands, though not without great cost to herself. She strides through the cloud, and wherever she sees the flashes of emotional and mental pain rend the fabric of his psyche, she heals the wounds with loving hands.

Time passes. As she finds her way deeper into the cloud, she comes upon a spot where there is an iron sphere seemingly exhausted and out of energy. Filled with sympathy and moved to action, she kneels down and lays her hands upon the sphere. A glow surrounds them both, there at the center of his all. The iron sphere seems to awaken as if from a deep sleep. It floats up and yawns slightly. Radiance spills forth from the slight aperture. Barely perceptible from her vantage point, she catches a glimpse of what is inside. Surrounded by a plush, crimson interior, is a delicate glass rose of such detailed, complex, and sorrowfully beautiful design it would make the heart bleed.

Time passes...

Prologue

They were red. Red like the angry wounds on his body. Red. The color of blood. The color of his bleeding heart as it was stripped of its last vestige of emotion.

He lay down in the field of flowers and curled on his side, bringing his knees to his chest and gasping for air against the pain that racked his body and his mind. Tears leaked out from between his eyelids. He couldn't stop them, couldn't help it. Thank goodness no one was there to see his weakness.

Slowly, the pain abated and went from stabbing agony to a throbbing ache. He trembled. He tried to remember his life before he'd come to live at the barracks. Something, anything that would help him hold onto his last shred of humanity. It was all that he had. All that mattered.

Nothing came to him. There was nothing to remember. Nothing that would help anyway. He had never had a mother hold him and whisper words of comfort when he was afraid. He had never had a father show him how to hunt and tell him he was proud of his son. He'd never had a gentle touch or a warm embrace. His whole life had been nothing but blackness. Why was he so adamant on holding onto the things that caused him to feel? He didn't even know, couldn't wager a guess. The only things he'd ever felt in his life were pain and abandonment. At one time, he had believed in hope, he supposed. Thought if he held onto that, one day things would be better, brighter...

What a fool he was. The others were right. This was what he was meant to be. He had been deluding himself to think otherwise all these years.

He was more than a fool to have held out so long against the commander. If he'd given in sooner, done what he was told, he wouldn't be suffering thus. He had no idea why he'd been so hard to train. Men with pasts much prettier than his had taken instantly to the training. Yet, he had wanted to hold onto his dismal, bleak existence. What for? To what gain? What did it matter if his emotions were stripped from him? He had no one who valued his heart. It had no place here. Why did he want to grip so solidly onto something that only brought him misery?

He didn't. Not anymore.

Hope did not exist. Not in his world. Not for him. Beauty was a myth. His fate was darkness.

He was so very tired...

Slowly, he opened his eyes as his breathing steadied and he calmed. The turmoil within his mind and heart fell away, abating slowly like the waves of the sea going out at low tide as he accepted what he had, up until now, fought against so viciously. He let his gaze focus on one of the undying, perfect flowers around him, and he reached his fingers out to tenderly caress the petals.

The only thing he had ever found comfort in. The only thing that ever brought him peace. Something supposedly legendary, mythical...and they grew outside the gates of the worst imaginable place ever created.

The amaranth. So delicate, so beautiful...

So unlike the taint that existed within him.

He was so unworthy of their radiance.

Like a slow poison running a course through his body, he felt his heartbeat balance, then grow mechanical, beating out of necessity. Not out of desire. Cold venom took over until the hurting stopped, the ache stopped, the confusion stopped. Everything stopped.

All he felt was numbness. Darkness.

And untold wonder as he gazed upon the flowers that still sought to give him comfort when he no longer needed any...

Chapter One

-Twelve years later

He despised this city. It sickened him. Riches and wealth elaborately and flamboyantly displayed every direction one looked. A golden plating to cover over the most corrupt of societies. Decadence and debauchery were accessible and available at every turn, and while a place tarnished by greed and excess generated Jaide quite a bit of work, he found the overall aura of it completely repulsive.

He stopped at one of the more popular taverns and looked up at the sign that swung gently out front. The Devil's Lair. He snorted. This tavern prized itself for having the strongest drinks and the best-looking women. Jaide took a glance at several of the bar wenches who were doing their best to entice patrons inside. They seemed to be arguing amongst themselves, all casting furtive glances back at him. One with black hair and dark eyes was finally pushed forward by one of her companions, and after shooting a scathing look back at her, the woman sauntered over to him.

"Well, good evening, handsome stranger," she purred, wrapping one arm around his shoulders. "In the mood for a bit of fun tonight?"

He slid his gaze over the woman's features. She was comely, but nothing special. None of them were. He pushed her arm off of him. "I highly doubt you would be game for my idea of fun," he muttered. "Go find yourself some other pleasure monger and leave me be. I have no need or desire for your rehearsed smile." He stepped away from her and pushed the door open to the tavern, letting his eyes scan the room until he found the purpose of his visit. He had business to attend to. He wouldn't set foot inside the establishment otherwise. He wasn't fond of crowded places.

With a sigh, Jaide made his way to the back of the tavern where a richly-dressed nobleman sat at the bar. He had his hand halfway down the front of a bar maid's dress and she was giggling like a ridiculous, blushing virgin. Jaide reached out and grasped the woman by the arm, hauling her none too gently off of the man's lap and all but shoving her aside.

She squealed in protest and shot an irritated glower at Jaide.

He barely even glanced her direction. "I have business with this man that outranks yours," he stated. "Come back later." The woman flounced off, and Jaide turned toward his client, leaning nonchalantly against the bar.

His client gave him a petulant scowl. "I'll have you know that she is, by far, the best wench in this entire tavern," he groused. "Men fight for her attention. It has taken me all evening to get her to come to me."

"Flash some more gold at her," Jaide said dryly. "I'm sure that will prove to be better incentive than your ever-engaging wit and charm." He raked his eyes over his client. Raglan Marden, the lord of the province. Rich, arrogant, much too young to hold the power he wielded. The man was an idiot... But he paid well, which was the only reason Jaide continued to have any dealings with him whatsoever. He was more corrupt than everyone else combined. He held the entire city of Dother in the palm of his hand, and his triple alliance with the three lords of the surrounding territories made him, quite possibly, the most powerful man in the entire country. He was no warrior by any means, but he was a conqueror in his own right. Raglan was of the mindset that anyone could be "persuaded" to align themselves with his way of thinking if the gold was enough. He claimed everyone had a price. For the most part, he was right.

"Sit down, Sideth. Have a drink," Raglan offered, indicating the stool next to him. He frowned and brushed a lock of his light brown hair off of his forehead. "Sideth... What kind of a name is that anyway?"

"One you don't want associated with yourself if you're not on the paying end of my blade. What do you want, Marden? I didn't come here to socialize with you," Jaide spat.

Raglan smirked and threw back his drink. "No, of course not. You never do. All right, we'll cut to the chase then."

"Please do."

Raglan turned his blue eyes up to Jaide and a malicious smile twisted his lips. It was a smile Jaide recognized. It meant gold was headed his way...and lots of it.

"As you well know, I am a very motivated man," Raglan began.

Jaide arched an eyebrow. "If that's what you want to call it."

He held up his finger and grinned. "Motivated and ambitious."

"Whatever helps you sleep better at night."

Raglan ignored Jaide's snide sarcasm. "I am of a mind to one day hold all of these territories in my power and become supreme ruler of them all."

Jaide heaved a sigh. "Well, there goes the neighborhood."

Raglan rolled his eyes. "Is everything a joke to you?"

"I wasn't aware that I was laughing. Now, could we please skip the part where I have to contend with your over-inflated ego and get to the job you're about to offer me? I am not someone who prefers to dither about in taverns." Truth be told, he didn't prefer to be any place where there were large amounts of people. He didn't like the noise, didn't like being closed in. It made him feel like he was suffocating. He just wanted to contract his job and return to the solitude of the outdoors.

"I do not have many enemies left."

Jaide frowned. "I didn't think you had any. Haven't I dispatched all of them for you?"

"All but one," Raglan said, leaning forward in his chair as if he had a secret. "There is still one, and he is proving to be the most difficult of them all."

Jaide motioned for him to continue.

"As you know, my power and control reaches all the way from Dother to the northern boundary of the province of Warset. Beyond that boundary is the sea, and beyond that is the country of Catlaan. Catlaan is not divided between lords as Warset is. It is ruled by a king. I have long had it in mind to take my army and seize Catlaan as my own, extend my power beyond the seas."

Jaide nodded. "Yes, and if I'm not mistaken, you led a campaign to conquer it last month and the king's forces wiped out your entire army."

Raglan's face grew dark and his eyes narrowed. "Yes," he snarled. "And that bastard king murdered my only brother."

Jaide remained silent. He knew of the incident between Raglan and the King of Catlaan. It had been the one time Raglan's unbridled arrogance had cost him more than a healthy sum of money. His brother, and commander of his army, had been killed in battle. It had been Raglan's first attempt at a real conquest. And he had failed miserably.

"I want him to pay," Raglan stated, venom dripping from his words.

Jaide gave a curt nod. "So you want me to get rid of the King of Catlaan. Is that what you're saying? That is going to cost you a very healthy fee."

Raglan shook his head. "No, I don't want to kill him."

Jaide frowned.

"He took what was most important to me, my only living family. I want to take what's most important to him, his daughter, Amara."

His frown deepened. "You want me to kill the princess?"

If it was possible, Raglan's smile grew even more malicious. "No, I want you to abduct her and bring her back to me. I want to keep her as prisoner until her father comes to rescue her. I will negotiate his daughter's safe return for his lands. Then, when he signs them over to me, I will kill her right in front of him. A life for a life, and a kingship for me." He sat back in his chair with a satisfied smirk.

Jaide scowled. "What do you take me for?" he spat. "I'm an assassin, not a kidnapper. I have no intention of trekking well over seven hundred miles across land and sea to abduct a woman and then play babysitter for another seven hundred. Find yourself another lackey." He pushed himself away from the bar and started to leave when Raglan plopped the largest bag of gold Jaide had ever seen down onto the bar in front of him. Needless to say, it halted his retreat.

He arched an eyebrow and met Raglan's eyes. In his line of work, gold was the only incentive that had any merit.

"I know what you are, Sideth, and I know what you do. No need to remind me," Raglan said, "but there are very few people in this world I can trust, and you have never once let me down. I know this is out of your usual realm of expertise, but let's face it, you're the best at what you do, and I never settle for less than the best. This job is important to me and I'm not going to hand it off to some amateur who will just botch it. I need to know it will be done right." He pushed the bag of gold toward Jaide. "Consider this a down payment."

Jaide took a long look at the bag of gold, then glanced back at Raglan as he considered his options. He didn't really have any. As much as he disliked the man, Raglan was his best client, and the opportunity to do a job that paid this well didn't come along too often. Besides, how difficult could kidnapping one spoiled princess be?

Jaide relaxed his posture and leaned against the bar again. "Let's talk specifics, Marden," he said. "When exactly do you need this to take place?"

* * * *

"Run, Jarinda! You have to run and hide from the dragon!"

The little girl squealed with laughter and took off as Amara headed toward her and the others. All of them shrieked and squealed as they ran. "He's coming!" Amara called, joining the children in their sprint across the courtyard. "Hurry! We must get to safety!" All of the children played along with her scenario until they had fled to the stables and all collapsed into the haystacks, out of breath and laughing.

"Did we escape?" one little girl puffed.

Amara looked over at her and grinned. "I think we made it just in time."

"Amara!" an exasperated voice shouted. "Are you in there?"

Amara winced and wrinkled her nose as she glanced back over at the little girl. "Maybe I was mistaken."

The little girl rolled with laughter.

A tall, hawkish woman tramped through the stables until she came to stand in front of Amara and the children. Her eyes widened and she put her hands on her hips. "Of all the—" She huffed and shook her head. "Amara, this is no place for a princess to be and is no way for a princess to behave! Rolling around in the hay like some vagabond with the kitchen staff!"

Amara rolled her eyes and sat up, picking straw out of her platinum hair. "I am not with the kitchen staff," she corrected. "I am with the children of the kitchen staff."

The woman huffed again. "You should be concentrating on your studies!"

"I am concentrating on my studies," she stated as she stood up and brushed off her gown. "I'm studying children's laughter and the effect of fresh air and exercise. It's much better than the studies in abject boredom that you subject me to." Why her father insisted on her having this terrible tutor was beyond her. She would have much preferred to study on her own, or have him talk with her and teach her like he used to. Things had changed so much in such a short time.

"Mathematics and history are important subjects for a young lady such as yourself," her tutor continued. "You are a very bright girl when it comes to academics, but I'm afraid that when it comes to manners and propriety, you are a very poor student!"

Amara motioned the children to stand up and she turned to them. "You all run along now," she instructed. "We can play again some other time."

"Sorry we didn't save you from the mean old dragon," one boy muttered, shooting a scowl up at her tutor.

Amara grinned and tousled the boy's hair as the children filed out of the stables.

Her tutor folded her arms across her chest and narrowed her beady eyes. "A dragon now, am I?"

Amara sighed and began to walk out of the stables as well. "Madam Gartner, we were playing pretend."

"Playing pretend," she scoffed as she followed. "Next I'm going to find you wearing scarves and bells and dancing around a fire like those nomad thieves who roam the countryside."

Amara rolled her eyes. "Playing a game with a group of children hardly qualifies me as a nomad, Madam Gartner, and I apologize, but I simply cannot stay indoors and pour over books all hours of the day. It is dull at best and exhausting at worst."

"The things that make us wiser are not always the things that are the most enjoyable, and a lady of your breeding has no place—"

She whirled as they came to stand just inside the castle. "Has no place where, Madam Gartner? On her own land? And the last time I checked, I was not a horse. I am a human woman with a mind of her own who can run across the court-yard and roll around in the hay if I want to. Now, please, I want to speak with my father."

Madam Gartner scowled. "Your father has more im-portant things to—"

Amara's eyes widened. "More important than his own daughter?"

"The king is in the middle of a very grave situation with that lord from across the sea and—"

"I am very aware of what my father has going on, Mad-am Gartner, and I will thank you not to act as his mouth-piece. You are my tutor, not the royal advisor. Now I will re-turn to my studies after I have seen my father. Good day, Madam Gartner. You are dismissed."

If her scowl got any fiercer, Amara was afraid her face might crack in half. "Now, you listen here, you impertinent—"

"Are you reprimanding my daughter, Madam Gartner?" a stern, booming voice came from down the corridor.

Amara grinned and looked up as her father strode into view.

Madam Gartner paled and swallowed. "No, your high-ness, but she is being difficult and is in need of discipline."

He slipped his arm around Amara's shoulders and pulled her up against his side. "I do not believe that is the job I pay you for, madam. When and if my daughter needs disciplin-ing, I will be the one to see to that. Now, you may go."

Amara knew Madam Gartner was far from finished, but she didn't have the gall to backtalk her father, so she settled with shooting a sinister glower at Amara and skulked off.

Her father chuckled and looked down at her. "What are you doing to that poor woman this time?"

Amara grinned. "I didn't do anything to her, Father. I just couldn't stand being cooped up in the castle any longer. I felt as if I would suffocate. I was playing with the children in the courtyard."

He framed her face with his hands and his hazel eyes reflected love and light. "Just like your mother," he murmured. "Wild and free, untamable."

She smiled and her heart filled with warmth, but it also twinged with sadness at the fact that she and her father no longer spent time together as they once had. "I know you mean well by wanting me to have a tutor," she said softly, "but I miss the way things used to be. I miss when you and I would go riding and hunting, or when you would read to me at night by the fire. I learned more from you by living life than I ever will by reading mindlessly all day in my chambers."

Her father smiled and smoothed her hair. "Ah, my daughter. I have done you a disservice by allowing you to run free all your life."

She snorted. "I would rather run free than be anywhere near that Gartner woman any day."

He chuckled. "I know you miss our time together, Amara. I feel the same, but there are grave matters that I must attend to."

She frowned and waved her hand. "I know that, Father. I hold nothing against you. I just miss you." He pulled her into an embrace and she sighed. "Are there any new developments with Lord Marden?"

He shook his head. "My scouts have not seen or heard anything. He is lying low right now."

"Maybe he will just leave us alone." Even as she said it, she knew that was a ridiculous thought, but she couldn't help but wish. Her whole life had turned upside down after Lord Marden had attacked Catlaan.

"A viper will always strike," her father said. "You just don't always know when. He'll make a move, rest assured. I killed his brother. He will retaliate."

A chill went through Amara and she wrapped her arms around herself. "I never thought war would touch my simple life," she murmured. "How naïve I have been."

He stroked her hair and bent to press a kiss to her forehead. "We were lucky to have such peace in our lands while you were young," he said. "It enabled me to raise you myself and not entrust your care to a maidservant."

"Yes, but it has made me spoiled and selfish because I want you all to myself." She gave him a playful pout, wanting to bring a smile to his lips.

He grinned. "The feeling is more than mutual, Amara, trust me." He gazed at her for a long moment then sighed. "You have grown into such a strong and vibrant young woman. Your mother would be so proud. I see her in you every second of the day."

Amara smiled, warm contentment washing over her at his words. Saying she was like her mother was the highest form of compliment he could give. He had loved her mother tremendously.

He shook his head and patted her on the shoulder. "Go on now," he said. "Continue torturing your tutor. Tonight, perhaps, we can read by the fire like we used to."

He winked at her and she grinned. She nodded and continued down the corridor. She thought about going to her chambers, but changed her mind. She wanted to be outdoors, enjoying the sunlight and fresh air. Plus, she knew that if she had to endure any more of Madam Gartner, she would lose her mind.

Turning back, she returned to the courtyard and went past the stables to the army barracks. She made her way to the armory and selected a bow and a quiver of arrows. Practicing her archery always made her feel better. She was sure today would be no different. Plus, it would help her burn off some of the frustration she felt at the impending war, her tutor, and all of the other variables in her life that she no longer had control over.

The winds of change were upon her. She could feel them blowing ever so gently, preparing her for things unknown approaching. She didn't want change, but it would come with or without her permission. She only hoped that, when it did, she could accept it and deal with it gracefully and with dignity, the way her proud and noble father had always taught her.

Chapter Two

It was dusk when Jaide finally returned to the forest to plan his strategy. He had been observing his target for the better part of the day, getting a feel for her whereabouts and how difficult she might be. Seemed easy enough, truth be told. Just a young girl, probably petrified of anything that went bump in the night. He had watched her running around in the fields with some children. Typical. No doubt she had any number of noblemen lined up for her hand, some rich idiot who would give her lots of rich, spoiled children.

He sat down against a tree and took inventory of his weapons for what was probably the tenth time. He didn't imagine she would need much brute force. She was slender, and he could overpower men three times his size. He didn't see why a weapon would be needed. The element of surprise would be best. Catch her off guard and knock her unconscious. It was the most efficient way, and less troublesome for him. If he didn't knock her out, she would scream and cause a fuss and alert the entire kingdom, and probably all the neighboring peasants. He had, after all, never met a woman who didn't possess the shrillest, most aggravating screaming banshee set of pipes. It was only one of the many reasons he avoided women more than he avoided all other people.

After making sure all of his weapons were accounted for and in their proper places, he leaned his head back against the tree trunk and closed his eyes. He took a deep breath, inhaling long and exhaling in the same manner. His heart rate slowed as he relaxed, and any muddled chaos that may have been in his mind fell away. He focused on the task at hand, the job that needed to be done. He rehearsed it in his mind, remembering the way to what he had deemed to be her quarters and the best way to get in.

A rustling in the brush not far from him brought him out of his planning, and he opened his eyes to survey the area. He had a clear view of the edge of the forest and beyond through the trees, and he ducked down somewhat to assure that his presence was not detected should anyone be lurking.

It didn't take long for him to spot her.

The princess of Catlaan was slowly making her way along a small forest path. Her platinum hair was in tangles all around her shoulders, and she was wearing a leather vest and breeches similar to what soldiers in these parts would train in. He raised an eyebrow in question, wondering what in blazes she would be doing dressing in such a manner.

She hummed to herself as she wandered along, trailing her fingers across the tops of some of the ferns and plant life decorating the path, and she finally settled herself on a large boulder in a tiny clearing. She sighed and toyed with her hair, gathering the thick mass into her hands and holding it up off of her neck for a few moments.

Jaide tucked himself closer to the tree, melting in with his surroundings so as not to be seen or heard. This was lucky, her wandering his way. Hopefully, he would be able to detect a prominent weakness, other than her already glaring femininity, that he could use to his advantage.

A lesser assassin may have been startled by the rustle of brush and the snapping of twigs off to the left of him, but Jaide remained stoic as he waited for whatever beast approached, human or otherwise. He glanced at the princess to see if maybe she was expecting someone, a secret lover perhaps that would cause him trouble in completing his mission, but she seemed as surprised by the sudden presence as he was.

She watched the area where the rustling was heard with intrigued curiosity, and when a large, white wolf broke into the clearing, Jaide drew in a small breath. He quickly grasped for his bow and lined an arrow up, getting the wolf in his sights. If the animal decided to attack, he would have to take it down. While that wasn't his way, he couldn't have a creature interfering in his assignment. Marden had already paid him a significant amount of gold...whatever good that would do him. Not like he had a home to call his own. The wilds were his home, and the only thing all the gold he received was doing was rotting away in his pack and making it heavier to carry.

Still, this was his assignment. This was what he did. This was who he was. He narrowed his eyes on the wolf as it stared the princess down.

The princess watched him for a moment, then did the strangest thing. She did not scream, did not run or cower as most women would. She smiled. Grinned, really. And she held out her hand.

"Well, hello there, sir. What are you doing out here all alone?"

The wolf put its head down, studying her for a moment, then crept closer.

"It's not right for a majestic creature such as you to be all by himself," she continued. "Don't you have a pack of your own?"

Jaide slowly lowered his bow as the wolf continued toward the woman's outstretched hand.

"A lone wolf, I see," she said. "By choice or by circumstance, I wonder."

Jaide's bow dropped even further and his brow furrowed as he watched the beautiful creature of the forest approach the woman with little fear. Its snout came in contact with her fingers, and she smiled as she let it get her smell, then easily drew her hand up along its head and ears.

"You are a beauty," she murmured. "Maybe just lost?" She framed its head with her hands and scratched along its ears. "There are many more wolves in my father's forest, mainly south of here. Go and find a place, lone wolf. You are not meant to be so isolated. Just stay clear of the deer, hm?" She smiled again, then sat back.

Jaide stared in wonderment as the damned wolf sat, lolled its tongue out at her for a moment, then turned to the south and trotted away like the thing had actually understood her. He watched it as it headed his direction, and when it smelled him, it stopped in its tracks, sniffing the air with its head low to the ground until it came upon where he was sitting.

As it spotted Jaide, it kept its head low, and they stared at one another for several heartbeats of silence before Jaide instinctively reached his arm out in much the same way the woman had done. The wolf jumped back and snarled instantly. The hair on the back if it raised and it bared its teeth, then it lunged forward and snapped at where Jaide's hand was.

Jaide recoiled quickly, missing the animal's jaws, and the wolf ran off into the heart of the forest. He stared after it for a while, feeling strange all of a sudden and not understanding why. He shook his head to regain his bearings, and scowled at the thought that an animal would cause him to lose his focus even for a second.

He turned his attention back to where the princess had been, hoping to glean more information about her, but the boulder and clearing where she had been were vacant, and as far as he could tell, she was gone.

* * * *

It had been a long day, but Amara was content as she entered her chambers. Her maidservant had drawn a bath and she dismissed her with a smile, eager to clean the sweat away from her earlier archery and sword fighting session. It had been pleasurable. There was nothing Amara enjoyed more as far as sport went than feeling the arrow fly free from her fingers as she pulled back the bowstring. She adored archery, had ever since she'd been small. Her father had taken her hunting and riding, had done activities that were usually only acceptable for boys to participate in. But seeing as how Amara was his only child and he had no sons to share the activities with, it had always been the two of them. She was grateful for it. She had many grand memories of the time spent with her father, and she loved the outdoors. Her father said he had ruined her for any potential suitor because no nobleman would want a wildling for a wife, but Amara didn't care. She would rather have the freedom to be herself than be shackled to a man. Although, she did have grand fantasies about what her wedding would one day be like when someone did decide she was not too much to live with.

After archery practice, Amara had decided to train a bit with her sword, something that would be frowned upon by most everyone she knew, but she did not care. She liked the feeling of the sword in her hand, slicing through the air. It felt like a graceful dance, not an act of violence. When she had expended her energy, she had taken a brief walk through the forest and then returned to her studies for several hours. She had eaten supper with her father, and the two of them had shared conversation by the fire in his study just as they had before Lord Marden had decided he wanted Catlaan for his own. It meant more to Amara than she could express. It was a touch of normalcy she had needed desperately, and it had enabled her to stop thinking about the pending war.

As she stripped off her clothing and stepped into the hot bath water, Amara let her mind return to the day of the attack. It had been terrifying. For as long as she had been alive, there had never been battles in her homeland. Her father was a good king. His people loved him, and he had very few enemies. The attack by Lord Marden had been unexpected and impulsive. Luckily, it had also been ill prepared and a move of arrogance more than strategy. Her father's army had obliterated Lord Marden's forces, but the young lord's brother had also been killed in battle, by her father's own hand. That event had changed everything. What could have been only a humiliating defeat became a quest for vengeance. Now she felt like they were all just standing by, biding their time until Marden made his move. It made everyone on edge, especially her. She worried for her father's safety, and for the people of Catlaan.

With a sigh, Amara let the hot water relax her and she tried to banish the troublesome thoughts from her mind. Fretting about what could happen would do absolutely no good, and she knew firsthand that usually what a person thought was going to happen ended up being the complete opposite of everything one expected.

She soaked a little longer, then stepped out of the tub and dried off with a yawn. A cool summer night's breeze blew in from the window and touched her skin, raising goosebumps all along her arms. She shivered and frowned. It wasn't really cold. The evening was warm, in fact, but something in the breeze chilled her right to the bone. She pulled on her night dress and combed out her long blonde hair, plaiting it into a braid. An owl hooted outside, it's call low and mournful. For some reason, that made her shiver also.

She frowned, wondering where her jitters were coming from. She hadn't been scared of the dark since she'd been five, and she usually found the sounds of the night calming and peaceful. She shook her head. She was probably just on edge because of her worrisome thoughts. It would do her well to get a good night's rest.

Turning away from her vanity mirror, she moved toward her bed, but stopped with a gasp when she saw a shadow pass across her window. Her heart stuttered in her chest then thumped hard against her rib cage. She blinked and kept her eyes on the window for several seconds. No other movement came. She debated on her course of action and knew she should leave her room and go find a servant or a guard, but she was no cowering child. Besides, she didn't even know if she had actually seen anything at all. She was exhausted and there was a very good possibility that that, coupled with all the worrying she had been doing all day, had made her eyes play tricks on her.

Taking a quick glance around her room, she snatched up a heavy silver candlestick. It wasn't the best weapon, but it was better than nothing. Clutching it tightly in her hand, she approached her window, which lead out onto a balcony. Tentatively, she poked her head out and scanned the area.

Nothing...

She breathed a sigh of relief and stepped out onto the balcony, letting her eyes gaze across the moonlit gardens of the castle.

Catlaan was a beautiful country, full of rolling hills and dense forest. Their kingdom was worth fighting for, and her father was a wonderful king. Benevolent and just, her father had ruled the lands with peace since before she had been born. She couldn't bear the thought of someone wanting to do him harm now.

She sighed, smiled sadly, and turned to go back inside, but instead of finding the open window granting her access into her chambers, she bumped into a solid object that caused her to gasp and stagger backwards.

She grasped the candlestick tight and raised it, ready to swing away, but her hand stopped in mid-air as her eyes fell upon the face of the stranger before her. He was very tall and dressed all in black, almost as if the night itself was cloaking him, and his face...it was wicked. Demonic almost in its darkness with green eyes that seared her...like jade fire.

His black hair framed a face harshly and cruelly beautiful, and shivers broke out all over her body. Shivers of fear. The menace that radiated off of him was almost nauseating in its intensity, and her shock abated into horror. Something clicked back into place in her mind and she swung her arm at him in an attempt to hit him with her weapon.

He shackled her wrist easily with his own large, gloved hand and he squeezed until she was forced to drop the candlestick. It fell to the ground with an echoing thump. His burning eyes never left her face and her heart hammered in fear as his sculpted lips broke into a malevolent sneer. He stepped up close to her, trapping her with his presence alone, and she felt a scream boil up her throat. She opened her mouth to release it, but no sound emerged. He grasped the back of her head and pressed a cloth to her nose and mouth, restricting her air supply and replacing it with something noxious, something that made her stomach turn and her vision go blurry. She squeezed her eyes shut and was vaguely aware of the fact that she was fighting against him, not that it did any amount of good. The stranger was as solid and unmovable as an oak tree. Slowly, her consciousness slipped into dim confusion. Then...darkness...

* * * *

The first thing Amara became aware of was her horrible, splitting headache. She grimaced against the pain then slowly forced her eyes open. The smell around her was damp and earthy, and it took her vision a moment to clear. Her mouth was dry and her mind was sluggish. She blinked several times, trying to bring her sight and her thoughts into focus. Wherever she was at was dark...

Dark...

Like the man on her balcony...

Suddenly, the events outside of her room came rushing back to her in vivid clarity and she sat up with a gasp, searching around her in all directions. She seemed to be lying in a cave, and her wrists and ankles were bound with thick rope. Her heart pounded as she scanned the area again. There was no sign of anyone. Immediately, she turned her attention to the ropes around her wrists, twisting and straining to try and loosen them. When she'd been small, her father had taught her how to get out of many different kinds of bonds just in case she ever found herself in a situation similar to the one she was currently in. She was a princess, and even though her family had been lucky for most of her life in that they had few enemies, her father had always taken the initiative to educate her on ways to survive if someone got it in their mind that she would be a good bargaining tool. His training would be more than useful now.

She continued to wiggle at the ropes for several minutes before she felt the hair on the back of her neck stand up. She froze and her heart started to beat double time. Someone was behind her. She could feel the presence as if it was a cold wind. Slowly, she turned her head to look over her shoulder, and gasped. It was him. He stood in the entry of the cave, holding an armload of firewood, staring down at her with an expression devoid of any emotion whatsoever.

"I wouldn't," he stated.

She glanced down at her wrists, then back up at him, chills working all along her spine at the deep timbre of his voice and the way his presence seemed to invade the entire cave and fill it with cold malice. She drew in a shaky breath and backed herself up against the wall of the cave, wanting to get as far away from his ominous aura as possible. "W-Who are you?" she stammered, her voice wavering. She swallowed and forced her fear away so she could at least sound brave. "Where am I? Where is my father?"

He continued on his way into the small space and put the load of wood down. "Your father, I imagine, is back at the castle," he drawled in a flat voice. "You're presently in a cave located in the mountains that border Catlaan, and as regards to who I am..." He met her gaze from across the room and she shuddered as hot shivers caused her to tremble. His eyes were pure fire, but they reflected a coldness that rivaled ice in the winter. They were beautiful and terrifying. "I am the man who is being paid to abduct you," he finished vaguely.

She frowned and retreated further. "Are you going to kill me?" she murmured.

He looked up from where he was beginning to assemble a fire pit. "I'm not, no."

She swallowed hard. "But someone else is?"

He nodded with an air of indifference, as if they were discussing the weather.

Her heart tumbled over in her chest and she felt tears burn her eyes, but she forced them away. Crying about her situation would do her absolutely no good. She couldn't let panic get its grip on her. She had to keep her wits. "Lord Marden," she assumed. "He is using me for his revenge."

The stranger glanced up at her again and regarded her for a torturous, silent moment. "Smart girl," he finally remarked.

She scowled. "He couldn't even do his own work? He had to hire someone to do it for him?"

He shrugged. "Lord Marden is not the type to want to dirty his hands with trivialities."

She snorted. "I would think that, if I am being used as a pawn in his war game, I would be slightly more than a triviality." He glanced up at her again, but said nothing. She sighed and brought her knees up to her chest, watching him as he stacked the wood and set to starting a fire. He did everything with a sense of purpose, as if even the simplest task of building a fire was strictly business. As he worked, she continued to discreetly twist her wrists, knowing that if she kept at it long enough, she would loosen her bindings and be able to escape when he wasn't looking.

Suddenly, her head started to swim and her stomach roiled like a turbulent sea, causing her to lean over and retch violently until her sides ached. When her stomach had finally calmed, she sat back against the wall of·the cave, laboring for breath and sweating. Her body shook uncontrollably.

"That's an after effect of the drug I gave you," her captor remarked absently, barely looking up from where he worked.

She winced as another wave of nausea passed over her. She took a brief look at her surroundings, trying to put together some kind of hasty plan of action if the opportunity to escape arose.

"We're traveling toward the country of Demrysk tomorrow," he stated, sitting down in front of the fire that now raged to life. "We have to marry before we cross the border. I know a man who will go about it quickly and with little difficulty."

She felt her face grow even paler than she knew it was

and her stomach revolted at his words. "Wh-What?" she stuttered. She shook her head. "I'm not going to marry you! Are you out of your mind? That can't have been part of the deal!"

He glanced up at her with a dismal expression. "Only citizens of Demrysk are allowed into the country without a visitor's pass. I do not have time to get a pass for you. I was born in Demrysk. If I marry you, you can enter the country without trouble."

Her heart beat out a painful and erratic rhythm. "But-But why are we even going to Demrysk? Is that where Lord Marden is waiting?"

He shook his head. "No, we must travel across the sea before we get to him. I am going to Demrysk to throw any search party your father might send off of our trail. He is no stupid man. He will assume this has something to do with Lord Marden. The quickest way to him is straight through the south of Catlaan and then across the sea. We are going north to Demrysk then cutting down through Lyanel. We can catch a ship there."

She felt the tears well up in her eyes again, and she wriggled her wrists with renewed vigor. She absolutely had to get out of there. She wouldn't marry a hired kidnapper with the disposition of a glacial wind just to gain citizenship into a country she didn't even want access to so she could evade her father's search party and better Lord Marden's chances of murdering her. It just wasn't going to happen.

She sought to continue the conversation, hoping that by doing so she could keep him distracted and free her hands. "But...why would you even do that? Bind yourself to a stranger?"

He shrugged. "It's not as if it is going to matter much after Lord Marden is finished with you. It's for legality only, and the expediency of our journey. The bloody thing is long enough as it is." He stood and grabbed a bow and a quiver of arrows, then strode toward the entrance. "Going hunting," he stated, then stopped and made a slow, predatory turn toward her.

Amara shrank back at his penetrating gaze and let out a small squeak when he reached down and yanked on the ropes binding her wrists, tightening them painfully.

"I thought I told you not to do that," he snarled.

She started to tremble against her will. She wanted to seem brave and strong, but the man was positively fearsome and he scared her to death. He radiated a power she'd never seen a person possess, even the strongest warriors of her father's Royal Guard. This man moved and acted as if he owned and commanded the entire universe. Danger clung to him like a second skin. It hadn't been as bad with him sitting all the way across the room, but having him in front of her was overwhelming and frightening.

"I would think carefully before you try and pull anything on me, princess," he hissed, kneeling down to burn his green eyes into hers. "I am not an amateur, and despite what I am presently doing, I am not a kidnapper by trade. This I am doing because the pay is good, but rest assured, if you were any other person I was being paid to handle, you and I would not be having this conversation right now. The only conversation you would be having would be with the worms in your grave."

She tried to retreat from his penetrating gaze and the menacing growl of his words, but it was impossible to move away any further. She trembled silently as he stared at her for several more agonizing seconds, as if challenging her to even breathe in a defiant manner.

When he finally must have decided she'd gotten the point, he stood in a slow, graceful movement and continued on his way out into the night. Amara immediately started to shake harder and the tears she'd been carefully trying to conceal boiled to the surface and spilled forth of their own free will. She pulled and tugged on the rope at her wrists, but he had tightened it to the point where she no longer had any room to maneuver. Her breath started to come in panicked gasps and she sobbed as she frantically tried to free her hands.

The rope bit harshly into her skin, and the pain of it brought her back to reality. She shook her head and forced some kind of control back into her body and mind. "Come on, Amara," she murmured to herself, closing her eyes. "You're no wilting flower. You're smart and strong. Stop panicking. Think." She took several calming breaths and pushed all terrifying thoughts of being forced to marry an assassin and then being murdered by her father's greatest enemy out of her mind.

She opened her eyes and scanned her surroundings while trying to position her fingers to untie the bonds around her ankles. That was also greatly impossible considering the way her hands were tied. One wrist was crossed over the other, probably to prevent her from doing exactly what she was attempting. Her eyes fell on a jagged rock jutting out from the far wall of the cave, and hope surged to life inside of her. She stood carefully and hopped over to it, then poised the rope across the sharp edge and started to saw. It wasn't long before the rope was severed and she immediately bent to untie her ankle bindings. With that accomplished, she threw a furtive glance over her shoulder to make sure her captor was not returning before she looked around for a weapon of some kind. She needed something to defend herself with. She wasn't stupid enough to go running off into the night without some sort of protection.

"Woman!"

Panic and fear consumed Amara at the baritone voice that suddenly echoed through the cave. She looked over to see her captor throw down his bow and arrows, as well as whatever animal he had killed. His scowl was black and he started to stride toward her with fury in every step. She looked down and picked up a rock. She hurled it at him with as much force as she could muster. He put his arm up to deflect it, and she grasped a burning log from the fire, swinging it at him like a sword as he approached. He narrowly evaded it and she continued to swing as she backed herself away from him and around toward the entrance of the cave.

He staggered backwards in retreat from her fiery weapon and adopted a predatory stance as he slowly circled toward her. The light from the fire highlighted the harsh lines of his face, and to say he looked menacing would be the worst kind of understatement. Her hand trembled, but she kept a hold on her weapon, glancing toward the mouth of the cave to try and gauge how far she would have to run to get to it. She and her captor were both about the same distance away, flanking opposite sides of the fire pit. He would easily be able to catch her if she tried to run now.

She looked back at him, her breathing ragged with fear.

Her body was weak from whatever drug he had knocked her unconscious with, and her legs wobbled threateningly as her stomach protested her vigorous movement. She ignored it. She could rest later, after she was away from this lunatic.

His eyes gleamed like a feral beast's in the firelight's glow, and he watched her movements carefully, stalking her as if she was prey. She swallowed hard and glanced back at the entrance again. Her eyes traveled lower until they landed on the dead rabbit and weaponry he had dropped upon his arrival. She drew in a sharp breath and her eyes widened. Throwing him another look, she flung the log down and bolted toward the entrance. He did the same with lightninglike speed. She reached for his quiver of arrows and managed to pull one free just as he caught up to her. She spun and drove the point of the arrow into his shoulder, causing him to roar with rage and pain. He took a step back, giving her just enough time to take off running.

She wasn't really certain of how much distance she covered. The terrain was treacherous and she had to follow a narrow mountain pass that weaved in and out of monolithic boulders. It was difficult to navigate in the darkness and she only had her thin bed slippers on. The rocks from the path bit into the soles of her feet, slowing her progress.

She heard him thundering after her, and she tried to run faster, but she couldn't. Her legs were weak as it was, and her body was sluggish. She shrieked when she felt him grab a hold of her from behind, and she drove her elbow back into his stomach. She heard his breath go out in a huff, but he didn't relinquish his hold. She screamed as he lifted her body and all but slammed her down onto the dirt path below. She coughed and gasped as the air was knocked out of her and the dust from their scuffle puffed up into her face. She tried to wiggle free, but his body pinned her to the ground with amazing strength.

"This was a very bad move on your part, princess," he snarled in her ear.

She cried out as he grabbed both of her arms and yanked them backwards, securing them behind her shoulder blades. Tears of anger, frustration, and fear leaked out of her eyes, and she screamed again as he hauled her roughly to her feet. She stumbled as he held her hands behind her back and pushed her back up the path to the cave.

Once they had returned, he pushed her down to the ground and firmly planted his knee on her back to prevent her from moving as he bound her wrists again, this time in the uncomfortable position between her shoulder blades. He also looped another rope from the binds on her wrists up to her neck, where he secured it around her throat, restricting almost any movement whatsoever. He shoved her aside and she landed hard on her shoulder, laboring for breath and coughing. She winced in pain and remained still, shaking violently.

"Try and escape now and you'll strangle yourself," he spat.

She squeezed her eyes shut, feeling the truth of that statement. If she moved her arms even the slightest bit, it caused the rope around her throat to tighten. Already her joints were aching from being tied in such an unnatural position.

"It didn't have to be this way," he said as he removed her shoes then secured a metal shackle around her ankle. "You chose to disobey me. Disobeying me has consequences. Stabbing me was not the best choice either."

She watched him as he took the chain that was attached to the shackle and slipped it through a metal stake of some kind, which he drove into the ground with the hilt of his sword.

"Now I'm going to have to do this every time we make camp, which is much more trouble than it is worth," he muttered.

He left her and she lay there on her side, watching him quietly as he removed his shirt to dress his wound. His body was muscled and honed in the way of a warrior, and he had many scars running along the expanse of his chest and torso. She studied the firm set of his jaw and the dark scowl that marred his otherwise handsome face. It remained the entire time he dressed his wound, and it remained while he skinned the rabbit and cooked it. It caused her to wonder if the man had ever smiled a day in his life. The lines of his face were stern and intense, as if his life had only ever been dark. She briefly wondered what it was that caused men like him to be the way they were.

He made some sort of stew out of the rabbit meat,

scooped some of it onto a banged up metal plate, and set it down in front of her. "Eat," he commanded.

She frowned. "Just exactly how do you propose I do that?" she muttered, her words fairly dripping with venom.

He turned toward her and sneered down at her. "You'll eat like a dog."

Her eyes narrowed. "And what if I don't? What if I starve myself?"

He squatted in front of her and grasped the rope behind her back, hauling her up into a sitting position and causing her to gasp as the loop tightened around her throat. He stared into her eyes with cold hatred, his face a hair's breadth away from hers. "You will eat, or I will force it down your throat." His voice was no more than a gravely growl, and it made her shiver.

He stood and retreated back to his side of the fire. Tears threatened again, burning her eyes, and a cold fist of grief clamped firmly around her heart. She leaned her head back against the unyielding stone of the cave and prayed that her father would come for her soon. Someone had to come for her. They had to.

They had to.

Chapter Three

Her arms and shoulders ached so badly she felt like they would snap right off, and her neck was rubbing raw from the rough rope that constantly grated against her skin. She had barely slept from pain and fright, and the food her captor had forced her to eat had been terrible, especially given the state of her stomach.

She had spent the entire day riding on the front of his horse as they traveled closer to Demrysk and farther away from her home. Being near him repulsed her and jostling around all day had made her joints hurt even worse. He hadn't spoken one word to her for the entire day. He remained in stoic, stone cold silence that he only broke when he spat a command at her.

They were still in the mountains at the end of the day; the mountain range between Catlaan and Demrysk was a long one. Her captor found them another suitable cave to make camp in at dusk and he pulled her down off of the horse then secured her shackle inside. This cave was smaller than the last and she cringed at the thought of having to be close to him in any fashion.

She shivered against the cool dampness of the cave and curled her legs close to her body. She'd only been in her nightclothes when he'd abducted her, and while the days were hot, the nights were cool and chilled her bare skin.

"I have to make a short trip to the mountain town of Delaney," her captor said suddenly as he secured his sword to his back. "I must speak with the man responsible for getting everything in order for our journey over the border. I will return in an hour, two at most." He shot her a piercing glower. "Don't try anything. I won't warn you again."

She swallowed, her mouth and throat dry. "Please..."

He stopped at the entry of the cave and frowned down at her. "What?"

"Can I please have a blanket or...something?" He hesitated for a moment and she pressed a little further, seeing a slight opening. "I have not given you any trouble all day long. Please, I'm not asking much. I'm cold..."

His eyes narrowed, but he pivoted on his heel and went back to his pack, pulling out a black cloak. He flung it haphazardly at her then disappeared out into the evening.

Amara blinked and her eyes welled with tears as she stared forlornly at the black cloth she couldn't even grasp to pull over herself. She twisted her arms, but the rope immediately pulled at her neck, choking her. Hot tears spilled down her cheeks and she rolled into a sitting position. She brought her knees up to her chest and rested her forehead against them, crying softly. Her heart broke as she thought of her father. He must be so worried.

Her thoughts strayed to her captor. How could anyone be so cold and unfeeling? Or so greedy to kill and abduct people for money? To not have any thought for a person other than what could be gained by them...it sickened her.

She twisted her hands some more, ignoring the way the rope bit into her neck. She had to get out of there. She had to! Otherwise she was going to end up married to that abominable man. She could do this. She was smart. She was strong, not some sniveling weakling like so many other girls. She just needed to keep working at it. The knots would eventually give way.

She jerked her arms and wrists with more determination and yanked so hard at one point that she made herself gag. More tears fell as a wave of panic and defeat washed over her. Who was she trying to fool? Even if she did get out of her arm bonds, she'd never be able to get out of the metal shackle. She let her shoulders slump, and she was able to draw in a decent breath even while her arms screamed in pain. It was useless. She was completely trapped. There was no way out. Unless...

She raised her head as an idea struck her, a memory of a hunting lesson she'd had with her father. Her captor wasn't a man. She had to stop viewing him as such, thinking he may

be capable of compassion or understanding. He was an animal, a creature existing on primal instinct. How did one entice a wild animal out in order to trap it?

She grinned and whispered to herself, "Make it think it
can trust you." She started to twist her wrists again, slowly
this time, and with deliberate, patient precision.

* * * *

Jaide dreaded returning to that cave. It felt like a prison,
like he was the one in captivity. He was an assassin for a
reason. In his line of work, all he usually had to do was
watch his victim for a while and wait for an opportunity. It
was a whole different game with a live person—a woman no
less—who flung rocks and burning wood at him, then
stabbed him with his own arrow. The woman was more trouble than she was worth. When they reached Dother and he
collected his pay, he was going to insist that Marden up the
amount. And after this job was done, he was never going to
do another kidnapping as long as he lived. It had only been
one day and he was ready to tear out his hair. He didn't deal
well with people. He was a solitary creature, had been for as
long as he could remember.

It was dark and the stars were out as he made his way
back to the cave. He stopped for one short second to look up
at them, sparkling and ever present, perfect in their infinity.
He sighed and closed his eyes, letting the moonlight bathe
over him for a short second. One tiny moment of beauty in
his hideous life. He loved nature and the wilderness. It was
the only thing he loved.

He snapped back to the present before his thoughts got
to wandering too much, and he continued on into the cave.
Everything was ready to go for two days from now. Although,
he was irritated that he had to wait that long. It wasn't smart
to stay in one place for too long, but they had to get over the
border, and his contact wasn't able to perform the ceremony
any sooner. He would just have to spend most of his time
outside and away from the confining cave. The woman would
be fine left to her own devices. It wasn't as if she could go
anywhere. He'd made sure of tha—

As he stepped into the entrance of the cave, he saw a fire

going, which was the first thing that alarmed him. The other was that there was a pile of rope sitting where the woman had been, but no woman. His black cloak was still in a crumpled heap where he had thrown it. For one split second, he was completely befuddled as to how she had managed to get out of her bonds, but the confusion was quickly replaced with supreme rage. He made a deep, growling noise in his throat. "Son of a—" He spun on his heel and almost barreled right over the woman, who was standing directly behind him, looking perturbed. He blinked, scowled, and glanced down at a plate of something she held in her hand.

"Your food tastes like hog slop," she spat, shoving the plate at him.

He took it because, if he hadn't, it would have gone all over the ground, or all over the front of him. He looked down at it again, then back up at her, his scowl growing deeper.

Her glare almost matched his in its ferocity. "Eat!" she shouted, throwing a crust of bread at him.

His lifted his elbow to deflect it then resumed his glower.

She put her hands on her slender hips and her white-blonde hair framed her face in gnarled tangles that had been pulled free from its braid. Coupled with the ferocious expression on her face, she looked like a wild woman, and he might have found the sight comical if he'd had a sense of humor. Unfortunately for her, he didn't. He opened his mouth to snarl something nasty at her about paying for her disobedience, but she cut him off before any words could emerge.

"What, are you confused?" she hissed. "It's not like I can go anywhere. I have a shackle on my ankle." She stabbed her finger down at her shackle. "And no shoes. Since escaping is impossible, I thought I could at least make something palatable to eat. Otherwise, I really am going to drop dead from your toxic cooking. Then you won't get paid, and I really don't feel like dying earlier than I have to."

For the first time in longer than he could remember, he couldn't form a rebuttal. His mind refused to wrap around the fact that she had, first of all, managed to get herself out of his bindings, but then had started a fire and cooked for the man who had abducted her and was transporting her to certain death. It went against the laws of human nature; it went against the laws of royalty. How did a princess, who had been babied and pampered her entire life, learn how to be an escape artist? And where had she learned to make a fire? And cook? He glanced down at the plate of food again then turned his glower back up to her.

He took a menacing step toward her and her eyes widened, but to her credit, she stood her ground. "Are you not afraid of me suddenly?" he queried.

"I'm terrified!" she cried, her voice wavering slightly. "You're absolutely horrifying, but I can't go anywhere. You have seen to that without ropes that choke me, which are useless anyway considering I was able to get out of them." She gestured toward her shackle again and her demeanor softened somewhat. "If I am to remain your captive, please at least allow me the freedom of movement," she implored.

He glanced down at where the chain was attached to the stake he'd driven into the ground. She had enough length to move freely, but not enough to leave the cave. And he had hammered it in deep enough that he doubted she would be able to yank free, regardless of how much she may try. Despite how much trouble she was, she still lacked the physical strength one would need to do such a thing. His eyes scanned over her flawless face, pale and perfect like an elegant sculpture. It reminded him of the calming moonlight...

He shook his head, banishing the ridiculous, unbidden thought and pointed his finger at her. "You *will* obey me," he ordered. The statement sounded more like a threat than anything else.

She swallowed hard and gave a slow nod.

He studied her for another several seconds and his eyes narrowed. "Are you going to stop throwing projectiles at me?" he muttered.

It looked as if she contemplated her answer for a moment before she raised her chin with pride and met his eyes full on. "I make no promises."

Again, he could think of no retort. Her complete honesty threw him as much as the fact that she had cooked supper for him. Were all women this way? He had no idea. He'd spent relatively little time around anything feminine. He'd imagined they were all the same—whining, shrill, annoying. He had no idea what this thing in front of him was. Certainly not a princess. Maybe he had kidnapped the wrong woman because none of this made any logical sense. He passed by her, growling out another intimidating snarl for good measure. To his delight and satisfaction, she retreated from him with fright in her large, gray eyes.

He flopped down in front of the fire and began to eat. He would have enjoyed it tremendously if her meal had tasted like sand, or sawdust, or rotten meat, but it was actually much better than anything he had ever prepared for himself. He frowned and glanced up at her as she sat across the fire, quietly eating her own meal. "What did you put in this?" He spat the statement out like it was a bad taste in his mouth.

She looked up at him, then pointed to his pack of supplies. He noticed her hand shook slightly. "I looked through your things. You had some dried meat in there, as well as some flour and a few wrinkled potatoes. I used some water to soften the meat and made gravy with the flour and the meat juices."

"You cannot make gravy from dried meat alone," he stated.

She chewed a bite of her meal slowly, then nodded. "Well, an unfortunate rat met his untimely demise. That helped."

He arched an eyebrow and pointed down at his plate. "I'm eating rat?"

She shrugged and met his eyes. "It's better than your rabbit."

He blinked and his frown returned. "How did you kill it?"

"It's a wonder what a large rock will do. I skinned it with one of your arrowheads, then roasted it on the shaft." She chewed on her bottom lip for a moment and looked as if she was debating with herself on something. Finally, she raised her chin in the most regal gesture he had seen from her thus far, and said, "It was stupid of you to leave your weapons in here with me, by the way, and you're lucky I don't bash your brains in the same way I did that rat."

He stared at her, unable to form a response, yet again. He wanted to rage and roar and frighten her to the point that she wet herself, but he couldn't deny the fact that she was absolutely right. He had underestimated his captive, something he should never do. Another reason why he would never kidnap another human as long as he lived.

A small smirk graced her lips and she pointed over to the back of the cave, indicating a wild plant that was growing out of the dirt. "That over there. That's sage. I'm pretty sure that's what made most of the difference."

He glanced at the plant again, then grunted and continued to mop up the remains of his dinner with the crust of bread she'd flung at him. He was painfully aware of her eyes watching him across the fire as she ate, but he didn't look at her. As far as he was concerned, she was a nuisance and nothing more. The sooner they were back in Dother and he was rid of her, the better off he would be. Then he could return to the life he was used to and he'd no longer have to concern himself with impertinent, prideful princesses who threw things at him, went through his belongings, made him eat rat for supper, and reprimanded him on his ability to do his own job.

"What's your name?" she asked him suddenly. Her voice was soft and melodic.

He glanced up at her with a glare. "My name is of no concern to you."

She was silent for one blessed second, but not long enough. "I'm Amara."

He huffed in frustration. "I know who you are," he barked.

She ignored him. "It's not my full name, though," she continued. "It's short for Amaranth. It was my mother's favorite flower."

The air slammed out of Jaide's lungs as if someone had kicked him straight in the chest. He stared down at his plate as a vision flashed through his mind. A vision of a field of flowers, comforting and safe, reaching their magnificent petals out to him, offering him the only solace he had ever known. He let out a shaky breath and swallowed hard, then cleared his throat, trying to force the image away. There was no room for that in his memory. Not anymore. He didn't need comfort. He didn't need solace. The only thing that could take care of him was himself. "Amaranths don't exist," he grumbled.

"Yes, they do," she countered. "I've seen them. When I was small. They're beautiful. Deep red...they seem to sparkle." She sighed. "My mother loved them... She died when I was little. I never saw the amaranth after that. They made Father sad..."

He swallowed hard, trying to get rid of a foreign lump that constricted his throat and made it difficult to breathe. He could see the flowers she described. See them as clear as if they were right in front of him. The only real beauty in his life. The only peace he had ever known...

Her name was Amaranth. Why? Why did the one woman named that in the world have to collide with him? Amaranths were perfect, they were undying, immortal in their radiance. It was the greatest tragedy to kill an amaranth...

He shook himself mentally. What was he thinking? She wasn't a flower. She was a woman. A human woman, just like any other...if a little bit unusual. She wasn't special, perfect, or immortal. She was a job. That was all.

But even as he banished the strange feeling that washed over him at the mention of her name, he found his lips moving against his own will. "Jaide," he rasped.

She frowned. "I'm sorry?"

He glanced up and met her eyes. "My name is Jaide."

She gave him a gentle, genuine smile that made her gray eyes sparkle in the fire light. "Jaide," she repeated with a small nod. "That's a nice name."

He frowned and averted his eyes.

"How did you become an assassin?" she queried.

His frown deepened and he remained silent, hoping she'd get the point and stop her incessant prattle. Apparently, that was too much to ask.

"What does your family think of your profession?"

He expelled a forceful breath and stood. "I have no idea what they think, as I do not have one. Now, enough talking."

She blinked up at him. "But—"

"I said, enough!" he bellowed. He pointed his finger at her. "Cease your gabbing, woman, or I will recant my decision to grant you mobility, and this time I will gag you as well." He knew his glower had to be sinister because fear came to life in her eyes and she visibly shrank back from him. He kept his gaze on her for several more seconds, just to make her uncomfortable and drive home his point, then he grabbed her plate and scraped the remains into the fire. He rinsed the dishes off with a bit of water, then readied himself for sleep, pulling out his bedroll and detaching his baldric and sword from his back. When he had finished, he made his way back to Amara, picking up the discarded rope he had used to bind her before. "Give me your hands," he commanded.

Her eyes widened. "But I obeyed!" she protested, moving away from him. "I stopped talking!"

He heaved a sigh and knelt down in front of her. He suddenly felt extremely tired. "Yes, you are learning. I am not going back on my word. I will let you move freely during the day, but I would be a complete imbecile if I let you free at night. You'd most likely stab me in my sleep or, as you so clearly pointed out, bash my head in with a rock like you did that rat. Now, come on. Do as you're told."

Her innocent eyes glistened with threatening tears, but she slowly extended her hands out to him. They trembled. He took one of her wrists and went around behind her. "I'm securing your arms behind your back, but I won't put the rope around your neck. Fair?" He had no idea why he asked her that and he instantly wanted to kick himself. What did he care if she thought she was being treated fairly? Her concerns and feelings were not his problem. Marden had ordered him to kidnap her. He hadn't put in the stipulation to make her as comfortable as possible. He rolled his eyes and briefly considered braining himself with the rock of death. At least it would put him out of his misery and stop his usually calm, rational mind from whirling out of control. Yes, after this, he was going back to contract killing and nothing else. Dealing with a living human was much too complicated to suit him.

"Fair," she whispered, her voice wavering.

He bound her wrists tightly, securing the bindings with knots only sailors would use. "All right, go to sleep," he commanded as he stood. He watched her curl on her side toward the fire. She stared into the flames for a second, her expression sad, then she closed her eyes tightly, as if to blink back tears.

He sighed and headed to his bedroll. He lay down on his side, his eyes falling on her slender, ethereal form. Another vision of the amaranth flashed in his mind, followed by a brutal memory of being beaten until most every surface on his body had been bleeding. He closed his eyes in an attempt to shut out the image, but it would not leave him tonight. Usually, he could force them out. Not tonight. Tonight, his demons were persistent. Slowly, as his mind continued to relive the torture of his early years, every scar and now healed mark on his body began to burn and ache as if it was all happening again. He could hear his own screams echoing through his head, and a wave of nausea rolled over him.

He sat up with force. He cracked his neck and rested his head in his hand. He closed his eyes, sucked in a deep breath, and let his ears fill with the popping of the fire. Somewhere in the distance, a wolf howled its mournful call. He sighed, and a very small bit of peace returned, as much as he was allowed anyway. He raised his eyes to Amara, who now slept in a contorted heap. He watched her for a long while, longer than he realized, before he stood and made his way outside. At times, sleeping in confinement was too much for him. It reminded him of the dingy cell he'd had to sleep in at the orphanage, and the tiny, constricted room he'd had to share with three other men when he'd been at the barracks. He needed open spaces. He needed the wind and the sky and the sounds of the night.

As he passed by Amara on his way out, he stopped for a second, then turned back and grabbed the cloak he had thrown at her earlier. He draped it over her then continued into the night.

Chapter Four

As Amara slowly came awake, she became aware of a wonderful smell that made her smile. It was wood smoke mingled with some kind of delicious spice. It took her a few seconds to realize that it came from the black cloak that covered her. She frowned and craned her neck to take a deeper smell of the fabric. Is that how Jaide smelled? If it was, the warm aroma greatly contrasted with his icy demeanor.

Her frown deepened as she tried to remember when she'd managed to pull the fabric over herself. She blinked as she realized that she hadn't. She'd gone to sleep curled on her side, trying to keep warm by the fire.

Had Jaide...?

It had to have been him. No one else would have put it over her. A smile touched her lips at that very small gesture. It would have meant nothing to anyone else, but coming from him, that tiny moment of thoughtfulness meant everything to her. It meant that, somewhere under his layers of ice and evil, he was a human being. It also meant that her plan was working. If she kept being pliable and obedient, kept luring him into thinking he could trust her, sooner or later, he would let his guard slip, and when he did, she would make her move. Although, being unable to stop the bashing his brain in comment from flying out of her mouth had probably hindered her progress somewhat.

She sat up and glanced over at his bedroll, but it lay untouched. He was nowhere to be seen and the fire had long since gone out. She winced as her stiff shoulders protested her movement and she hunched over, trying to stretch them out. At least she didn't have that awful rope around her throat anymore, and she had been granted mobility during the day. That was better than nothing.

Her father had always told her you got more bees with honey than you did with vinegar. Apparently that was true with cold-blooded assassins, as well. All men, regardless of their personality, usually thought with two things: their loins and their stomachs. She wasn't going near the first part of that equation, but cooking him a decent supper seemed to have worked in her favor.

She heard footsteps approaching and looked up to see Jaide stride through the mouth of the cave. He wore his ever-present scowl and had two dead rabbits gutted and slung over his shoulder on a string. She frowned. "Did you go hunting?" she queried.

He set aside his bow and arrows and threw the rabbits down, then gave her an insipid expression. "Obviously."

She rolled her eyes.

"I figured this would be enough meat for a couple meals. That way I'm not forced to eat anymore disease-ridden rodent." He stood and continued over to her, kneeling and untying her hands.

She let out a sigh of relief and shook her arms out to get the blood flowing and rid her joints of their stiffness. She ran a hand through her matted hair and made a face. It was so snarled she'd probably never get the tangles out. "When did you get up? It doesn't even look like you slept in here last night."

"I didn't."

She frowned. "Where did you sleep then?"

He huffed and fixed her with a dark expression. "Are you already intent on giving me a headache so early in the morning?" he snapped. "When and where I sleep is of no concern to you. Stop talking."

She glowered and brought her knees to her chest, wrapping her arms around them. She watched him as he strapped his baldric back across his broad shoulders. "Where are you going?"

"I have a job I must do," he replied. "I'll return by midday."

She felt her face pale and her stomach protested the thought of murder. She hugged her knees tighter.

He continued getting ready, then headed back toward

her. He reached down and unclasped her shackle, then grasped her by the wrist and hauled her up in a standing position, causing her to shriek. She tried to pull her hand back, but his grip remained firm. "What are you doing?" she cried.

"There is a shallow pool not far from here. I'm taking you to bathe and wash your clothes. Do it quickly. I'm on a schedule." He didn't even give her a chance to digest the information he had given her before he yanked her outside after him. The bright morning sunlight blasted her eyes and she blinked rapidly in an attempt to adjust her vision while she stumbled after him. The pebbles and stones on the ground bit into the tender flesh of her feet and she winced. Luckily, the pool he spoke of wasn't far away. He led her to the edge of it, then shoved her in its direction and stood back with his arms folded.

Amara glanced over her shoulder at him in question.

"If you even think about running, you will regret it a hundred ways from Sunday," he muttered with a sinister glower.

She heaved a sigh and looked down at the water. A bath would feel wonderful... She looked back over at Jaide. "Would you turn around?"

He snorted. "What do you take me for? Do what you have to do and be quick about it."

Her eyes widened. She absolutely was not going to strip her clothing off in front of this man. No man had ever so much as glimpsed her naked other than her father when she'd come out of the womb. She aimed to keep it that way. "I can't take my clothes off in front of you!" she cried.

He let out a rumbling, aggravated growl and strode forward, lugging her up into his arms and dumping her directly into the pool below. She fell into it with a splash and a gasp as the cold water attacked her skin. "Then bathe with them on," he sneered. "I care not." He stood there, arrogant and wicked, his arms folded over his chest.

She cast him her best threatening glare, although she was sure it paled in comparison to the one he had mastered, and quickly washed off in the frigid water. She unbraided her hair and doused that as well, relishing the feeling of being clean, even if it wasn't exactly what she was used to.

She finished quickly, as Jaide seemed to be in an even fouler disposition than usual, and she felt terribly exposed as he led her back to the cave. Her wet bed clothes clung to every curve on her body and the white material had become practically transparent. She may as well have just been naked for all that it revealed. As soon as they had reached the cave, she grasped his cloak and pulled it around herself as he secured her shackle.

He didn't so much as glance at her in her vulnerable state. He kept his eyes downcast and his attention diverted. She was grateful for that, if nothing else.

"I am leaving you untied while I am gone so you can prepare some kind of suitable meal," he stated. "Do not make me regret it."

She rolled her eyes. "Yes, yes, I know the routine. Growl, hiss, snarl. I understand." He stood and regarded her with a frown. She was beginning to think it was the only expression he was capable of. "Have a good day at work," she said snidely. "Hope your murder goes well."

He stared at her for a moment, as if he wasn't quite certain how to respond, then he pivoted on his boot heel and disappeared outside. Two seconds later, the tromped back in and snatched up his bow and quiver of arrows. He shot her a pointed look and swooped out of the cave again.

Amara heaved a sigh and pulled off the cloak, folding it and setting it aside. She then combed her fingers through her wet hair and went around to the rest of his things, searching through them to see if there was anything she could use to unlock her shackle and escape. There wasn't. She tried to pry the stake out of the ground. That didn't work either. He had managed to hammer it in rather solidly with the hilt of his sword.

Finally, after pacing restlessly for a long while and getting virtually nothing accomplished, she lay back down and closed her eyes, dreaming of home and aching for the life she had once known. It seemed lost to her now, so far away...

* * * *

She had been awake for a while and had prepared lunch when Jaide returned. His shirt was covered in blood and she had to turn away for fear she would retch. Her mind filled with hundreds of terrible images that she tried to banish, and she was reminded, once again, of how unfeeling and evil her captor really was.

He discarded the soiled shirt, ate in silence, then bound her wrists again as he claimed he wanted to take a nap. Amara was aware of the fact that he tied the rope with some kind of tricky knot, but she wasn't thwarted. She'd managed to get out of them again in a little over a half an hour. She wasn't going to sit there with her arms aching while he snored away. And she couldn't stand the thought of that horribly stained shirt lying there, gathering flies while it crusted and dried.

Quietly, so as not to wake him, she grabbed a cooking pot and poured water in it from a water skin. His shirt was still close to where he slept and she swallowed, trying to gather her courage to approach him. She closed her eyes and steeled herself, then crept over to his sleeping form and looked down at him. She was going to reach for the soiled shirt next to him, but her progress was halted for a moment as she studied his face. Such strong, masculine angles and planes... He was almost breathtaking in his beauty, however cruel it might be. She had to smirk at the fact that a small wrinkle marred his brow. He even frowned as he slept.

There was something strange about Jaide, something she couldn't quite place. He was fierce and harsh, and he was being paid to transport her to her death. He killed innocent people to make his living. He should be revolting to her, completely unredeemable and no better than the Devil himself, but...

She frowned. She couldn't find a name for the elusive feeling in her heart, but somewhere deep within her, she got the distinct impression that there was more to him than met the eye...much more.

Shaking her head to disperse her wandering thoughts, she reached down to collect his shirt. Her fingers closed around the material and, without warning and with hardly any movement, his hand came up to clamp firmly around her wrist. She shrieked as he knocked her onto her back with the sheer force of his body, and he had pinned her to the ground with his hands around her throat before she could even think. She held her hands up to show she was unarmed. "I was only going to wash your shirt!" she cried, tears hovering on her lashes.

The power in his grip was undeniable, and he wasn't even applying much pressure. He stared down at her, his jade eyes flashing fire. Jade...like his name. He looked like a demon, like a messenger of death, and she wondered if this was what his victims had to look at before they met their end. A face of malevolence. A face of stone.

She shook her head as she trembled beneath his unrelenting form. "I was only going to wash your shirt," she murmured again.

His expression instantly shifted to ferocious anger. "Are you insane?" he shouted, pushing himself into a standing position. "What kind of idiot sneaks up on a sleeping assassin?"

She scrambled to her feet and put some distance between them. "I wasn't sneaking!" she exclaimed. "I was going to wash your shirt!"

He glanced at her, then over at the cooking pot with the water in it. "In my drinking water?" he snapped, stabbing his finger over to the pot.

Amara swallowed, and glanced up at him sheepishly.

He let out a great aggravated, snarling huff and ran his fingers through his hair. "And is there any point in actually tying you up? Is there any kind of knot that you can't get out of?"

If he hadn't been so terrifying when he was furious, she would have found the situation funny. But he was terrifying, and she shrank back, giving her head a small shake.

He roared in frustration and kicked at the nearest object, which happened to be the cooking pot. It clanged against the ground with a clamor and water flew everywhere, making Amara jump.

He spun and fixed her with a black scowl. "Do you think you could at least pretend that the bonds I put you in are effective so that I can feel like I am actually doing my bloody job?" He bellowed the last part at her in a volume that threatened to send rocks crashing down from the mountain.

Amara averted her eyes and, not knowing what else to do, she crossed one wrist over the other as if she was bound. She glanced back up at Jaide. He stared at her for a long moment, and she could have sworn she saw the rage just deflate straight out of him. He heaved a great sigh and closed his eyes, putting his hands on his hips. An angry muscle still worked in his jaw, but his fury seemed to abate into a seething kind of frustration. "Wash the shirt, if you must," he ground out.

She chewed on her bottom lip, wondering if she should even say what she was thinking. She decided she had nothing to lose. She cleared her throat. "Well, I would, but—" She cleared her throat again. "You kicked over the water I was going to use."

He sighed again. "We can go back to the pool. I need to bathe anyway." He started to stride past her. He stopped and made a slow turn toward her. "Do not sneak up on me again," he said, pointing his finger directly in her face. "The next time you do, I'll slit your throat. You understand me? There comes a point when the money just stops mattering. I'll slit it." He drew his finger in a threatening line across his throat to show her he meant what he was saying.

She swallowed hard and nodded. As he bent down to unclasp her shackle, she just couldn't help herself. "Is that what you did to your unfortunate victim? Slit his throat?"

He heaved another exasperated sigh and looked up at her. "It was a cow," he stated.

She blinked in bewilderment, wondering if she'd heard him correctly. "You assassinated a cow?"

"In a manner of speaking." He went over to the stake that was attached to the chain and pried it out of the ground with the blade of his sword. "I owed a favor to the man who is helping me with the border legality. He had a cow he needed to slaughter in order to feed his family. He is crippled and has no sons. His eldest daughter couldn't bring herself to do it, so he asked me if I would do it in return for his services. So, I did."

She blinked, then gave a curious frown. That was almost...kind.

"I never double book myself on jobs. That is a recipe for trouble all the way around." He looped the freed end of the chain around his belt and secured it, then reattached the shackle to her wrist.

Amara glanced down at the shackle with a frown, wondering how a device that went around her ankle could still fit around her wrist.

"It's adjustable," he stated. "Never know how big or how small someone's ankles are going to be."

She arched an eyebrow. "Resourceful." She met his eyes and smiled out of habit.

He looked taken aback by the gesture, but immediately replaced the perplexed expression with his usual menacing glower. "Yes, and because I just happened to be enlisted to kidnap the only princess magician I've ever had the unfortunate pleasure of meeting, I'm going to have to secure you to me like this at night to make sure you don't go running off." He shook his head as he headed toward the mouth of the cave, tugging her along behind him.

She smirked. "If you thought I was just going to lie down and accept the fact that you're transporting me to my slaughter, you're sadly mistaken. If someone is being paid to bring me to an early death, rest assured I'm going to make him work for his money." He snorted in a way that actually caused her to grin. It gave her a small measure of satisfaction to know that she could frustrate him so well. It was the only card she had to play, but it was better than nothing at all.

* * * *

He had no idea what to do with this woman. No idea whatsoever. She defied any kind of preconception he'd had. Currently, he was soaking in the cool water of the pool she had bathed in that morning. He had secured her chain underneath a large rock that she would not be able to move by herself without quite a bit of fuss, and she had washed his shirt at the far end. It was drying on a rock in the sun, and she sat atop a large boulder, combing her fingers through her long, lustrous, golden hair. She looked very much like royalty at that moment. Elegant, graceful, noble... He would be completely lying to himself if he didn't admit that she was beautiful. It didn't greatly matter, but it was true nonetheless. It only intrigued him because he had never before found a woman alluring in any way. He knew pretty women when he saw them, but that was all they were. Amara's beauty was different. It seemed to shine from within like a luminescent light. He had never before encountered a human with that kind of light.

But then again, his entire world existed in dank darkness.

He watched her as she stretched her arms above her head and the sunlight illuminated the silhouette of her body through the sheer fabric of her white chemise. He swallowed and frowned as he realized his throat was dry. With a scowl, he averted his eyes. He rested his head back on the rock he was leaning up against and sighed, closing his eyes.

"Jaide!"

Her sudden exclamation made him jump, and he jerked into a sitting position. "What?" he barked. "What's wrong?" He looked over to see her scrambling down off of the boulder, and he glanced around to see if there was a wild animal or some other kind of threat anywhere nearby.

"Jaide, look! I told you they were real!" He frowned as he watched her kneel down at the base of the boulder and point at a small, dark crevice in between the boulder and a smaller rock. She looked up at him and grinned. "It's an amaranth!"

He sucked his breath in and his whole body went rigid for a moment before the tension dissolved into shivering ripples.

"Come and see!" she urged, motioning him over with childlike glee.

He frowned and forced himself to get out of the water. He didn't want to go, but he couldn't make himself stay. As much as the amaranth pained him because it made him remember a past he'd like to efface from his mind, it also called to him like an enchanting spell that he was powerless against. It was the only thing that he'd never been able to resist.

Amara moved aside as he approached and pointed down to where the tiny flower grew. He gazed at it, his heart reminding him that it still existed by twisting painfully. Most of the time, he didn't feel it at all. Only a dull, empty chasm where a heart should be. But now, it reminded him.

He hated the reminder.

He frowned as he looked down at the one flower that had always been his only beauty and his only weakness. It grew in the shadow of the boulder and looked as if the petals on one side were being marred by an unyielding rock that trapped it. He reached out on instinct to try and dislodge the rock.

"What are you doing?" Amara asked, grasping his wrist to stop him.

He pulled away from her touch instantly. He didn't like to be touched. His frown deepened. "That rock is going to crush it." He reached out to the rock again, intent on getting rid of it if he had to pry it out of the ground.

Amara shook her head and grasped his wrist again. "No, stop. It's not going to crush it. It's protecting it."

Jaide wished he could frown harder, but it was physically impossible. He yanked his wrist out of her hand again. "Stop grabbing me," he grumbled.

She ignored him and pointed back down at the flower. "Don't you see how it's growing? The rock shelters it against the elements." She looked up at him with her large gray eyes. A graceful smile curved her full lips. "It may seem harsh and unyielding, and it may look like the flower is being crushed, but it isn't. It's being protected. Don't remove the rock. The amaranth needs it to live."

For some reason, her words made his stomach clench in a way that was almost nausea, but not quite. It was something different. Something foreign...and he didn't like it. He glanced away from her and back down at the beautiful flower. So perfect, so pure...

He reached his fingers out to caress the petals, and warmth washed over his blackened heart.

He saw Amara watching him out of the corner of his eye. "You lied to me, didn't you?" she questioned softly.

"How so?"

"When you said amaranths didn't exist. You've seen them before."

He swallowed hard and nodded slowly. "Yes," he whispered. "Long ago..." Her eyes remained on him and he glanced up at her, his gaze meeting hers. Her eyes were filled with quiet curiosity and a gentleness he couldn't handle. There was nothing gentle in his world. Nothing soft at all. His entire existence was and always had been made up of things harsh, cruel, and painful. The gentleness in her stormy-eyed gaze made him feel filthy, like he wasn't even worthy of looking at her, like he wasn't worthy of touching the flower below him. He was surprised the ever-blooming petals didn't wilt and turn black. He was so full of taint. He did not deserve gentleness or beauty in any fashion.

Slowly, Amara's gaze traveled lower and her eyes widened in alarm as she must have just come to realize that he was completely without apparel. She let out a shout of surprise and covered her face with her hands, pulling back so quickly that her foot caught on the edge of a small stone and she went tumbling toward the ground.

Jaide reacted on pure reflex and caught her by the wrist to keep her from falling, but he pulled harder than he'd meant to and she crashed into his body, overturning his balance and sending them both into the water. He landed hard on his back, and because of the shackle around her wrist, Amara twisted slightly as she fell, her shoulder planting itself with force right into his sternum.

Pain sliced through Jaide's body and water splashed in every available direction. He winced and let out an annoyed, growling grunt. "For goodness sake, you act like you've never seen a naked man before," he muttered between clenched teeth.

"I haven't!" she cried.

He looked down at her, lying half on top of him and flopping the other half of her body in the water to try and sit up. The position made it so that she was almost nestled against him and it was, quite possibly, the most uncomfortable moment of his whole entire life. He would have even taken the merciless beatings he'd received at the barracks over the feel of her soft, velvet skin rubbing against his. "Kindly get off of me!" he barked.

"I'm trying!" The tension of the chain attached to her shackle made it almost impossible for her to do anything useful with her right arm so she wiggled around, trying to get some kind of footing. She attempted to pull herself out with the chain, but Jaide must not have secured it under the rock as well as he thought because it went flying out from under it at the pressure of Amara's body weight, sending her crashing back into him again. This time, her elbow made contact with his stomach.

Jaide wasn't sure if he was angry, or just completely overwhelmed and bewildered. It didn't matter much either way considering anger was the only emotion he was actually capable of showing. It was the only one that hadn't been eradicated from his being. "Get off of me!" he bellowed. He couldn't handle her nearness. It made him feel like he couldn't breathe. People, physical contact, made him feel like someone was slowly choking the air right out of his body.

To make matters worse, she didn't even seem to register what he'd said. She didn't retreat at his command, fearful of what he might do if she didn't obey. Instead, she did something so unexpected and strange to him that all he could do was stare.

She dissolved into laughter.

And she rested her forehead against his chest.

Like she was comfortable with him.

Like he wasn't evil incarnate.

Like for one short second in time, she completely forgot who he was and why she was there with him.

She raised her head and looked down at him, her flawless face fairly sparkling with her joy. He felt something foreign wiggle around in his hair and he frowned. She squealed with even more laughter and shook her head. "Y-You have—" She wrapped her arms around her stomach as she tried to get the words out between laughs. Tears streamed down her cheeks. "You have a frog- a frog in your hair."

He heaved a sigh and suddenly felt about twenty years older than he was. This woman had aged him twenty years in two days. He had no idea how he was going to last the rest of the journey. "Get it out!" he snapped. He reached up to try and swat at the top of his head where he felt the creature moving.

She giggled and pushed his hand away. "Stop! You'll kill it!"

He rolled his eyes. "Did you forget who you're talking to?"

She shot him a halfhearted scowl as she untangled the frog from his hair. "You're a contract killer. And while you may assassinate cows now and again, I don't believe anyone paid you good money to murder a frog." She sat back, cupping the creature in her hands, and she met his gaze with a grin.

Jaide stared at her in silent wonderment. Her golden hair hung in damp, curling strands around her face, and her gray eyes held mischief. He couldn't wrap his mind around it. Her laughter, her joy. It made no sense. He was escorting her to her death. In a way, he would be responsible for killing her.

How could she laugh? How could she act as if he was any other man and not the monster that he knew he was?

She opened her hands enough to show him the tiny, green frog. It sat there for a second, then leapt off of her palm and back into the water. She giggled in a way that reminded him of a free-spirited little girl.

He sighed and sat up. Strangely, he didn't feel angry as he should. He wasn't irritated at her, didn't want to punish her to show her who was boss. He just felt weary. He looked up at her. "I think that perhaps I am the fool in this entire equation," he muttered.

She frowned in question.

He combed his fingers through his dripping hair. "I was told I was being hired to kidnap a harmless princess. I think I may have been double-crossed, and you are actually an assassin come to do me in."

She laughed again. "Would I make a good assassin?" she teased.

He grabbed a hold of her chain to keep her from trying to escape, as he knew she would if given the right opportunity. "You'd make a clumsy assassin," he muttered as he grasped his shirt and pulled it over his head. "But what you lack in finesse, you'd make up for in the sheer ability to drive your captive mad." He slid his eyes over to hers, and she flashed him a grin that gave him that strange feeling in his gut that he didn't like. He frowned. "All right, close your eyes so I can put my pants on," he said. She obeyed, and he dressed quickly, then held his hand out to her. "Come on," he said. "I believe we've had enough excitement for one day. I'm hungry."

She stared at his outstretched hand then turned her eyes up to him in surprise. He swallowed hard, then scowled furiously and dropped his hand, wondering what in the world kind of demon madness had possessed him. He cleared his throat and stepped away from her, yanking harshly on the chain around her wrist. "Get up. Come on," he barked.

She regarded him for a moment, and it made him feel like his skin was crawling. He felt as if her eyes were stripping away every layer of his being so she could glimpse something hidden deep within that terrified him more than anything else in the world. Something he'd thought had been annihilated long, long ago. Something he refused to let her look upon. He turned away, as if doing so could hide his soul from her penetrating gaze.

She stood silently and stepped out of the water. He donned his boots and headed back to the cave, hoping she would remain silent.

For once, she actually did.

Chapter Five

A storm had rolled in over the course of the night, a summer rain that brought lightning and thunder and washed everything clean. Jaide had kept the shackle around Amara's wrist instead of her ankle, and had secured her to himself so if she tried to move too much or escape, he would awaken. It made her wish that she hadn't been so cavalier about her ability to escape the rope. It would have been difficult to escape her ankle shackle, but it might have been a possibility. There was no way in the world she'd be able to get around Jaide, and she remembered all too well his reaction when she had startled him awake.

Amara had lay awake for a long while, listening to the storm and watching the fire cast its shadow shapes on the walls of the cave. Jaide's eyes had been closed, and he'd been breathing rhythmically, but she got the distinct feeling that he was not asleep. She had no proof. It was more like a sensation, but it gave her the impression that he was lying there, listening to the storm just like she was.

There was something so wild about Jaide. Wild and untamed like a feral animal. She wondered what kind of life he had known, wondered what sort of things had happened to him to make him so hardened and callous. More than that, she wondered about the fleeting glimpse of humanity she had seen in him when they'd been at the pool. The way he'd touched the amaranth, with reverence and tenderness. And then with the way he'd offered her his hand to help her up before he'd realized what he'd done. It intrigued her.

Her father had always told her she had a gift for taming the wild things. When she'd been a small girl, she had always sought to take care of creatures she found that were wounded or sick. There was nothing that had frightened her, and nothing, her father claimed, that she couldn't get to trust her. He had also told her that the reason he believed she was so good with wild animals was because she didn't try to tame them. She'd taken care of them, nursed them back from the brink of death even, but she'd never tried to make them her pets. She'd always had a healthy respect for what they were, and never tried to mold them into something docile and domesticated.

Jaide reminded her of one of those wild things, made ferocious by a life of cruelty and suffering. She wondered what lay beneath all of that. Vicious animals attacked because of being frightened. They sought to protect themselves against anything and everything because they had been so abused they'd lost the ability to tell the difference between friend and foe. To them, all were their enemies. She saw that in Jaide. She saw the uncertainty buried deep within the burning flame of his eyes. He knew coldness. He knew death. He knew the ugly things in life. He would not know how to react to kindness or love. He would not know how to trust. It pained her heart to think of such an existence. Even though he would never admit it, deep down he must be so very lonely.

After spending quite some time contemplating the man she was chained to, she finally fell into a restless sleep.

It was still drizzling in the morning and Amara ate her breakfast in silence, stealing glances at Jaide as he went about packing up his things for the next leg of their journey. He'd put his horse in a stable in Delaney when they'd first arrived, and he informed her that he had instructed the stable boy to bring it to him that morning.

Just as she was beginning to wonder when the stable boy would come, Amara heard hoof beats outside of the cave. Jaide immediately stood and went out. She could hear several men's voices, but she could not make out anything that was being said.

Suddenly, Jaide returned with an older man who hobbled on a cane. She frowned and stood.

The man stopped just inside and glanced at Amara. "Is this the woman?" he asked Jaide.

Jaide nodded. "Yes. Can we make this as quick and painless as possible?"

The man chuckled and gave a nod. He looked at Jaide. "Say yes," he stated.

"Yes," Jaide replied.

The man turned his attention to Amara. "Say yes."

She frowned and her heart picked up its pace. "Are you out of your mind? I don't know you. I'm not going to blindly say yes when I don't even know what I'm saying yes to."

Jaide heaved a sigh and met her eyes. "Amara, do you want me to tell you what is going on?"

She snorted and folded her arms across her chest. "Of course I do!"

Jaide looked back to the man and held his arms out as if in question.

The man shrugged. "That works well enough for me. I now pronounce you husband and wife. Here is the legal document you must show to border patrol." He handed Jaide a slip of paper.

Amara's eyes bulged and her heart plummeted in a sickening way. "Wh-What?" she stammered.

Jaide met her eyes as he ushered the crippled man back outside. "I told you, we had to marry in order to cross into Demrysk."

He continued to escort the man outside and Amara's legs buckled. She fell to the ground and started to shake as fat, hot tears rolled out of her eyes and down her cheeks like rivers. No, it couldn't have happened like that. Not like that. She had so many dreams about her wedding. She was supposed to wear a beautiful gown and have flowers in her hair. Not soiled and torn bedclothes that she had been abducted in. She was supposed to bind herself to a man who would look at her like he worshipped her, who loved her and cared for her. Not a cold-blooded assassin who treated her like an object and a job. She was supposed to say her wedding vows with love in her heart, not be tricked into them by a stranger who was doing her captor a favor because he had butchered his cow. It was all wrong. It was sickening. She felt sick. Sick to her stomach and sick at heart. He had taken everything from her. Everything she loved. He had robbed her of everything. Her home, her family, her dreams...her life. At the end of it all, he would have destroyed everything that she was.

Jaide strode back into the cave, intent on packing up his

horse and heading on to Demrysk, but he was halted as he caught sight of Amara. She looked like a frightened child. He frowned, and as she looked up at him, she curled in on herself and burst into sobs, pulling her knees to her chest and burying her face.

He blinked in bewilderment and put his hands on his hips. "Why are you so beside yourself? I told you this was going to happen." Her eyes snapped up to his at his words and, had he been anyone else, he would have retreated a step from the inferno that blazed in her gaze. A ripple of warning shivered along his spine and he glanced at the chain he had not bothered to secure to anything that morning. He'd been in the cave with her. She would have been easy to catch if she'd tried to escape. Now, he cursed his foolhardiness. Especially as she stood, and with impressive force, hurled the nearest, and not the smallest by any standards, rock at him with an ear-splitting and rage-filled scream.

He sidestepped her projectile, but had to cover his head with his arms as various items continued to rain down upon him. More rocks, some sticks, a decent-sized log of firewood, and even his own satchel, full of not so light things.

"I *hate* you!" she shrieked with wrathful venom. "You have destroyed *everything*! Everything in my life!"

Her screams were laced with bitter sobs and he pulled his arms away from his head just in time to almost get decapitated by a flying plate. It crashed against the far side of the cave with a ringing clatter. He scowled and strode his way toward her with purpose, intent on stopping her violent tirade before she made her way to his weapons.

She held her arms out to him and stared at him like a cornered rabid animal, her eyes alight with fear and rage. "You stay away from me!" she shouted. "Don't come near me or I'll claw your face off with my own two hands!"

She flung something else at him, he didn't know what, but he was able to sidestep around it and snatch her by the arm. She let out a yell as he yanked her toward him, and she struggled with more strength than he ever would have given her credit for. "Amara!" he roared. "Stop this, woman!" He grasped her by the shoulders and gave her a harsh shake, but she wrenched one arm free of his grip and struck him hard across the jaw with the back of her fist. His head jerked sideways and his ear actually rung with the force of her blow.

He shook his head to rid himself of the stinging pain that coursed down the side of his face, as well as the surprise that clouded his mind. He grabbed hold of her arms again and pinned them to her sides, giving her another violent shake. "Stop this!" he commanded. "Stop this ridiculous display or you will suffer the consequences!"

She stopped struggling, but her eyes burned into his with a kind of fury he had rarely seen. It was alarming in its intensity. "What are you going to do?" she hissed. "Kill me?" She snorted. "You already have." To accent her point, her spat directly in his face.

A strange and foreign wave of cold washed over Jaide's body, and he went silent and still, gazing into her gray eyes full of rancor and wrath. Another pair of eyes flashed through his mind. Black eyes, the eyes of a demon. And he heard his own voice ring in his ears as the blunt club that had been his commander's favorite weapon descended onto his midsection. He felt his own limbs strain against the shackles that held his wrists and ankles.

"See what happens when you disobey? See what happens when you don't do as you're told? One of these days, you're going to end up dead because of your stubbornness."

Jaide stepped away from Amara, shaking his head to banish the voice. He clenched his teeth the same way he had back then.

"Kill me then. There is nothing left within me to live for." His own voice was bitter, defiant even in his pain.

He drew in a gasping breath, then quickly forced the memory away and banished it back into the dark recesses of his mind, into the locked and barred place he never opened. He let his eyes fall on Amara, who was now crying softly, hugging her knees to her chest like a frightened child. He swallowed hard then left her where she was and went about packing up his horse.

She didn't fight him when he came back in to collect her. All traces of her dangerous fury had abated and she just stared ahead blankly, doing whatever he told her with out of character docility. It should have pleased him. He should have been ecstatic to see that she was finally broken and pliable, but strangely, as he rode with her in front of him on their way to Demrysk, all he could see was her laughing, joyous face from when they'd been at the pool. And all he could feel was the foreign sensation of having her rest her forehead against his chest and laugh with abandonment as if, for that one small moment in time, he had been a man like any other.

He felt cold as he traveled. Colder than he had ever been.

He cursed the rain for that, as it was the only reasonable explanation for the feeling.

* * * *

Getting over the border to Demrysk had, as predicted, been little trouble. He'd presented the certificate of marriage to the border patrol guard and they'd been let into the country in a matter of seconds. Jaide had opted for an inn instead of making camp out in the open, as it was still raining and they were out of the mountains. There would be nowhere that offered adequate shelter and, as much as he hated staying anywhere near a large amount of people, he didn't feel like catching his death out in the cold.

Because of staying at the inn, he had eaten dinner in the tavern below instead of making anything for himself. Amara hadn't eaten, even though he'd offered to bring her something. She'd sat herself in a chair, pulled her knees to her chest, and had stared out the window at the gray clouds and drizzling rain for the remainder of the day.

She hadn't so much as spoken a word to him all day, and she was still silent now. He lay on the only bed in the room, staring up at the ceiling, listening to the gentle rhythm of the falling rain outside. It was late so the tavern had quieted down, thank goodness. It had been so full of drunken revelry earlier that his jaw was aching from how hard he'd clenched it to try and block out the noise of so many people... Or perhaps it was aching because Amara had socked him a good one. He couldn't actually tell. All he knew was that, whatever else he might think of her, that slender, weak-looking girl threw a mean backhand. He had to respect her for that. It was the only language he understood.

His attention shifted as he heard Amara stand. He watched her stiffly make her way over to the bed and stand in front of him. He frowned slightly. "What is it, Amara?"

She stared at him, then swallowed hard and squared her shoulders. She bent her head, and with shaky fingers, started to unlace her chemise.

His frown deepened. "What are you doing?"

She met his eyes and fear reflected in hers. "Well, I am your wife now..." she murmured, her voice wavering.

He sat up with force. "What kind of man do you take me for?" he snapped. He grasped his cloak from where he'd flung it on the end of the bed earlier and stood to wrap it around her pale shoulders, pulling it snug against her body.

She looked up at him in bewilderment, sincere confusion etched into her face. "A man like any other, I suppose," she said softly. "Probably worse."

He gazed at her there in front of him, looking lost and forlorn, and a lump formed in his throat. He heaved a sigh and guided her down to sit on the bed. "Our marriage is legality only," he said. He met her sad eyes with purpose, so she knew he spoke truth. "Whatever else I may be, I am not that. Understand?" His voice sounded unnaturally soft to his own ears.

Her eyes searched his for several agonizing seconds before hers narrowed into a disgusted glare. "No, you're just a killer with no conscience," she muttered. "You've shown me no discernible decency. Why would you expect me to think you would be decent about this matter?" She hugged her arms around herself and averted her eyes. Her bottom lip quivered and she put her face in her hands, dissolving into tears and quiet sobs. He watched her cry and ran his hands through his hair. His chest was strangely tight and he felt like the walls of the room were closing in on him. He stood to put some distance between the two of them, then made a few restless paces before he turned toward the door.

"Where are you going?" she questioned.

"Away," he rasped. He shook his head. "Downstairs, I don't know. Just...away." He put his hand on the doorknob, then doubled back and pointed at her. "Don't try anything or, rest assured, you will regret it." His usual menacing tone sounded hollow and flat, void of any real threat.

She looked up at him, tear stains marking trails down her alabaster cheeks. "Do you want me to sleep on the floor so you can have the bed when you return?"

Her voice was so meek, so submissive. It should have brought him relief, but it only added to his aggravation and to the oppressive weight that was crushing him. He shook his head. "No, you sleep on the bed." He pivoted on his heel and grasped the doorknob again.

"Goodnight, Jaide," her weak, watery voice called after him.

The tightness across his chest increased to the point of pain. He paused at the door, but didn't look back at her. "There is nothing good about it." He rasped it out past the ever-growing lump in his throat, and he yanked the door open. He locked it behind him so she could not get out, and he knew the window in the room was too thick to break. They were constructed that way to keep unruly, drunken patrons from shattering the glass if things got out of hand. Even if she did manage somehow, they were up much too high for her to try and jump out.

He all but ran down the stairs and to the bar in the tavern, motioning the bartender over with vehemence. The bartender gave him something strong. Jaide didn't know what it was. He didn't care. He just threw it back and let the fiery liquid scorch a path down his throat and incinerate the lump that was restricting his airway. He let out a long, soothing breath, then motioned the bartender to give him another. A tavern wench started to swagger his direction, but he sent her scurrying away with a well placed glower and a low growl in his throat.

He downed his second drink also, then made his way outside into the rain. He upturned his face to the sky and closed his eyes, letting the water roll down his body. He'd hoped it would ease some of his turmoil, but his relief was minute. He couldn't erase the image of Amara's sad eyes. The look in them was too familiar. It was the look of someone who had given in, who had surrendered to the awful truth of their situation. He knew it because he had experienced it. He knew what Amara felt. He knew it a hundred times over and a hundred times worse. She had not yet crossed the point of no return, but the fact alone that she had surrendered at all...

It was his doing. He was the cause of it.

It made him no better than the man who'd held the club, and the whip, and the chains. It made him no better than the one who had stripped him of every last piece of his soul.

It made him sick.

He forced air into his lungs and frowned, trying desperately to get a handle on his chaotic thoughts. "She's a job, Jaide," he muttered to himself. "She's nothing more than that. How she reacts and what she feels is not your concern. Marden is going to kill her anyway. Get a grip on yourself." He repeated it mentally several times, and slowly, his cast-iron control slipped back into place. The torturous memories of his past went back into their chamber, and his breath came freely once again. He forced himself to remember the look in her eyes, to confront it within himself and dare any part of him to feel sorry for her, or to feel anything at all for that matter. He played the image over and over in his mind until it no longer bothered him, until he felt the comforting numbness that kept him sane.

But, still, he could not bring himself to return to the room where he knew she slept.

Chapter Six

Jaide didn't return all night. Because of that, Amara didn't sleep all night. She had no idea why. She was exhausted and just wanted to close her eyes and block out the world, block out everything that had happened. She wanted to escape into unconsciousness if no other escape was available to her.

But sleep would not come. She lay on the bed, listened to the rain, and waited for him to return. She didn't know why. She hated him. She loathed the very sight of him, and it was sick to think that a small part of her had actually been worried about his welfare. Not only was it sick, but it was stupid. The man was a trained killer. She doubted there were many situations that he couldn't get himself out of.

Yet, there she remained. All night.

She'd come to terms with her current situation. There wasn't much else she could do about it. She was married to her captor. She would have to ask her father if anything could be done about it once she escaped. Maybe there was some kind of loophole that would free her from the bond.

Because she would escape. She had to. Her life depended on it, and so did her father's. The people of Catlaan depended on it. Her father was a good king, but she knew he would bargain for her life. If Marden ruled Catlaan, the people would suffer greatly. And she knew he would kill her father as soon as he killed her. Her own life mattered little, but she could not allow any harm to come to her father.

She didn't resent Jaide half as much as she had the day before. She wasn't one who held onto anger for long, and though he had wrecked everything in her world, she really couldn't fault him for it. He was doing what he always did. He was being who he was. Maybe his way was not her way, but he was not her. He was an assassin. How should she expect him to behave? He was doing what he was used to and what had gotten him by in life. He wasn't the most pleasant person on the planet, but he wasn't a monster. He was just a man. Different from her, that was all. He survived the way he knew how.

She was lying on the bed when he returned. She had washed herself to the best of her ability with the water in the pitcher and the small wash basin, and she had plaited her hair back into a braid. She had his cloak pulled over her, enjoying the smell of it, when he stepped into the room, carrying several packages. His eyes slid over her momentarily, but he said nothing as he closed the door behind him and headed over to his pack.

Amara sat up. "Where have you been?" she questioned.

"My whereabouts are not your concern," he muttered. He stuffed the supplies he had gotten into his pack, stopping to throw her a look over his shoulder. "Decide yet what you're planning on pitching at me this morning? Should I start wearing battle armor?"

She rolled her eyes, but didn't form a reply. She wished she'd been able to throw something at him that had done some damage. So far, all she'd been able to do was fuel his temper.

"My jaw may never be the same," he grumbled with great sarcasm.

She smirked at that. She knew she couldn't have really hurt him much considering he was a great deal stronger than her, but she had hit him hard. For a second, it almost sounded like he was trying to joke with her, but that was something he wouldn't do so she tossed that thought aside. The man had the sense of humor of a hungry troll. "Well, you deserved it," she spat. "You tricked me into marrying you."

"I didn't trick you!" he said in frustration as he continued to load up his pack. "I told you straight out what the plan was. It's not my fault if you didn't want to believe it."

She scowled and crossed her arms over her chest, then heaved a sigh and directed her attention out the window. Every time she thought about the fact that she was married to him, her stomach turned. Tears pricked her eyes, but she blinked them away. "It's just disappointing is all," she murmured. "It's not the way I'd imagined my wedding..." She averted her eyes to the ground in sadness, feeling as if she was literally watching every dream she had burn to bits around her.

He snorted. "Life is disappointment, princess," he muttered. "The sooner you accept that, the better off you're going to be."

She stared at his broad-shouldered back in annoyance. "The better off I'm going to be?" she repeated in irritation. "How is accepting that going to make me better? I'm going to be dead!"

He spun on his heel to face her. "Then accept it and stop talking," he commanded.

Her eyes widened. "You're the one who started talking to me!"

"Well, now I told you to stop it. Put these on." He shoved a pair of black riding boots at her.

She blinked in bewilderment and frowned as she looked at the boots. She turned her questioning eyes up at him.

His brows drew together in a deep frown. "I can't have you running across land and sea with no shoes on, and I can't have you wandering around taverns in your bedclothes either, so here." He shoved another package at her. "You're going to start attracting unsavory attention unless you dress with some decency, and you'll freeze to death once we get on the ship if you're still wearing that." He folded his arms. "Can't have you die before I deliver you to Marden."

She rolled her eyes as she started to pull the brown paper off of the package. "Oh no. Dead before my own murder. No, we can't have that."

He cocked his head to the side in a curious gesture. "Does death not frighten you?"

She arched an eyebrow.

"You make light of it as if it doesn't matter."

She shrugged. "I don't want to die, but you've made it rather clear that I don't have a choice in the matter. If I am refused a say, I don't see any point in being a baby about it. It is what it is." Her response seemed to puzzle him, but he said nothing else. She unwrapped the package and pulled out a dress.

An absolutely ugly dress.

It was brown with a bodice that looked like it was made out of rabbit or fox fur. It laced up the front and had a high collar that made absolutely no sense. The sleeves were long and made out of the same material as the skirt, and she had a feeling that the entire thing would make her look like some kind of half-crazed wild woman who trapped animals and made a living off of their pelts. She blinked and was unable to stop the grimace that crossed her face.

Jaide snorted and put his hands on his hips in an agitated gesture. "Well, I'm sorry it's not up to your standards, your majesty," he mocked, "but if you think I'm going to indulge your tastes for silks and satins, you are sadly mistaken. It serves its purpose well enough. I care not if you think you'll look beautiful in it. Lord Marden won't care what you look like."

She glanced up at him and fought the urge to smile. He almost acted offended that she didn't like the dress. The fact alone that he had gotten her clothing and shoes baffled her. It was thoughtful, and the man in front of her was anything but. It contradicted his personality in the worst way.

She gave him a small smile. "Thank you, Jaide," she murmured. "Will you turn around so I can put it on?"

He scowled, but obeyed. She dressed quickly, then smoothed the fabric of the skirt and cleared her throat. He turned and she held her arms out. "How does it look?"

He blinked and stared at her for several seconds in silent contemplation before shaking his head. "You were right in making that face, Amara," he said dryly. "That is, by far, the most hideous gown I have ever seen."

She giggled, unable to stop herself. She wished she could say something cruel, or make a rude remark, but it wasn't her way. Besides, there was something different about Jaide this morning. Something...not softer, but maybe a slight bit more pliable. He was still surly and sour, and she had no doubt that he would make her life miserable if she tried to cross him, but for the moment, some of his malice was gone. It made the air in the room considerably more breathable.

He heaved a sigh and shook his head again. "Well, now I know why I became an assassin and not a tailor. I obviously have atrocious taste in clothing," he muttered.

She giggled again, delighting in his small display of humor, however grumbly and snide it may be. "You could always kill the garment," she suggested.

He raised an eyebrow and the smallest trace of a smile touched his lips. "You want me to kill it for you?" he offered.

She nodded with a grin.

"Well, it's going to cost you."

She sighed in an exaggerated fashion. "Darn it, I left all my gold in my good pair of pantaloons back home."

An unexpected chuckle was torn from his throat and her eyes widened in surprise. It must have surprised him just as much because he lowered his head and stifled it almost immediately. It was the first time she had ever heard him make any sort of sound even remotely resembling a laugh, and for some reason, it warmed her heart.

A little more of her resentment toward him slipped away.

He raised his head again once he had smothered his laughter, but the remnant of a smile still played around his sculpted lips. "I'm afraid I can't help you then," he stated.

She held her arms out to the sides. "Well...you could always take me back home. I can give you your pay there."

His lips upturned at the corners. It was a wry, slightly sadistic smile, but it was a smile nonetheless. He shook his head. "Sorry, princess, but I'm afraid you are worth much more than that sorry excuse for a garment. Have to go where the gold is." He shrugged. "My apologies."

She knew he wasn't sorry in the least, but the small bit of banter brightened her mood ever so slightly.

"Put your boots on," he commanded, all traces of playfulness leaving his face and his voice. "We have a lot of territory to cover."

She obeyed, and soon she was shackled to him again, being dragged down the stairs of the tavern and outside like a purchased slave. Jaide handed the key back over to the innkeeper and retrieved his horse from the stables. He was leading it out when Amara noticed three absolutely terrifying men making their way toward them. They were all swathed in black and seemed to walk in unison, as if they were of all one mind with one sinister purpose. Something about them set off every bad feeling in her body and her stomach churned in protest. She glanced at Jaide. He was attaching his pack to the horse's saddle and didn't notice them. He was a bear, all teeth and claws, but at the moment, she would rather have the bear than whatever kind of beasts those other three were. "Jaide," she whispered.

He looked over his shoulder at her and she pointed to the advancing men. Jaide followed where she gestured and his face grew dangerously dark. He spat out several different oaths and Amara shrank back behind him. That couldn't be a good sign. For once, she was grateful to see the air of malice return to her captor.

"Well, look who we found," one of the men called tauntingly. "Long time no see, Jaiden."

One of the other ones snorted. "Don't you know, his name is Jaide now? Jaide, the big, bad, lone wolf assassin. Too good for his pack mates."

Jaide's body grew rigid. "You're not a pack, you're a disease," he snarled. "When you're infected with a diseased limb, you have to cut it off."

One of them arched an eyebrow. "You hear that?" he said to the others. "He just called The Rezzegard a disease." He snorted and shot a malicious glower at Jaide. "You weren't too good for it when they were training you." He let out a loud, obnoxious, mocking laugh. "Oh, wait, I forgot. You were one of the ones who didn't take too well to training, weren't you? Wanted to hold onto his humanity." He snorted. "Pathetic. While all of us were rewarded for our obedience, you had to have your rebelliousness beat out of you."

Amara frowned and glanced up at Jaide. The muscles in his jaw were working angrily and his body was coiled tight. She turned her attention back toward the men and shrunk back with a shudder as one of them met her eyes and leered.

"Hey, Jaiden, after we kill you, we're going to take the wench off your hands for you." He chuckled.

"Is she a job of yours?" one of the others queried.

"Of course she is," the third scoffed. "Jaiden Sideth would never trouble himself with a woman unless there was gold involved." He nodded in Amara's direction. "Hey, don't worry, honey," he called. "We'll take you back home."

She frowned, a ripple of uncertainty running along her spine.

"Don't listen to a word they say," Jaide's voice came, low enough so only she could hear. "These men are not men, in any fashion. They will not return you to your father. Men like them are not to be trusted."

She turned her eyes up to him. "You mean men like you?" she challenged.

He met her gaze and, to her shock and bewilderment, she saw a small glimmer of sadness in the deepest part of his amazing eyes. "Precisely," he answered. "Trust them as much as you would trust me." He reached down and un-hooked her chain from his belt. "Run if you must," he muttered quietly, "but know that I will find you."

He met her eyes and a shiver went along her spine. Not a shiver of fear. A shiver she didn't recognize, but it was produced by the deadly look in his eyes and the rigid set of his features.

He pulled his sword free of the baldric on his back and went out from behind his horse to face the three men. He sighed. "So, how much is the bounty up to now?" he queried. "I have to be worth a decent amount considering you've been trying to catch me for the past ten years and still haven't managed to get it right." He gave a derisive snort. "And you say I'm the one who's pathetic?" He twirled the sword he held into a ready position as the other men started to disperse and circle him.

"You're worth enough that we tracked you all the way here," one of them muttered. "It's dangerous to come back home to Demrysk. That's much too close to the Rezzegard for you to remain safe."

Jaide gave a dry, non-joyous chuckle. "I haven't had a home since I was born." With those words, he attacked the man closest to him. His blade swept through the air and crashed with his opponents'. Then, all hell broke loose. The other two men lunged at Jaide with deadly intent, all of them swinging their swords with expert skill and precision. Amara drew in a shaky breath as she watched in morbid fascination.

Jaide moved with more speed than she had ever seen another living creature move, and his strong body rippled with power and elegance. It was different than the way the other three fought. While they were lethal in their force and strength, Jaide moved with an agility that was almost beautiful. For several heartbeats, she couldn't look away. He was breathtaking in the most primal, dangerous way.

She shook her head, regaining her wits, and turned. She ran back to the door of the inn and burst inside, the chain attached to the shackle around her wrist clanging along behind her. "Help!" she cried. "I need help!" She ran to the innkeeper and stabbed her finger toward the door. "There's some men outside. They're um...the Rezzegard? They attacked my companion!"

The innkeeper's eyes came alight with anger and he strode toward the door, grasping a sword as he did so. Amara watched him, then listened as he bellowed, "You there! Rezzegard are not welcome on this property! Leave before I summon the authorities, you mercenary scum!"

Amara swallowed, then made haste to the back door of the inn. She ran out into the city streets and kept running, hoping she could put enough distance between Jaide and herself to find a suitable place to hide. She hadn't been running that long when she began to hear the distant pounding of hoof beats. They grew louder as they approached and she ran faster until she was laboring for breath and her legs began to tingle.

The hoof beats grew to a deafening crescendo until she found herself being hoisted off the ground by the back of her collar. She didn't struggle, didn't even bother to scream. She just silently cursed her bad luck as she was flopped onto the front of Jaide's horse, his strong arm tight around her waist. His alluring, spicy scent assaulted her senses and she breathed it in before turning her eyes up to his stoic face. She briefly reflected on the thought that it was a good thing she was wearing the monstrosity of a dress he had gotten her. At least the material was durable. Otherwise, he might have ripped her head clean off of her body.

He glanced down at her as they continued out of the city. "I told you I would find you." His voice was flat. Not harsh, not gentle. Just matter-of-fact. It wasn't his voice that made strange, warm shivers work throughout her body. It was his eyes. Those eyes of death and magic. They raked over her like a touch you didn't want, but couldn't resist.

She swallowed hard. "I had to try," she rasped.

His eyes met hers: impassive, baleful, bottomless. "I know."

It was the simplest of statements, but it said more than

any other words he had uttered since her abduction. It said he wasn't angry with her for trying to escape. No more than she was angry with him for kidnapping her. He understood that she was doing what she had to do, just as she understood the same of him. It was a strange and twisted impasse, but strangely, it brought relief to her soul. They were two people unfortunate enough to have to cross paths, but it didn't change the situation for either one of them. It was as she had said earlier that morning. It was what it was. There wasn't much else that needed to be said.

With a weary sigh, she relaxed her body back against him. She was exhausted and had no idea how long he intended to travel. She yawned. "Jaide?"

"Hmm?"

She glanced up at him. "Can I lean against you and close my eyes? I'm very tired." She remembered what he'd said about not liking to be touched, but she really couldn't get around it. She was tired and there was nowhere else for her to go. She'd fall off the horse if she tried to lean forward.

She felt his body tense slightly and he glowered fiercely. "Do what you will," he grumbled.

She gave him a small, gentle smile. "Thank you." She rested her head back against his shoulder and sighed, closing her eyes. His body was warm and strong, and for some absurd reason, she felt very safe in that moment. Maybe she knew that he wouldn't let anything happen to her because, if he did, he wouldn't get paid. His reasons didn't matter. She just knew he wouldn't let anything happen to her, and that brought her comfort.

Sometimes comfort was found in the strangest places.

She slept.

Chapter Seven

Amara enjoyed the sounds of the forest at night. They were soothing to her. She had never been afraid of the wilderness like so many other women. She thrived on the untamed.

She sighed as she sat next to Jaide. She was chained to him again, and he sat as far away from her as he could get given that fact. It made her smile just slightly. It must be so strange for such a solitary person to have to be in close proximity to someone else.

She let her gaze wander around the forest they had made camp in as her mind replayed the day's events. She still shuddered when she thought of those three men. They had known Jaide. And they had said some things that made her exceedingly curious about her captor. She wanted to ask him about it, but...

She stole a sidelong glance at him. She never knew when it was all right for her to talk to Jaide. He was touchy and unpredictable. She tried to observe his body language to get a feel for his mood. He'd been absolutely silent ever since he'd recaptured her in the city, and while he was usually silent, this was a different degree. He seemed far away, lost in dark thoughts that made his ever-present scowl even more menacing. He stared into the fire, unmoving like an aloof statue. It would probably be in her best interests to remain silent.

But sometimes, Amara didn't do what was in her best interests. She was curious in a way that defied her fear of the man she sat next to. Besides, she wasn't nearly as afraid of him as she had been. Jaide snarled a lot, and he couldn't care less about what she felt emotionally, but he'd only ever hurt her physically the first night he'd captured her when he'd practically yanked her arms out of their sockets.

She took a deep breath. "Jaide?" she murmured.

He glanced over at her.

She bit her bottom lip. "Who were those men today?"

He stared ahead into the flames, his face impassive. "Demons," he finally muttered.

She arched an eyebrow. "The Devil has a bounty on your head?"

His lips turned up into a lopsided, sardonic smirk and he slid his gaze back over to her. "Something like that."

She waited for more, but nothing else came. She sighed. Speaking to this man was like trying to converse with a stone. "They called you Jaiden. Why?"

"Because that used to be my name."

This was getting her nowhere. "What's the Rezzegard?"

He swallowed and seemed to contemplate whether or not he wanted to answer her. Finally, he said, "It's a company of mercenaries."

She frowned. "You mean, people can hire them out?"

"As a unit, yes. They train mercenaries there, and when they complete their training, they are sent on assignments. They do what I do, only their profit goes directly to the Rezzegard."

She continued to watch him carefully. She wanted to know more, but she didn't want to overstep and send him into a fit of rage. "You used to be part of that?"

He nodded slowly and his body seemed to tense up as he sat there.

"How did you end up there?" she prodded. "Why don't you work with them anymore?"

He shot a dark scowl her direction. "Why do you want to know?" he snapped. "What does it matter to you?"

The firelight played across his face and she drew in a soft breath. His features were so strong. Everything about him was strong and unyielding, but she saw the faintest glimmer of pain buried deep within his eyes. This was, obviously, not an easy subject for him to discuss.

She pressed forward anyway. "Well, because..." She shrugged her shoulders and looked down at her lap. "If I'm really going to be killed when I am given over to Lord Marden, that means you are the last person I'm ever going to know. I...I want to learn about you." She glanced back up at him. "Please, let me know you...at least a little bit." He was such an enigma, a puzzle that she wanted to solve. There was more to him than the heartless man she saw every day. She felt it in the deepest part of her, and she was rarely wrong about wild things.

Her words seemed to catch him off guard and, for a fraction of a second, confusion and uncertainty flashed through his eyes before he averted his gaze to the ground. He was silent for a long while before he finally muttered, "Well, as I told you, I was born in Demrysk. I have no parents. None that I ever knew. My mother was probably a whore. I have no idea. I was raised in an orphanage. In the Demrysk orphanages, when a child is not adopted by the time he or she is fifteen, they are sent to train at the Rezzegard barracks. In Demrysk, which is a free and independent country, but with minimal resources, the Rezzegard is the closest form of military they have. "

She blinked, and her heart twisted at the information he delivered. He had been alone for his entire life. No wonder he was so cold. He'd spent the entirety of his life with the belief that no one wanted him. That was horrible... And he'd been sent to become a mercenary without a say in the matter. His whole life had been forced upon him.

"I didn't take very well to the training there," he said, his voice taking on a harsh, bitter edge. "So I left when I was twenty."

"And that's not allowed?"

He shook his head. "When you are trained by the Rezzegard, you become one of the Rezzegard. They operate as one united, lethal force. When soldiers desert, they are hunted down and dispatched."

Dispatched. She shivered at the way he said that. As if life had absolutely no value. "So, they've been hunting you?"

He nodded. "For ten years." He slid his gaze over to hers and the faintest glimmer of amusement crept into his eyes. "They underestimated me."

She smiled. "Obviously." His mouth twitched at the corners ever so slightly before he grew silent again. She watched him, her heart aching with the knowledge he had given her. She began to see him in a different light. He was not someone who killed innocents because it was what he wanted to do. It was all he knew. He'd never been offered a choice. She sighed. "What was it like there?"

"Where?"

"At the Rezzegard barracks?"

The air around him seemed to grow dark and his face took on a black, stonelike expression. He stared into the leaping flames of the fire for a long, silent moment. "When I met with Lord Marden to discuss his proposition for your kidnapping, we met at a tavern called The Devil's Lair," he stated. He shook his head. "It made me laugh."

She frowned, wondering what that had to do with anything. "Why?"

He slowly turned his gaze back up to hers, his green eyes glittering with malevolence and dark things. "Because if the Devil has a lair, I've been there...and it doesn't come with tavern wenches and liquor."

A shiver went along her spine at the way he delivered the information. His eyes held a thousand things, black, painful things that made her heart twist in empathy for him. What kind of life had he known? Something terrible, something not even fit to be called a life.

He let out a derisive snort and turned his gaze away from hers. "What's wrong, princess? Your delicate stomach turning at my sordid history?"

She frowned. He'd obviously mistaken her look of concern for one of fear and loathing. She shook her head. "No..."

He slid her a sidelong glance. "Must be a pretty despicable creature to someone like you."

"Not at all!" she stated emphatically. It was enough to make him shoot her a curious frown. "Jaide, you're not despicable for living a life you were forced into."

He shifted back to face her. "You mean you do not find fault with me for my occupation? For my lifestyle?"

He seemed genuinely surprised, and she shook her head.

His frown deepened. "You do not find me hideously repulsive? I kidnapped you and forced you into marriage, destroyed everything in your life, as you so vehemently shouted at me, yet you find no fault with me?"

He almost sounded angry, as if it irritated him that she didn't abhor the very sight of him. She heaved a sigh and glanced down at his hands. They were resting in his lap, strong hands...hands that could so easily end a life. Hands that had shed innocent blood.

She reached out and slipped her fingers across his wrist. His entire body tensed at her touch and he tried to yank his arm away, but she was persistent. She shackled his wrist with her fingers and held on. The man had never known gentleness, had never been shown any sort of kindness or understanding. She knew it was foreign to him, and probably unwelcome, but she had to try. It was her way. It was her nature. Take care of the wild things... It was what she had always loved.

She knew he could very easily remove her hold from him, but surprisingly, he didn't. He curled his fingers into a fist and his entire arm went rigid, but he allowed her to continue touching him. "I find no fault with you, Jaide," she murmured.

He drew his breath in sharply and stared at her as if she'd managed to manifest a third eye or an extra limb...like she was completely and totally out of her mind.

She met his eyes with purpose. "How can I find fault with someone who is doing the only thing he's ever known?" She shook her head. "You're not repulsive. You're not a monster. You're a survivor. You've done what you must to survive. That is all."

He stared at her for a long, silent moment, his eyes searching her face and reflecting stunned uncertainty. Her heart beat out a peculiar rhythm as she gazed into his eyes. They looked so haunted, like they had witnessed more than any living soul should have to. They were magnificent, and dangerous, and she wanted to drown in them. It should have alarmed her, but it didn't.

He cleared his throat and tore his gaze from hers, jerking his wrist out of her grasp. "Stop touching me," he rasped. "I don't like to be touched, especially by my captives."

Her lips turned up at the corners. "How many captives have you had?"

"You're the first and the last," he stated. "I'm not in the kidnapping business. The only reason I did this job is because the money was irresistible." He glanced back at her with an evil glint in his eye and he gave a wry smirk. "You're probably worth more than I am."

She smiled. "So, how come you don't like to be touched?"

He huffed and met her eyes with an exasperated expression. "Do you never shut your mouth, woman? Am I in an interrogation?" His brows drew together in a disgruntled scowl. "I have already told you more than you need to know. Enough talking."

"But—" She was nowhere near satisfied.

"I said, enough!" he barked. "Do as you're told!"

She rolled her eyes and sighed. "Yes, master," she grumbled. She turned her attention back to the fire and watched the flames leap and dance for several minutes before she said, "For the record, I don't have a delicate stomach. If I did, the first meal you ever cooked me would have killed me instantly." He made some sort of growling noise that she imagined was supposed to be threatening, but it only made her smile. She pulled her knees up and rested her chin on them. "I always enjoyed cooking. You're lucky for that. At least you'll know what real food tastes like for a little while before I'm killed."

He snorted. "Where did you learn to cook amidst all your frills and finery?" he grumbled sarcastically.

She shot him a petulant look. "I'll have you know that I spent more time hunting, cooking, and playing in the meadows with the servants than I ever did in any kind of frill or finery." She turned her attention back to the fire and a pang of grief stabbed at her heart as she thought of home. "My father loves the outdoors," she said quietly. "I did everything with him. He taught me all he knew." A painful lump constricted her throat and she grew silent. She missed her father so much. He had to be worried sick. She wondered if she would ever see him again.

"Feeling sorry for yourself?" Jaide scoffed.

She bristled, then turned to meet his eyes brazenly. "No. Why? Are you?"

He raised an eyebrow in mild surprise. "I never feel sorry for myself," he muttered.

She lifted her chin with pride. "Well, what do you know? We have something in common. Neither do I." He said nothing and returned his attention to the fire and the dark forest beyond. Her eyes narrowed. "How many wives have you had?"

He slowly shifted his attention back to her. "You're the

first and the last," he grumbled sardonically.

She snorted. "Till death do us part," she mumbled. "How sickeningly poetic." She sighed and held up her left hand, letting her eyes graze over it for a second. "You didn't even get me a ring," she nettled. He heaved another exasperated huff and opened his mouth to speak, but she giggled and put her hand up. "I know, I know. 'Enough talking. Shut your mouth, woman.' I get it. Fine." He tried to snarl at her again, but she just smiled. He was all prickles and spines, but he seemed slightly more human to her now that she knew a bit about his past. He had reason to be the way he was, and she accepted that. It was easier to handle him if she knew some of what had caused his disposition. In order to understand something wild, you had to see the world from its eyes.

She stretched out next to the fire and sighed, letting her gaze travel across the great expanse of the cloudless sky. The stars twinkled merrily at her, and she smiled as she picked out all of the different constellations. As a small girl, she had loved finding them with her father and listening as he told her their stories.

She glanced over at Jaide, and even though she knew she should probably just leave him alone, she didn't. Something within her hated how isolated he was and had always been. It must be such a lonely existence. To never know companionship, or friendship, or any kind of love. To only ever know how to be cold, and how to kill, and how to survive. It chilled her to the bone. That was no life. That was barely even an existence.

"Jaide."

She saw his shoulders move with a large sigh before he slid his gaze back over to her. "Yes?" he drawled.

She smothered a smile. "Do you know where Ulyxes is?"

He shook his head in complete exasperation. "What?"

She bit her bottom lip in order to keep her rebellious grin under control. Well, at least she knew that, by the time they reached her executioner, she would have done everything in her power to drive her captor out of his mind. There was a small amount of comfort in that. "Ulyxes." She pointed up at the sky. "It's a constellation. He's a warrior."

He glanced up at the sky then shook his head with a scowl. "I must have missed the day they taught astronomy at the Rezzegard barracks," he muttered, his voice saturated in sarcasm.

She rolled her eyes. "Come here, I'll show you."

"I can see fine from here. Besides, I thought I told you—"

"Enough talking. Yes, I know. But this is different."

He raised an eyebrow. "Is it? Because from where I sit I still hear your voice and see your jaws flapping."

A giggle was torn from her throat before she could sensor it and he frowned in disapproval. She couldn't help it. His frustration was amusing. She met his eyes and smiled. "Just come look, Jaide," she coaxed, her voice soft. "I'm not going to bite you." She looked back up at the sky. "They tell a story."

He stared at her for a long moment, then finally heaved an enormous, snarling sigh and moved to lie down beside her. "Do not touch me," he commanded.

She held her hands up in an innocent gesture and turned her attention back to the sky as he lay down. "All right, look. See that cluster of stars off to the right? That's Ulfarr, the wolf. He's the greatest enemy of Ulyxes, the warrior." She drew her finger in a slight arch across to the left side of the sky. "Ulfarr keeps looking for him, you see." She glanced over at Jaide to see him actually paying attention to what she was saying. She smiled. He was still frowning. He was always frowning. "And down here is Elendria." She drew her finger in another subtle arch to a cluster of stars below both of the others. "She is Ulyxes' one true love, but she's chasing Ulfarr. You see?" She pointed back up to the wolf constellation. "She chases him to avenge the wrong he's done to Ulyxes, but Ulfarr is chasing Ulyxes." She drew her finger back to the warrior. "And Ulyxes is chasing after Elendria." She circled her finger between the three. "And they never catch one another because they're always ahead of the other. They travel in a circle across the sky every night...for eternity." She dropped her hand and sighed. "It's depressingly beautiful."

"Why is it depressing?" Jaide questioned.

"Well, because. Ulyxes will never be able to catch his love because she's always ahead of him. They can never be together."

"But he's eluding the wolf. He's staying alive. Isn't that the important thing?"

She turned her head to look at him. "But what is life

without love?"

His frown deepened and he met her eyes. "Life without love is life. Period."

She heaved a sigh. "Well, maybe one day you will think differently when you have something you love."

He arched an eyebrow and snorted. "Heaven help that unfortunate thing." He sat up. "Go to sleep, Amara. I'm finished with your never-ending prattle and your fairy tales."

She rolled her eyes and turned on her side, knowing it was fruitless to attempt to talk to him anymore. He was done. She'd pushed him to the limit and she knew better than to try her luck. She smiled as she drifted off to sleep because, despite his grumbling, she had actually succeeded in getting him to converse with her. It was a small battle to be won, but it was a victory nonetheless.

Chapter Eight

This woman was going to put him in an early grave. She never stopped talking. Ever. And while she may not converse more than the average human, to him that was much more than he was used to. He was always by himself and the most conversation he ever shared with another was when he was negotiating a job. This woman talked just to talk. About everything.

All day he had traveled with her on the front of his horse, rattling on about this and that and whatever. He knew the names of all of the kitchen staff that worked at her home. He knew all about her horse in more detail than he would prefer. He knew that when she'd been five she'd fallen out of a tree and broken her leg, and against his will, he knew all about the dreams she'd had of her wedding before he'd destroyed everything; her words, not his. She'd stopped listening when he told her to be quiet, or she would be quiet for a few blessed minutes and then start on a different subject. He didn't know if she was doing it on purpose to deliberately make him want to tear his hair out, or if she was just doing it for herself. Maybe it made her feel better to talk. If she *was* doing it with the sole purpose to drive him insane, he almost respected her for it.

Whatever her reason, by the time they'd found a place to camp for the night, he was so tense his teeth hurt from how much he'd been clenching them all day. It was a couple hours away from sunset and he just wanted to get off of his horse, tie Amara down to something, and disappear in the forest for a while. The *silent* forest.

"Jaide?"

He gnashed his teeth together again, causing a pain to

shoot along the line of his jaw. "Confound it, woman," he grumbled as he began to unhook his pack from the horse's saddle. "Do you never cease talking?"

She smirked as she stroked the horse's nose affectionately. "How come you don't go by Jaiden anymore?"

He heaved a weary sigh. "Because that man no longer exists."

She frowned in curiosity. "What happened to him?"

"He died." His voice had more than its share of bite to it, but she seemed completely unperturbed by it.

She arched an eyebrow. "He died?" When he didn't respond further, she put her hand on her hip. "You're going to have to elaborate on that one."

He rolled his eyes heavenward and forced himself to stay put and not strangle her on the spot. He slowly turned his eyes to her. "Jaiden was not conducive to helping me live my life," he muttered. "I killed him to survive. You understand?"

She stared at him for a long moment before something that resembled sadness came to life in her eyes. "Yes, I understand," she murmured.

He gave a curt nod and turned back to his pack.

"What was he like?" she all but whispered. "Jaiden?"

His movements stilled and his heart made an uncomfortable flip, reminding him, once again, that it still existed. He swallowed and stared straight ahead, remembering the boy in the field of amaranths. Barely eighteen, broken, beaten... "Weak," he snarled. He scowled, yanked his pack off, and flung it to the ground. The sudden movement startled his horse and it danced away from him with a surprised whinny.

Amara immediately took it by the bridle and reached up to soothe it, running her delicate hands over his nose and ears while whispering soft words. Jaide watched as the horse eased almost instantly at her touch. Its ears twitched back and forth and he bunted her in the chest, making her giggle.

Jaide's eyes traveled over her face and curling, platinum hair. Every line of her body was etched in grace and ethereal beauty. Even in that terrible dress. Even in her less than favorable circumstances. Light radiated from her like the sun's rays. She smiled even when she knew she was sentenced to death. She found joy even as he tried to rob it from her. It made no sense to him. None at all. How could someone have their entire life destroyed in a matter of days and then find happiness by merely patting a horse? How could a woman rest against her captor, tell him tale after tale about her life, and show him stories in the stars?

She threw things at him, hit him, stabbed him, spit in his face and told him how much she hated him, yet she claimed she wanted to know him. She asked him questions about his life as if he mattered when he knew he didn't. And she touched him as if she cared when he knew she couldn't.

His wrist tingled at the mere memory of her touch the night before. It was the only gentle touch he had ever known, despite how unwelcome it had been. She told him she found no fault with him for what he was and what he did. How could that be? He had ruined her entire existence, and yet, she found no fault with him? She accepted that he did what he did to survive? How? How could she see past the horrific fiend he knew himself to be?

She giggled again as his horse searched her palm for treats. "Do all creatures bring you such pleasure?" he found himself asking.

She turned her soft eyes up to him and nodded with a smile. "My father used to call me Amaranth of the Wild Things."

He arched an eyebrow and folded his arms across his chest. He snorted. "What, you tamed them all and made them your docile pets?"

She shot him a glare. "Of course not! I don't want to tame them. I accept them for what they are and respect them." She reached up to pat his horse on the nose. "In return, they respect me as well. We understand one another."

"But that horse is tame."

"No, he isn't," she protested with a shake of her head. "He just does what you say because he likes you."

Both of his eyebrows came up on that one. "He told you that, did he?" She flashed him an impish grin and nodded. Something about the look made his stomach clench in a foreign way. He immediately tried to force the feeling away and replace it with coldness. "Don't be ridiculous," he grumbled. "He's just an animal."

She looked absolutely affronted and her glower could have rivaled one of his. "How dare you say that. He is not just an animal. That's like saying you're just a stupid oaf with no personality. While it may be true, it's not all there is to you, is it?"

He frowned, pretty sure he should be offended, but he let it slide for the moment. "I take care of him," he countered. "I feed him."

"Do you pat him like this?" she asked as she continued to lavish affection on the animal.

His frown deepened. "I brush him."

She stared agape at him. "That's all? You're trying to tell me you've never touched your own horse other than to brush him?" She snorted. "He'll only take that for so long, you know. Sooner or later, he's going to trample you in your sleep."

"Is that so?" This woman was out of her mind. Talking to horses...

"Yes, it is so. Now, come over here and show him you care."

He blinked in bewilderment. "Excuse me?"

"Come on," she urged, stepping aside.

"He's liable to bite my fingers off!" he exclaimed. He'd never touched anything with kind intent in his entire life. Only the amaranth. That was the only thing he had ever bestowed a caress upon.

"Jaide!" she snapped. "What are you, ten years old? You're a big, mean assassin who is afraid of your own animal? Come touch your horse!" She shoved her hands on her hips and her voice snapped with a definite royal command.

He scowled at her, although he knew his scowl had to look more perplexed than menacing. "I do not take orders from my—"

"Coward," she interrupted.

He bristled and felt a steely kind of calm come over him. He slid his gaze over her, hoping to make her squirm with the dark warning he knew his eyes possessed. "I am no coward," he growled.

She didn't shrink away, didn't even flinch. She just retained her challenging posture and stared him straight in the eye. "Do it then."

He hated her right then. Hated her more than anyone he'd ever come in contact with. He hated her because she didn't fear him as she should. He hated her because she saw straight through him and knew exactly how to get what she wanted. No one had ever been able to do that in his lifetime. *No one.*

His horse must have sensed his anger because he tried to shy away from him. Jaide turned and grabbed the bridle, causing the horse to jerk his head back and make a noise of surprise. Its nostrils flared and its ears twitched back and forth uneasily. Jaide stared into his great black eyes, feeling furious and foolish and overwhelmed. It was stupid that he didn't even know how to bestow kindness upon something as simple as his own beast, but life... He'd been taught not to value it in any form. He'd been taught not to care, not to feel for any living thing. He'd only been taught violence and survival. Not once had his fingers of death ever touched anything with kindness other than the petals of the one flower he could not resist.

His horse made an uneasy nicker and a tremor went along Jaide's spine. He wasn't even sure what emotion caused it for he had banished his emotions long ago, but he was pretty certain it had something to do with self-loathing. He let out a long, defeated breath and felt the anger melt out of him. An ache settled in his chest and he slowly raised his hand to place it on his horse's nose. He slid his fingers up to the animal's head, then back down. The horse instantly eased and nudged him in the chest the same way he had done to Amara.

Jaide felt the corners of his mouth twitch and he reached up to scratch the horse's ears, which caused him to whinny and lift his front lip, showing all of his teeth. Amara burst out laughing and a chuckle that he couldn't help rumbled through Jaide's chest.

Amara came to stand next to him and she reached up to rub the horse's ears also. "See, I told you. You made him smile."

A wry smile curved Jaide's lips. "Is that what that was?"

She nodded with a giggle and ran her hand down the horse's nose as Jaide was running his up. Their fingers brushed over one another briefly and Jaide pulled his hand away as strange, fiery tingles worked their way up his arm. He frowned and curled his fingers into a fist, trying to banish the unwelcome sensation.

He glanced down at Amara, standing so close to him, her eyes alight with her joy. It was the second time she had brought him laughter, even in such a small form. Two times in a few days from one woman when nothing had brought him laughter in well over twenty years. He didn't know what to do with it. Laughter felt strange when it lived within him, like it should be squelched immediately. He looked at her and wondered what it felt like to be so free to laugh. Would it be liberating? Or would it be a weakness someone could use to their advantage?

She turned her eyes up to him and grinned. The sunlight reflected on her hair, turning it golden. Her eyes grew soft for a moment and she shook her head, then reached up and tucked back a rebellious strand of his hair.

He drew his breath in sharply and retreated from the touch, shooting her a look that he wanted to seem like a warning, but he knew it reflected more surprise than anything.

Her eyes widened as if she'd just realized what she'd done and she held her hands up, taking a step away. "I'm sorry," she said. "I know, no touching. I'm sorry." She shook her head. "It was just...instinct, I guess." She looked down at the ground with a puzzled frown.

He cleared his throat and took several steps away from her until he realized they were still chained together. He unhooked the chain from his belt, then looped it through the metal stake and drove it into the ground. "Make camp," he ordered. "I'm going hunting." He strode away from her and disappeared into the trees.

* * * *

"He's going hunting, but he forgot his bow and arrows," Amara murmured to herself as she watched Jaide's proud, powerful form melt into the thick of the forest. She sighed and set about preparing the camp.

She had no idea what had come over her to make her reach up and touch him the way she had. It was just...the way he'd smiled. She'd rarely seen him smile at all, and had never seen him look as if he was actually experiencing joy.

The smile he'd given at the horse's theatrics had been small, but it had reached his cold eyes, and that tiny gesture had softened every harsh line of his cruel, magnificent face. She couldn't help herself. Seeing the roguish strand of ebony hair falling across his forehead had prompted her to act without any forethought. She'd called it instinct, and that was what it had to have been, but for some reason she had trouble comprehending, she still felt like a hundred birds were fluttering in her stomach.

She shook her head, banishing her strange thoughts and feelings, and started to gather wood for a fire. The horse whinnied suddenly and Amara looked over to see him dancing in place, as if something troubled him. She stood slowly as the hair on the back of her neck prickled in warning the way it had the night Jaide had abducted her. She shivered and glanced around at the trees. All seemed normal, but a strange, foreboding sensation drifted across her skin like an ominous breeze, causing her body to go cold all over.

Something was wrong. Something was coming.

Chapter Nine

Touch. It was something so unfamiliar to Jaide. He tried to remember a time in his life when he'd been touched with anything other than cruel intent, but he couldn't. Not really. The tavern hussies who would occasionally sling their arms around his shoulders or plop themselves into his lap didn't count. They were as fake as their perfume and rouge.

No one had ever touched him kindly in the orphanage. That place had been no better than a prison. He'd had no friends, and all of the other boys had only liked to try and beat on him for a laugh. Then at the barracks...

He shuddered. There had been no such thing as gentleness there in any form. The only sort of touch he had been taught was the kind that hurt, the kind that stung, the kind that bruised, the kind that burned, and the kind that caused blood to flow. Those were the only touches he had ever known.

He'd never had anyone attempt to offer comfort the way Amara had the night before, and he'd never had anyone do something so simple and insignificant as to reach up and brush the hair back from his face. Her smile...

It had seemed so second nature for her. A smile of exquisite and unsurpassed beauty bestowed upon someone so filthy, followed by a tender touch that would mean nothing to everyone else.

Everywhere she touched burned.

But it wasn't a burn like he was accustomed to. It was painful, but not in the way he knew. It was a different kind of pain. It didn't mar his flesh, didn't bruise, didn't cut. It stabbed and sliced straight through all he'd become, all he'd made himself into in order to survive. It moved through solid, impenetrable walls of iron and stone, wrapped around the heart he'd locked away behind bars, and squeezed until he couldn't breathe.

It was the most excruciating pain he had ever experienced.

With a heavy sigh, Jaide rested his head back against the trunk of the tree he sat under. The birds sang in the treetops, cheerful and oblivious to the torment of the human below them, and he let his ears fill with their joyous, carefree song. For some reason, it reminded him of Amara.

He knew they were there long before the popping of a twig sounded their approach. He could feel their presence like an evil wind.

"Sleeping on the job, *Jaiden*?" one of them sneered. He snorted. "You're getting sloppy."

"I knew you were there," Jaide muttered, his eyes remaining closed. "You've been following since Demrysk." What did these fools take him for? He had been one of them. He knew their tricks. He'd known it was only a matter of time before they made their move. He hadn't slept the entire night before because of it, and he'd escaped into the trees under the guise of hunting to draw them away from Amara. She was not part of this battle. "What I'd really like to know is why one of you didn't just fire an arrow into me when my back was turned? Wouldn't that have made the entire affair that much easier and faster?"

"And deprive one of us of the privilege of feeling our sword slice through your body?" another scoffed. "Now that isn't very nice at all."

Jaide opened his eyes and stared at the trio in front of him. His stomach turned. Smug, arrogant curs with no souls to speak of. Even less than he possessed. They were the worst creatures in the known world, not even fit to be called men. It made him ill to think he had, at one time, been one of them. It made him even more nauseous to think that part of him always would be. The taint of the Rezzegard had been ingrained into him. It was like a slow moving, poisonous parasite that would always live within him.

All was silent for several heartbeats as the four of them seemed to assess the situation. Then, with the speed he prided himself for, Jaide pulled a dagger from his boot and sent it spiraling into the chest of the middle man, dropping him to the ground instantly. The other two barely even registered the fall of their companion and Jaide jumped into a standing position, pulling his sword free from its sheath and blocking the blows of the other two with a clamorous ring.

* * * *

Amara's eyes widened as she heard what distinctly sounded like steel against steel coming from deep within the trees. Her heart leapt up into her throat and hammered there, threatening to choke her. "Jaide," she whispered. Her mind filled with visions of those hideous men at the inn in Demrysk. Had they followed them after the innkeeper had dispersed the quarrel? She shook her head. Of course they had. They were being paid to bring Jaide down. Jaide didn't halt in his purpose, didn't falter. If that was the way he operated, these men would be that much worse. They had hunted him for ten years. They would not stop because one innkeeper had thwarted their battle. It would only be a small delay to them.

Jaide is in danger. The message echoed through her mind and her heart, sending panic coursing through her like icy ocean waves. Without thinking, she began to take off in a run toward the trees, but was halted by the shackle around her wrist. It bit into her skin as the chain pulled tight, reaching the end of its length, and she stumbled as her progress was abruptly stopped. She turned with a scowl and tried to pull the stake free of the ground, but he always hammered it in so far. It was impossible to get a grip on it. She scanned the area for something within her reach that she might be able to use to pry the stake out, but there was nothing.

More ringing of steel sounded from the forest and fear seized her heart. *Jaide is in danger*. It kept repeating in her mind, becoming all consuming and the only thing she could concentrate on. She had to help him. It didn't matter that he was a skilled assassin. Luck only lasted for so long. Those men were brutal and evil. They were motivated by greed and hatred. She had no doubt in her mind that Jaide could hold his own, but she refused to sit idly by and wait, just hoping that the person who emerged from the trees when the battle was over happened to be Jaide and not one of those terrible mercenaries. She would take Jaide one hundred times over, even with his foul temper and apathetic heart. At least he didn't hurt her. There was no telling what those other men would do. She didn't want to find out.

And she didn't want to find out what they could do to Jaide if they got the upper hand. She didn't want him dead. She didn't want him hurt. He was surly and irritating, but he'd been hurt enough in his life. All he'd ever known was battle. All he'd ever known was fighting alone. He deserved someone at his right hand. He deserved to know that someone cared...because she did. More than she should.

With determined focus and a kind of power she didn't even know she possessed, she wrapped the chain around both of her arms for leverage and braced her feet solidly on the ground, then pulled with every ounce of her might. She yanked on the chain over and over, screaming her frustration, until the stake began to wiggle free of the earth and, finally, broke loose. She grabbed the slackened end of the chain up in her hand so it would not trip her as she ran. She then slung Jaide's quiver of arrows over her shoulder, grasped his bow in her free hand, and dashed into the trees.

＊ ＊ ＊ ＊

"You've gotten slow, Jaiden," one of the men taunted. "You never used to be this slow when we sparred as boys."

Jaide glowered, continuing to defend as the other two attacked from in front and behind. He was constantly turning, constantly moving and trying to deflect attempts to run him through in the front and the back. It was next to impossible with only one sword, especially with the way they kept circling, and he would be lying to himself if he said he wasn't growing weary. These men were not average men. Two average men he could handle. Two soldiers even. Two Rezzegard mercenaries were a different story. They were faster, deadlier, and had absolutely nothing to lose. He was lucky he had killed the first with his well-thrown dagger. Otherwise, he probably would have been dead long before now. Being outnumbered by the Rezzegard was a recipe for fatality.

"He wasn't slow back then because he was terrified of his

punishment," the other man continued. "Every time he turned around, he was getting beaten by the commander." He shook his head. "Hardheaded weren't you, Jaiden? We all knew how much the commander enjoyed torture. We all learned early on not to disobey him. You were a poor study."

Jaide blocked a swing intended to lop his head off and sweat trickled down the side of his face from his exertion. He ignored the mockery, knowing it was meant as a distraction.

"Why did you disobey for so long?" the first one asked in a tone that held genuine wonder.

Jaide met his eyes briefly and saw a small opening in the fact that the man was momentarily concentrating on the conversation and not his sword. "Because I am not a mindless dog to be told how to live and what to do," he muttered. "I was not like you then. I am not like you now. It doesn't matter how much I am beaten. It doesn't matter how much I fight like you or act like you. My independence and my freedom are my own. No one will ever take that from me." He anticipated that the man attacking him from behind was going to swing high, as he had been alternating between the two for the last several seconds. As he raised his arm, Jaide kicked him in the stomach, sending him crashing back against a tree trunk. It left him open for a slash across the arm from the blade of the other, but it gave him enough opportunity to out-maneuver him and drive his sword through his mid-section.

He pulled his sword free as his one-time companion crumpled to the ground, and was in the process of turning to finish the battle with the other when a searing pain tore through his back and the left side of his body. He roared with the agony of it, then looked down to see the blade of a sword protruding from his chest and dripping with his own blood. The blade twisted in a way that dropped him to his knees, then was yanked free, tearing another pain-laden cry from his throat.

He dropped his weapon as his right hand came to clutch at the wound and he squeezed his eyes shut against the pain every ragged breath caused. He was done for. It was inevitable.

"The great assassin finally falls," the man snarled, raising his sword high. "And you did me the favor of taking care of the other two for me. I thank you for that. That means the gold is all mine."

Jaide closed his eyes, waiting for the killing blow. It was typical that his death would be at the end of a Rezzegard blade. He would never escape them. Even his death could not be his own.

"Jaide!"

He heard a great trampling rustle come from the trees beyond and he turned his head toward the noise, as well as the sound of his name. He felt as if he was moving exceedingly slow, and his fingers dripped with his own blood from the gaping wound he had his hand over. Sounds were dulled and his vision was not as clear as it should be, but he did make out one very important and unexpected thing.

Through the trees Amara crashed, bursting into the clearing like a warrior goddess, her blonde hair cascading around her shoulders in wild, unruly tangles. She didn't look frightened or uncertain. She looked fierce. A heavy length of chain she held in one hand dropped to the forest floor as she reached behind her and pulled an arrow free of a quiver and aligned it with the bow. The arrow flew, and found its home in his would-be executioner's shoulder. Another one flew, and another, and while it felt to him as if everything took a much longer length of time than it should have, it must have only been a matter of seconds.

The last Rezzegard mercenary fell to the ground.

Jaide watched as Amara flung the bow aside and ran toward him, and he was aware of her calling his name, but it sounded muffled to his ears, and his vision blurred and swam threateningly. He groaned and slumped forward, still clutching his bleeding wound.

"Jaide!" she cried, falling down on her knees in front of him and taking him by the shoulders.

He howled in pain at the sudden movement and white spots danced before his already hazy vision.

"Jaide, oh my gosh," she whispered.

He heard a rending tear and smothered another roar as a great amount of pressure was suddenly applied to both his chest and his back.

"Was that all of them?" she questioned.

He nodded, though it seemed to take a great amount of effort to do that simple movement. Breathing suddenly felt very difficult. "Where...did you lean to shoot like that?" he gasped.

"My father. Jaide, we have to get you back to camp. Please, can you stand?"

"How did you get free?" He closed his eyes as waves of dizziness washed over him.

"Stubbornness. Jaide, please, I need to get you back to camp. You're going to die if I don't."

He heard panic in her voice and he thought it was strange. He opened his eyes, and though her face was blurred, he saw the concern mirrored in her gray eyes. Concern for him? How? How was that possible? He frowned. "I...I don't understand. Why...why did you—"

"Jaide!" she cried, her voice snapping like a whip and holding a faint note of hysteria. "Please, I can't move you by myself. Help me!" She looped his right arm over her shoulders and tried to lift him. He did his best to assist her, but his legs didn't seem to cooperate. His entire body felt so horribly heavy.

He was tired. Good lord, he was so incredibly tired... The pain in his back and chest dissipated until all he felt was the tremendous need to sleep. His vision distorted and darkened. He couldn't help it. He was too tired. He had been so tired for so long... Finally, he could rest...

Chapter Ten

"Jaide!" Amara cried, tears filling her eyes. "Jaide, please!" She put her head to his chest to see if he was alive. It still rose and fell with shallow breaths, but his face was terribly pale. Panic threatened to consume her and her chest constricted to the point of pain. Her thoughts spun wildly in her head, not connecting in any sort of rational way. She brought her hands to her head and tangled her fingers in her hair, trying to get control of herself.

Her eyes fell on Jaide's face and pain squeezed her heart. There was no way she could get him back to camp. His blood was everywhere, staining his shirt, the fabric she had placed to his wound, and the ground. She had to act quickly. He was dying!

Forcing her hysteria away, she pressed the fabric she'd torn from her dress deeper into the wound, then brushed her fingers across his face. "Hold on," she whispered. "Please hold on." She found the key for the shackle around her wrist attached to his belt and she unlocked it, flinging it away from her as far as she could. She would run faster without the chain weighing her down.

She tore through the trees, sprinting until her chest labored for breath. She broke through into the small clearing where their supplies were, gathered Jaide's pack and slung both it and herself into the horse's saddle. She spurred him into a gallop and dodged through the trees back to Jaide, praying he would still be alive. He couldn't die. Not now. Not like this.

As she neared where the battle had taken place, she didn't even wait for the horse to stop completely before she fell out of the saddle and scrambled back to Jaide. He was still breathing, but he looked even more ashen than before. She took a quick look at her surroundings and her heart slammed against her rib cage as she only counted two Rezzegard bodies where there had once been three. She stood and grabbed Jaide's sword immediately, scanning the area and listening closely to the sounds of the forest, but nothing seemed out of the ordinary. She swallowed hard and shook her head, trying to push her fear away. There were more important things to attend to right now. Wherever the man was, he was gravely wounded and not in the position to attack any time soon. She would just have to keep a very close watch, especially during the night.

With as much speed as her trembling fingers would allow, Amara hastily made a fire and gathered supplies from Jaide's pack. She wrenched the dagger free of the dead man's chest and wiped the blade clean, then placed it in the flames of the fire.

The blood flow coming from Jaide's wound had slowed enough to buy her several precious minutes, but time was of the essence and she knew that.

She unbuckled his baldric and slipped it off of his body, then tore his shirt straight down the middle. She cleansed the wound to the best of her ability with some of the drinking water, but knew that bandaging it would not be enough. The blade of the sword had been twisted in a way that kept it from closing. She would have to cauterize it.

She was amazed and grateful that the sword had some-how managed to miss any vital organs. Just an inch to the left and it would have pierced his heart. She imagined that's what the mercenary had been going for.

Once the blade of the dagger was red hot, Amara re-moved it and slid the flat over Jaide's flesh, cringing at the sound and the smell. It was only after the wound had been sealed that she was able to take a full breath. While he was far from out of danger, at least she knew he would not bleed to death.

She brushed back some of his ebony hair in a gentle ca-ress and tried to make him as comfortable as possible by pil-lowing his head on some bunched up clothing and covering him over with the horse's saddle blanket. It was the only blanket he had and she knew the cloak she slept with would hardly be adequate.

Once she had done as much as she could with what she was given, she set about the task of dragging the two dead men far enough out of the camp so that wild animals and scavengers would not venture near. She flung dirt over the spilled blood and searched the forest plants until she found several herbs that held medicinal properties. She ground one into a paste and placed it over Jaide's wound, securing it with a makeshift bandage made from strips of material she'd sliced out of one of his shirts. It was the second shirt she had destroyed, and he would probably holler at her for it when he found out, but she would welcome his hollering over his eternal silence. She also cleaned and applied some of the herbal remedy to the gash along his arm. It was shallow, but still needed tending.

When she had done everything she could for Jaide, the sun had set and night had descended. She tethered the horse, fed him, and made something passable to eat, even though she didn't have much of an appetite. She made a tea with the other plant she had found and forced some of it down Jaide's throat, hoping it would help to combat any fever or infection. She spread his bedroll out next to him and sat on it, propping herself up against the trunk of a sturdy tree. She gripped Jaide's sword tightly in her hand and had all of the other weapons close by.

Amara was not someone who was afraid of the dark, or afraid of the forest. She enjoyed the outdoors, but tonight, her heart refused to stop pounding. And her fingers refused to stop shaking. Nothing in her life had ever seemed as black and ominous as this night did. Especially when she knew that, somewhere out there, a deadly mercenary might still be alive.

She glanced over at Jaide. He was so still and pale. Tears stung her eyes and she bit her bottom lip. She reached her hand out and touched his skin, needing to feel its warmth and know he lived. Even though she could see his chest rise and fall with his breath, she needed to touch him. She needed to reassure herself.

She threaded her fingers in his dark hair and studied the texture of the silken strands.

Her eyes traveled across the planes and angles of his

face and a soft sigh escaped her lips. She had seen many handsome men in her life. Many of the soldiers who belonged to the Royal Guard had been strong and striking. Jaide made every single one of them seem like a scrawny, naïve youth. Every sinew of his body, every strong curve and line, reflected complete masculinity. He was dominant in every way, his presence dwarfing even that of the strongest men she had known. It pained her to see him lying so helpless.

She trailed her fingers across his forehead and down his cheek, wondering why his life seemed to matter so much to her. True, she was not someone who thought any life of little value, but for some reason, her heart ached at the thought of something happening to Jaide. It made her wonder when, in all of his snarling nastiness, she had come to care for him at all. She'd hated him three days ago, hated him for destroying her life, her dreams, and everything she had ever known. He was transporting her to a man who would end her life. She should abhor the very sight of him. She should have let the Rezzegard mercenaries do away with him and then run back to Catlaan where she would be safe.

But she couldn't do that. The thought had never even entered her mind. When she'd heard the battle break out in the trees, the first thing she had thought of was to help Jaide. Nothing else. Then, when she'd seen him lying bleeding on the ground, the thought had intensified. Not for one brief second had she even considered leaving him to die. He didn't deserve to die. Jaide had never known anything but suffering and cold violence. He deserved to know what beauty life could hold in it before it was brutally snatched from him. She never would have been able to live with herself if she'd left him to bleed to death, slain by the people he hated above all others.

Her attention snapped to him and she drew her breath in sharply as he turned his head and his brow furrowed. His eyes opened slowly and he glanced around, looking disoriented. When his gaze of gorgeous jade came to rest on her, all she could do was stare.

"Amara?" he croaked. He winced. "I'm...still alive?"

She swallowed and shook her head, relief flooding over her. "Yes," she whispered. "Yes, you're still alive." She stood quickly and went to fetch a cup of the tea she had brewed, taking it back over to him and lifting it to his lips. "Here, drink some of this. It will help combat infection." He seemed skeptical for a second, but relinquished. She had to hold his head up for, even though he was conscious, he seemed far from alert, and the sheen of sweat on his forehead concerned her.

"The Rezzegard..." he murmured, laying his head back down with a grimace.

"They're dead," she supplied, leaving out the part where one had managed to escape. She would tell him about that when he wasn't busy fighting for his life.

"I'm dead," he rasped.

She blinked then frowned. "No, you're not," she stated. "And I did not go to all this trouble to have you give up on me now."

He shook his head. "I've been dead... They killed me long ago." He drew in a pained breath, and with his soft confession, slipped back into unconsciousness.

Amara stared at him for several long moments, her heart twisting at what he'd said. She reached out and caressed his hair again, her stomach knotting at the fact that his skin felt hot to her touch. That was not a good sign. She had been hoping to avoid a fever, but with a wound as gruesome as his, plus with the shock to his body of cauterizing it, it was probably inevitable.

She stood and returned to the supplies, dousing a strip of cloth with the drinking water. She returned to Jaide and applied it to his forehead, hoping it would cool his skin slightly. She sat back against the tree and listened to the crickets and the far away hoot of an owl. Exhaustion set in, and even though she knew she should remain awake and alert, her eyelids grew heavy and sleep overtook her.

* * * *

He didn't want to go. At least at the orphanage he could hope that one day someone would come for him, that someone would care. Here, at this dark edifice he was staring at, he had the feeling that he would never have the chance to know compassion or love. Ever. A frightened tremor went along his spine and he swallowed hard.

"Come on, boys! Don't stand there and gawk! Get a

move on! I don't have all day!"

Jaiden was shoved forward by a harsh hand on his shoulder and he stumbled toward the barracks with his three companions. All of them were fifteen. All of them had failed to be adopted. All of them now had to serve here, at this place that looked like death. The Rezzegard barracks...

They were taken inside. It stank of grime and filth. The orphanage worker handed them all over to a tall, menacing man who stripped them of their clothes, shaved their heads, threw cold water on them and gave each of them a sound lashing across their backs before they were thrown into a tiny cell and told that their training had begun. Jaiden had never been so frightened in all of his life as he was while he shivered and bled in that dark hole. He curled on his side, clutched his knees to his chest, and cried.

* * * *

Amara was pulled from her sleep by something unknown. A strange kind of urgency tugged at her and she glanced over at Jaide. Her eyes widened. He was covered in sweat and his brow was furrowed. He tossed his head back and forth as if having troubling dreams, and she immediately went to fetch another cool cloth.

She had no idea how long she had been asleep, but the fire had almost completely died out. She revived it, then went back to Jaide, applying the cloth to his forehead and wiping the sweat away. She swallowed hard and worry pooled in her stomach as she felt how hot his skin was. He was burning with fever.

She tugged the blanket down and washed his chest as well, then changed the bandage over his wound, applying more of the herbal compress in hopes to fight any infection that might be trying to take hold.

* * * *

Jaiden's hand shook badly. His ears filled with the angry shouts of his commander. "Kill him!" he was demanding. How could he? He didn't even know who this man was. Had he committed a crime? Had he done something awful? His hands were bound. He was completely unarmed, and he was begging for mercy.

He glanced over at his fellow men-in-arms, two of which were the boys he had come to the barracks with. The third had died shortly after arriving a year ago from an infection. All of them had a person they were supposed to kill. A few of them even had women, and one of them had a child. They'd been told nothing of the people's pasts or histories. All they'd been told to do was to kill them. Without a thought. Without question. Here you did what you were told or you suffered the consequences. Jaiden knew that. He already had several scars to prove it.

"Just do it, Jaiden," his nearest companion whispered. "You know what they'll do to you if you don't. What does it matter? It's just one pathetic man's life."

Everyone else had done the assigned task with no qualms, even the one who'd had the child. He had been praised above all the others. Jaiden looked back at the man and he grimaced as he felt his commander's whip slice across his shoulder. He raised his sword and tried to banish his reservations, but he couldn't. This wasn't right. This wasn't who he was. He didn't want to become what these men were trying to force him to be.

At the orphanage, there had been some boys and girls with pasts the same as him. They had been just as alone, just as abandoned. They had been found by someone who wanted them, loved them... Couldn't he have that too? Couldn't all of them? He couldn't have that if he became...this. He wouldn't deserve it if he became this.

With a determined scowl, he flung his weapon down and turned to boldly meet the eyes of his commander. "I am not your dog to beat and give orders to," he spat. Immediately, both of his arms were seized by two men, and his commander struck him hard across the jaw as he was dragged away.

"Take him to the dungeon and strap him down!" the commander barked. "By the time I'm finished with him, he'll be begging to do my bidding."

The memory swirled and turned into various scenes of torture and pain. In his subconscious, Jaide was forced to relive every lash of the whip, every slice of a blade, every hit with a blunt weapon. He couldn't escape the visions. They swarmed and plagued him, all bursting free of the locked and barred door he kept them behind. In his memories, a young Jaiden screamed with fear and pain, desperately trying to hold onto the person he was inside. Someone good. Someone redeemable. He clung to his last shred of humanity even as wicked people tried to beat it out of him. He couldn't let them claim the last bit of himself. He wouldn't.

As the horrific visions barraged him, Jaide felt fiery pain tear up the left side of his chest and he heard an evil laugh. Black eyes loomed before him. Eyes that had haunted his worst nightmares.

"You stupid fool," his voice hissed. "Do you honestly think we can't break you? Every human has their breaking point. I will find great delight in the day you reach yours. You are nothing. Nothing but the dog you keep insisting that you aren't. A dog that bites the hand of its master. Insubordinate boy, you will pay for your disobedience!"

Pain unlike anything he'd ever experienced tore through Jaiden's body as his limbs were stretched to the point where both of his shoulders dislocated. Still he saw the black eyes. They were dark and sinister, and they laughed at him.

"Every human has their breaking point."

With a mighty roar, Jaide broke free of the restraints his former self had been placed in, determined to master this hellish vision that would not let him rest. His body felt on fire, but he ignored it. He was not that weak child any longer.

The images around him dissolved, but the eyes remained. He launched himself at where he knew the throat should be. His hands latched on and squeezed. This nightmare would leave him. He would force it to! He would kill him once and for all and banish him even from his subconscious. The man would never lay a hand on him again in reality or in memory.

* * * *

Amara gasped and her eyes widened as suddenly, and with a tremendous amount of strength, Jaide sat up and grasped her around the throat with both of his hands. Her hands came up to clutch at his, but his grip was unyielding as his fingers bit into the flesh of her throat. Her airway constricted and blinding panic consumed her. His eyes...they were terrifying. Cold, lifeless...she knew he was looking at someone else, someone from a life long past, someone he abhorred with all his strength. She wanted to look away, but she couldn't. She was forced to stare into eyes that sentenced her to death with pure hatred.

She clawed at his unrelenting grip and croaked his name in desperation. "Jaide," she rasped. "Jaide, please... It's Amara. It's Amara." Her vision blurred and swam, and she fought to take air into her lungs. Tears leaked out from her eyes, and just as she thought her life was over, he released her and fell back with an agonized-sounding groan.

Air rushed into Amara's lungs and she gasped it in, choking and coughing. She brought her hands up to her throat and squeezed her eyes shut, trying to get a grip on the all-consuming terror that tried to take hold of her. She glanced back at Jaide, who was shaking and muttering incoherently under his breath. He let out a scream full of wrath that made her jump.

She put her hand over her mouth and tears welled in her eyes as the fear over him almost strangling her abated into the deepest kind of sorrow. Jaide was strong and powerful, he was an indomitable force that no one crossed. It was horrible to see him suffering so much. What kind of terrible memories was he being forced to experience? What kind of demons had taken hold of his dreams?

Shaking her head, she steeled her resolve and crawled back over to him. She couldn't leave him to combat this alone, despite how frightened she may be. She placed her hands on his shoulders in an effort to keep him from thrashing around and injuring himself further. "Jaide," she murmured softly, applying the cloth to his face again. "Jaide, it's all right. You're safe."

* * * *

The evil eyes of his commander vanished right as Jaide was sure he'd been about to end him once and for all. Anguish consumed him and he wanted to cry out in rage. Would he never gain mastery over it? Would even his dreams taunt him for all time? He smothered a roar as all of his old injuries seemed to come alive and burn with renewed pain at the recollection of them. He curled his fingers into fists and fought for some kind of control against the relentless barrage of torture that came after him.

"Every human has their breaking point."

He flinched at the sound of the arrogant voice.

"Hold him down!" The snap of a whip. The blow of a club. He felt one of his ribs crack. "We'll make a mercenary out of you if it kills me...or you."

Jaide fought for control. He fought against the pain that lanced through his body. He trembled with the effort it took not to cry out. He wouldn't give him the satisfaction. He would never have that satisfaction again.

Suddenly, the tumultuous visions swirled into one clear, distinct image. It was himself. Jaide. Not Jaiden. Jaide. He was standing over a corpse. The first man he'd ever killed. The day he'd sold his soul to the Rezzegard and continued forward with his training. The day he had ceased to be everything other than an empty shell.

"Well done, Jaiden."

It was the voice of one of his companions. He looked over to see his entire faction watching him, staring at him. The one who spoke wore an arrogant smirk. "Can't say you're the weak little boy any longer, can you? Welcome, brother. You should be proud." He indicated the body. "Look what you've done."

His voice repeated the statement over and over, becoming more of an echo than an actual voice. Jaide brought his hands up to stare at his palms. They were covered in blood. The voice grew louder, taking on an otherworldly quality.

"Look what you've done!"

Around him, darkness began to swallow everything in its path, coming closer and closer. He knew soon it would envelope him too. He wished for it, ached for it, prayed for it. He just wanted some peace.

"Jaide..." A soft voice on the wind.

He drew in a great, gasping breath as light shattered the impending black and he found himself lying in the field of amaranths outside the barracks. The soft breeze tousled his hair and he closed his eyes.

"It's all right, you're safe... You're not alone." That voice...

Who was it? Who would offer him comfort? No one ever had. He'd always been alone.

He slowly opened his eyes and let himself bask in the splendor of the red, immortal flowers that surrounded him. Slowly, his pain abated, as did his tormenting visions. They were so beautiful...

* * * *

Amara continued to press the cool cloth to Jaide's face and forehead, but she really wondered if it was doing any kind of good. His skin was still on fire and he was still delirious. He kept muttering under his breath, things about a commander and about how he would never break, never give him the satisfaction. Her heart ached as she tried to care for him. What kind of horrors had he endured to create such violent, terrible nightmares?

He stilled suddenly and his eyes came open, unseeing once again. He was far away, locked in a delusion that would not let him go. She sucked her breath in and retreated slightly, afraid he would try to attack her again, but something else happened that shocked her even more. His green eyes rested on her and filled with so much tenderness it robbed her of air. He let out a slow, sad-sounding sigh and reached trembling fingers up to her lips. She remained still, unable to move, lost within the unfathomable beauty and depth of his mesmerizing gaze.

"Amaranth."

The word left his lips in a whispered caress and his fingers feathered across her lips, then trailed up to her cheek. Amara shivered and burned all at the same time, something strange blazing to life within her at his kind touch and soft voice. She stared at him, dumbfounded, her own shaking hand coming up to rest over the one he placed against her cheek.

"So...beautiful..."

Tears welled up in her eyes and spilled down over her skin. She knew he wasn't seeing her. He was locked in some memory, no doubt of the undying flower he had lied about never seeing. It didn't matter. It didn't matter because, regardless of what he was seeing in his dreams, in that moment, he was looking right at her. He was touching her and gazing at her in a way that made her heart crumble. His eyes were so haunted, so pained. She wanted to erase that pain. She wanted to heal the scars. It was her way. It had always been her way. Take care of the wild things...

With a pained groan, Jaide's arm dropped and his eyes drifted closed. He curled himself onto his side and grimaced. Amara placed her hand over her chest and forced a full breath into her lungs as her tears continued to fall. She brought her trembling fingers to her lips. They tingled where he had touched.

Jaide muttered something else about just wanting to know what peace was like, and Amara moved to his side. "Jaide," she whispered, combing her fingers through his dark hair. "It's all right. You're safe. You're not alone. Please, you need to rest." She gasped in bewildered surprise as he curled his body around her and brought his head up just enough to pillow it in her lap. She blinked down at him, stunned and unsure of what to do. He looked so troubled, so agonized. It stabbed at her heart like a hundred knives. She tentatively returned her fingers to his hair and he seemed to ease ever so slightly. It puzzled her that a man who hated touch so much could be comforted by it in his delirium. Especially from someone like her.

Then again, he didn't know it was her. Heaven only knew where he was in his mind. She hoped he found his way to someplace lovely. Somewhere he could rest, if only for a moment. "Shhh," she soothed. "No one will hurt you while I'm here. I won't let them." She smiled at her own words, thinking they were kind of ironic. Jaide was the fiercest man she had ever known, yet she was vowing to protect him. He was a warrior, a trained assassin. She was no one to him. No one of importance anyway. Only a job, a contract. He had destroyed her entire life. Anyone else would have left him to die. They never would have saved his life then cared for him in an attempt to banish his troubling nightmares. She was probably out of her mind, but she didn't care. She never could have left Jaide to die. No matter how horrible he was, for some sick reason that she couldn't explain, his face would have haunted her for the rest of her days if she'd left him to save herself.

Slowly, Jaide stilled and his breathing became slow and rhythmic. She continued to caress his hair, and continued to apply the cool cloth to his face, hoping that his fever would break soon and his visions would stop tormenting him. She wished it as much for herself as she did for him, because her heart could not take seeing him in such turbulent pain. It killed her inside. She didn't know why. She wasn't sure she even wanted to know why. She just knew that it did, and she wanted it to stop.

Chapter Eleven

The first thing Jaide became aware of was the smell of smoke. Wood smoke drifting listlessly on the morning air. It was a wondrous smell, one he enjoyed above all others. It was wild, untamed, perfect.

His eyes opened slowly, though he didn't want to rouse himself from the warm, contented feeling he seemed to be wrapped in. It was the first time in his life he'd ever awakened in such a manner. He felt completely and totally at peace.

With a heavy sigh, he lifted his head and frowned as he glanced at the brown material beneath him. Blinking to try and clear the fog from his brain, he trailed his eyes upwards until they fell on the sleeping form of Amara, leaning awkwardly back against the trunk of a tree, clutching his sword in her hand as if her life depended on it. Smoke drifted by in the hazy morning light, no doubt from the fire that had gone out and still smoldered. Her mane of golden hair fanned out around her shoulders, blowing ever so softly with the breeze, and he suddenly became aware of her fingers tangled in his hair. His eyes widened and the previous day's events flooded his mind with a vengeance.

He bolted off of Amara's lap, disoriented and confused, and a red-hot pain sliced through both his back and his chest, causing him to cry out and slump over, clutching at his wound while it continued to burn in protest of his hasty movement.

"Jaide!"

She came awake instantly and he felt her hands on his face. He jerked away, causing more pain to tear through him, and he glared up at her, more perplexed than anything else.

"Jaide, it's Amara!" she cried, holding her hands up in a gesture of peace.

He scanned the area, his mind still spinning, and he recognized the clearing where he had fought the Rezzegard mercenaries. He frowned. "What?" He shook his head and tried to make sense out of a hundred mottled thoughts. "Why was I sleeping on your lap?" he rasped. "What-what happened?" His chest ached with the effort it took for him to breathe.

Her gray eyes came to rest on his and they filled with a gentle light he didn't understand. "You suffered a grave wound," she explained. "You were delirious with fever. You were having dreadful nightmares. You..." She glanced away and her voice grew soft. "You almost killed me."

His eyes widened slightly. "Killed you?" As if some part of him knew what he had done, his eyes went to her throat, where dark bruises were forming.

She swallowed and gave a meager nod, bringing her hand up to cover the telltale signs of his assault. "I think you were seeing someone else. Someone you must have hated a great deal..." She cleared her throat and glanced away. "Anyway, I was trying to get your fever down and you just kind of flopped over into my lap. For some reason, you seemed to settle there and your nightmares stopped so I just let you stay." She eyed him warily, as if uncertain of what he would do or say.

Jaide winced and positioned himself to lean back against a tree. The small movement took as much effort as trying to move a boulder. His chest heaved with his effort to breathe, making his wound throb painfully. He closed his eyes and swallowed. His throat felt like the desert.

"Here, Jaide," Amara's soft voice murmured.

He opened his eyes to see her kneeling in front of him, handing him a cup of water. He reached out with his right hand to take it. Her eyes were so tender, full of compassion and care. It made him feel dirty, and he frowned, taking a sip of the water. "What happened to the bodies?" he questioned.

"I moved two of them into the forest so animals would not be drawn near our camp," she replied. She hesitated a moment before continuing. "The third... Well, when I returned from fetching the horse and supplies, he was gone."

Jaide's eyes snapped up to hers. "Gone?"

She nodded. "The one I took down..." She averted her eyes, but he didn't miss the way they glistened. "I thought I'd killed him. He had three arrows in him!" She shook her head in self-disgust. "I'm sorry, Jaide. I-I didn't know."

He frowned. Why was she apologizing? She had burst into the clearing right as he'd been about to meet his end like some kind of valiant warrior. She hadn't even hesitated to fire arrows at his assailant. Most women would have been squeamish, or would have been cowering and waiting for it all to be over. It was incredible, the strength she possessed.

"So, one of the mercenaries not only escaped, but did so with his plans foiled after you turned him into a human pincushion." He heaved a sigh. "That will mean that we have to be extremely cautious for the rest of this journey. He'll be back, and he'll be back with more men and a score to settle."

She bit her bottom lip in apprehension, but said nothing. Instead, she stood and went about starting up the fire. "Well, I imagine he can't come back to finish us off right away," she said. "He's injured and will have to tend to his wounds before he returns. We aren't going anywhere for, at the very least, another day. You are in no condition to travel. You almost died."

To say he was bewildered and confused at the fact that she was idly talking about finishing the journey to Lord Marden would be an understatement. What was she even doing there? Why hadn't she run away when she'd broken free? Why had she come back to help him at all? It made his stomach twist. "You saved my life," he stated. His voice sounded feeble and surprised even to his own ears.

She glanced back at him. "Of course."

His stomach knotted even more at her simple, direct reply. "Why?" Astonished was a weak word. There had to be a better word for what he felt. She frowned as if she didn't understand the question, and he shook his head, refusing to believe that she had done what she had selflessly and out of kindness. It made no sense. No normal human being would do such a thing. "I am your captor!" he continued. "I kidnapped you, hurt you, imprisoned you. I am taking you to meet your death. Why would you save my life? Why would you even care? You broke free! You could have run back to your home. You could have been done with me once and for all."

She looked bewildered, like what he was saying was insane. "Jaide, I couldn't just leave you to die!"

He stared at her and a wave of cold washed over him.

She shook her head and left the fire to come and kneel before him. "I could have run away, yes. I could have left you to die in a pool of your own blood slain by your greatest adversary, but I never could have lived with myself. You don't deserve to die!"

He stared at her in shock and horror for the words she spoke were worse than any kind of wound, or any kind of malicious statement. She really was so purely good that she would overlook his purpose in being with her, along with the kind of vile thing he was, to save his sorry existence. He couldn't cope with that. He didn't know how. He knew harsh things, cruel things. He couldn't handle anything good or kind. Amaranth of Catlaan was a deadly weapon he had never been taught how to deflect.

"Jaide," she murmured, reaching out to gently caress her fingers over his.

He sucked in his breath and everything inside of him screamed to pull away, but he didn't. He couldn't. Not at that moment. Her touch burned like fire all the way from the back of his hand up his arm. *Look what you've done!* The voice from his dream reverberated in his mind and shook his heart. He had so much blood on his hands, and now he would be responsible for the death of her. Someone so selfless, so caring. No one was like that in the world. He could justify his way of life by sticking to the philosophy that everyone was inherently evil and no one deserved to live any more than the next person, but this woman...this woman was an anomaly. She was something he couldn't understand, something he couldn't categorize, and he knew that he would never be able to rationalize her death away.

"Jaide, listen to me," she continued, squeezing his fingers. "I don't care what you think you are, or what you think you deserve, and I know that you probably don't even understand where I'm coming from, but your life matters. Your life is just as important as anyone else's."

He snorted. "Who could my life possibly matter to?" he spat.

"Me," she replied, her voice wavering ever so slightly. "It

matters to me."

He stared at her, and his heart, his blackened, barricaded heart, trembled in fear like that of a little child. He would never let her see it, would never tell her, but it did. He didn't realize until he saw her eyes widen as she looked down that his hand had turned to touch his fingers with hers. He inhaled sharply and yanked his hand away. Traitorous appendage. He scowled and swallowed hard, trying to force his heart to return to some kind of normal beating pattern. He could still feel the soft touch of her hand. It was like flower petals...

Amara studied him quietly for a long, agonizing moment, and he kept his gaze carefully averted, feeling completely ridiculous. What was wrong with him? Where had his composure gone? His self control? He never gave way to strange emotion. He never sought comfort, or touch. Why did his heart and body betray everything he had taught himself to be?

A small smile curved Amara's lips. "I have to change your bandage," she said. "Otherwise your wound could get infected. Then your arm would fall off or something, and a one-armed assassin just loses some of its appeal, don't you think?"

The light teasing in her voice caused a rare and fleeting smile to cross his lips. He met her eyes, allowing himself to bask in their tenderness for a moment before he gave a curt nod. "Do what you will."

She stood, finished with the fire, and returned to him with strips of cloth, a bowl of water, and some strange, green paste on a plate. He frowned. "You going to make me eat that?"

She giggled and shook her head, reaching up to remove the cloth from his wound. "It's just a plant ground into a paste that will help keep infection away."

He watched her quietly as she cleaned and dressed his wound with tremendous care. It stung, but her deft fingers made it bearable. She went out of her way to be gentle, trying to keep his level of pain to a minimum. It was strange and bizarre to him, completely out of his realm of experience. A delicate touch... It was the most foreign thing in his world. "You cauterized that yourself?" he found himself asking.

She glanced up at him and nodded. "It was disgusting."

He smirked because she stated it extremely matter-of-fact. There was no whine in her voice, nothing that sounded like she wanted pity for the task she'd had to perform. It was just disgusting. Period. "You dragged those bodies away from the camp all by yourself?"

She nodded again.

"That must have been difficult." Amara was slender and graceful. Those men had been large and sturdy.

She shrugged. "It had to be done."

Again, she stated it as if discussing a business transaction. Another smirk found its way to his lips. "You are not a typical woman," he muttered.

She looked up at him and gave him a playful, soft smile. "You are not a typical assassin."

He arched an eyebrow. "How many assassins have you known?"

She grinned. "Probably about as many as the women you've known." She glanced up at him from underneath her lashes and her smile was all devilment. She finished with his wound, then moved away from him. "You should rest, Jaide," she murmured. "I'll make something for breakfast."

He watched her swagger back over to the fire and he swallowed hard. He wanted to say thank you to her for the kindness she had given him, but the words stuck in his throat. The fact that he wanted to say it was what shocked him the most. What was the matter with him? He had to be losing his mind.

With a sigh, he leaned his head back against the tree and closed his eyes. It was weariness that was making him think such foolish thoughts. It had to be. He would never be so completely passive if he was at full strength. Letting a woman take care of him... It was absurd.

"Here, Jaide, lie down," her melodic voice came. He opened his eyes as she approached and straightened out his bedroll. "You can't rest comfortably against that tree."

He moved to lie down, the small amount of exertion causing sweat to form on his forehead. It was agony trying to breathe, and he squeezed his eyes shut as he came to rest on his back. Her fingers moved up to touch his forehead. He jerked away instantly, causing more pain to tear through his chest. He grimaced.

"Jaide!" she scolded. "For goodness sake! I'm only checking your temperature."

He opened his eyes and met hers, which held a clear, un-spoken reprimand. He watched as she pulled the blanket up over him, and he frowned. "Why are you doing this?" He couldn't wrap his mind around it, no matter how hard he tried.

She heaved a sigh and sat at his side, gazing into his eyes for a long, uncomfortable moment. "Because I want to," she finally replied. "Is that so difficult to comprehend?"

Difficult? No. Unfathomable? Yes. He drew in a shaky breath as bits and pieces of his nightmarish hallucinations of the night before barraged his mind. He didn't understand. What kind of normal person did the things she did? She was royalty, yet she fired arrows like a skilled archer. She was re-gal and elegant, yet she fought like a caged tiger. She knew plants in the forest that could be used as medicine. She did not flinch at the sight of a dead man. She cauterized wounds, cooked extraordinary meals, laughed when others would des-pair... And she selflessly took care of a man who had kid-napped her, forced her into a marriage in order to gain access into a country, barked and snapped at her, treated her any-thing but kindly, and had almost throttled her in his delusions. She claimed his life mattered to her, that she wanted to care for him. It was ludicrous. She defied any kind of logic.

"Are you a mad woman?" he queried. At her raised eye-brow, he snorted. "Why do you do any of this? What kind of a lunatic does the things you do?"

A small smile tugged at the corner of her mouth. "This kind of lunatic." The breeze pulled at her flaxen hair and she studied him for a moment before shaking her head. "I know no other way to be. This is my way. This is who I am." She sighed. "One day, wild assassin Jaide, you will come to realize that not every person in this world exists with only cruelty in their heart." She chewed on her bottom lip for a second, as if contemplating something, then very carefully reached her hand out and stroked his hair away from his forehead. "And one day you will come to realize that not all touch is bad."

He sucked his breath in and would have moved away, but something stopped him. He didn't know what. His eyes closed against his will and tingles worked throughout his body as her fingers moved down the side of his face in the lightest, most compassionate and non-threatening touch he had ever received. It was perfect, like something he would only find within a torturous dream of beauty he would never know. Because of that perfection, he found the touch terrifying.

"Get some rest," she instructed. "I will save some of the meal for you. You can eat when you wake."

Jaide was not someone who took orders from anyone. He was a law unto himself who only answered to himself, but as exhaustion overcame him and every muscle in his body began to protest the mere fact that he was conscious, he took her advice.

* * * *

Jaide slept all day and Amara was grateful for it. He needed to rest in order to recuperate. She checked on him periodically, and he seemed to sleep comfortably, at least as comfortably as he could, considering his hideous wound. The main thing was that he did not seem to be having any troubling dreams, and that was mattered the most.

Amara spent most of the day doing mundane things, tidying up the camp and caring for the horse, and she'd slept a great portion of the day as well, considering she'd slept so poorly the night before. By nightfall, she'd hunted down a pheasant and had it roasting over the fire when she realized Jaide was awake again.

He didn't say a word and barely moved. He just gazed up at the stars as if deep in thought. She frowned curiously and went over to him. "How long have you been awake?" she queried.

"Awhile," came his vague response.

"What are you looking at?" She glanced up at the sky.

He heaved a sigh. "I was just wondering if Ulyxes will ever manage to escape Ulfarr, or if one day, Ulfarr will catch up to him."

Amara frowned, confused as to why he was contemplating the constellations, but then she realized that he was saying something much deeper that had absolutely nothing to do with the actual stars. She had no idea how to respond, so she said the only thing that came to mind. "I need you to sit up. I have to change the dressing on your wound again.

Twice a day is best." She hated the ridiculous words that flew out of her mouth. She hadn't even acknowledged what he had said. Instead, she just barked an order at him, much like he would do to her. She cleared her throat and frowned as he quietly pushed himself up into a sitting position.

She met his eyes, pale and eerie in the moonlight. They looked as if they held a thousand dark things that a normal man would shrink in fear at. She took a deep breath, trying to banish the empathetic pain that stabbed through her heart as she gazed at him. She was unsuccessful. "I think," she said softly, "that Ulyxes will just keep fleeing from Ulfarr, and Ulfarr will continue to pursue him for all time unless Ulyxes turns and faces him. He has to confront the demon that chases him, or else he will always be running."

His eyes narrowed as if he was mulling over her words, and she took the opportunity to return to the fire, turn the pheasant on its spit, and fetch the supplies needed to clean and dress his wound.

He was still silent as she removed the old bandage, and remained that way while she cleaned it. She was happy to see that the wound, though angry-looking, did not seem to have the appearance of any infection. "You're very lucky, Jaide," she murmured. "Just a little to the left and the blade would have pierced your heart."

"Impossible," he muttered.

She frowned and glanced up into his brooding, moody face.

"It's impossible to pierce something that doesn't exist," he stated.

She thought she detected a faint note of bitterness in his voice, and she shook her head. "You have a heart, Jaide," she said softly, brazenly placing her palm to the middle of his chest. "I can feel it beating."

"Imagine that."

His tone was flat, but his voice held something strange. A deep rasp that almost sounded like...emotion. She bit her bottom lip and looked at her hand on his chest. Her fingers were right over a long, jagged scar, and that was only one of many on his chiseled upper body. She marveled over his masculine beauty for a moment, then wondered about all of his scars. How had he received so many? Part of her was exceedingly curious. Another part of her didn't want to know. Without thinking, she slowly traced the line of the scar across his chest.

His right hand came up to grasp her wrist, pulling her hand away from his body. It wasn't a harsh touch, just a reminder that she was venturing where she was not allowed. She swallowed hard. "What did they do to you there?" she found herself asking.

"Where?"

She looked up into his dark face and licked her lips, wondering whether or not it was wise to continue with her current conversation. She decided to press a little further. "At the Rezzegard barracks." A black shadow passed over his features and she almost instantly regretted asking.

He was silent for a while before he turned his eyes to hers. "Tell me, Amara, do you still fear me?"

She frowned, wondering why he wanted to know, and why it even mattered. She swallowed hard as she gazed into his eyes, those incredible eyes full of sinister mysteries. "Absolutely," she replied.

His brows drew together in a quizzical frown. "Yet you seek to find the answer to questions you know are dangerous to ask?"

She gave a small shrug. "Fear is merely one emotion in a spectrum of many. Sometimes it is great. Sometimes it is small. Right now, it is minimal considering you can't do much to me in the condition you're in." A small smile touched his lips, so small that only she would notice, and it brought one to her own. She sighed and removed her hand from his grasp as she set to bandaging his wound. When she went around to his back, her eyes fell on many more scars. Some she could tell were lash marks. Others were different, more hideous, and it made her heart twist in her chest.

There was one set of scars in particular that drew her attention. Six long, thin scars in vertical rows across his right shoulder blade. They looked like claw marks, but no animal had that many claws on one foot, and she had yet to see any that attacked in such a precise manner. Unable to stop her questing hand, she reached up and lightly ran her fingers along them, causing his body to tense. She frowned and worried her bottom lip between her teeth, knowing she was treading on treacherous ground. She pushed ahead anyway. "What are these?" she asked softly. When no reply came, she murmured, "Please, will you tell me?"

She braced herself for his biting reprimand, but none came. Instead, he was silent for a long moment before he heaved a sigh. "At the barracks, boys in training were forced to kill unarmed civilians in order to prepare them for their life as a mercenary. How many they were forced to kill depended on how many the commander thought it took to rid them of their conscience..."

His voice trailed off and Amara glanced up at him. He had his head down, the firelight reflecting off of his dark hair. She waited for more of the story, but when he said no more, she tried to put the pieces together herself. She looked back at the scars and frowned deeply, repulsed by the conclusion she came to. "You mean they carved a line into the boys' flesh every time they murdered a civilian?"

Another long moment of silence stretched between them before he said, "Not every boy. Just me."

Her eyes went wide at that atrocious bit of information. "Why?"

He swallowed. "He said it was to remind me of who I was, of who I would always be. I was difficult to train. He said that this way, I would never be able to return to who I once was, and I would always bear the mark of the Rezzegard."

She put her hand over her mouth and tears burned just behind her eyes, but she needed to know more. "You spoke of him in your dreams. The commander. Who was he?"

"A demon wearing flesh as a disguise." He spat the words like poison. "A man who had once been the greatest mercenary at the Rezzegard, but who had faltered once. His skills were too valuable to dispatch him, so the commander at the time removed him from field work and made him his personal slave for however many years. When he retired, he handed over his position, but what is an office of honor in any other military unit is seen as lower at the Rezzegard. To have to train young boys instead of being out doing what you were trained to do...let's just say the commander took all of his anger and bitterness at both the Rezzegard and himself out on the boys he was forced to train."

"That's awful... And it took you six men to rid you off your conscience?"

"Three men, two women...one child."

Amara's stomach churned in protest and she felt bile rise in her throat at the horrendous thought of killing an innocent child. Her first instinct was to get as far away from Jaide as possible, to be revolted and repulsed by his mere presence, but as she looked at him, with his eyes staring straight ahead, his face stone-cold, as if it took every ounce of his self control just to speak about the things he confessed, she forced herself to remain where she was. She drew in a deep breath in an effort to calm herself. "And...what happened if you didn't do what you were told?"

"Three broken ribs, two cracked, two dislocated shoulders, several lashings, several beatings with a blunt instrument, a knife blade across my chest, a knife blade across my back, one session of water torture, two weeks with no food, and a month's worth of solitary confinement."

She stared at him in absolute horror, having difficulty wrapping her mind around how someone could do any of that to another person. "All of that happened to you?" she asked.

He slowly turned his gaze to meet hers over his shoulder. "I told you, I was difficult to train."

The firelight reflected in his eyes, making him look dangerous and untamed. Shivers worked along her spine. He had endured all of that because he'd rebelled. He hadn't wanted to be a coldhearted killer. It had been forced upon him, just like everything else in his life. He'd been tortured into obedience. It was absolutely despicable. She had no idea what to say to him.

His lips turned up into a wry, slightly twisted smile. "Repulsed again?" he muttered, some of his usual sarcasm slipping back into his voice.

She shook her head and tried to clear the tears from her vision, coming around to face him. "No..." she murmured. "Jaide, I..." Her words trailed. There was nothing she could say that would even be remotely adequate. "How many times do I have to tell you that I am not repulsed by you?"

His gaze met hers and he regarded her quietly. A thousand different things flashed through his eyes, none of which she could name. "You're a fool," he stated.

A soft sigh escaped her lips and she shrugged. "So be it." Confusion crossed his features for a brief moment, and then it was gone. "Are you hungry?" she queried, changing the subject. At his nod, she went over to the fire and pulled the pheasant off the spit. She let it cool, then pulled the meat off and divided it between the two of them.

They ate in silence and Amara's mind wandered, touching on many different subjects. She thought of the last time she'd eaten pheasant. She'd been at home in the castle. It had been just her and her father enjoying a peaceful meal together. Pain stabbed through her heart at the memory so she immediately shifted her attention to something else. She contemplated the escaped Rezzegard mercenary for a moment, wondering if he'd managed to survive, and if he was in the dark of the forest right now, watching and waiting for the perfect time to make his move.

She couldn't believe that a place like the Rezzegard barracks actually existed. It seemed so horrible to her, to take boys and train them to be nothing more than killing machines. A deep, aching pain set into her heart as she thought over what Jaide had told her. It was a pain even worse than that at her remembrance of home. She couldn't imagine what he must have gone through. The torture and the loneliness. He had been difficult to train, he said. That meant he hadn't wanted to be what they'd sought to make him into. He'd wanted to hold onto his identity, to his humanity, to his heart and soul. It made her wonder what Jaide would have been like if he'd been able to remain Jaiden.

She glanced up at him and studied him for a moment as he ate. So stoic. So cold. He was difficult to read, always keeping anything he might feel carefully guarded. But she saw things now and again, small glimpses of things that led her to believe that, somewhere deep down within him, a man still remained. A man with emotions. A man with a heart. Maybe it was scarred and calloused, but it was there. It glinted every so often like a piece of glass hidden among pebbles. It needed the right amount of light shining on it in just the right way for it to be seen. Even then, it could only be seen by someone who was looking.

"You are unnaturally silent this evening, Amara," Jaide said suddenly.

Amara blinked at him. He was still eating, still had his eyes averted to his plate. She arched an eyebrow. "That should make you extremely happy," she said wryly.

He paused for a moment. "It should." He didn't look up, and his voice really held no inflection, but his words made Amara frown. He hadn't said, "It does." He'd said, "It should." As if he knew that her silence should bring him joy, but it didn't. Did that mean he wanted her to talk to him?

She sighed softly as empathy took over her heart once again. She imagined maybe he preferred even her talking over the visions and memories that no doubt plagued his mind. She had a feeling that all of his nightmares had unleashed things he'd kept carefully locked away for many years. When things like that surfaced, it was probably difficult to put them back.

"I could tell you the story about the girl who thought she was a warrior," she offered.

He glanced up at her. "Another one of your fairy tales?" he drawled.

A smile spread across her lips and she giggled. "No, this one has a little more truth to it considering the girl was me."

He regarded her for a moment, then looked back to his plate. "Tell me."

His voice was the same neutral tone it had been before, but Amara couldn't stop her smile over the fact that he wanted to hear her story. "Well, when I was younger, the Royal Guard at the palace would have these annual tournaments, competitions between one another and so forth. They allowed outsiders to enter as well. You didn't have to be an exclusive member of the Royal Guard to participate. You just had to pass a series of preliminaries, and if you were skilled enough, you were allowed to compete. It was something that all the men did for fun, and all the ladies would come and cheer for their favorite. You know how things like that go." She waved her hand. "Anyway, I was fourteen years old and an extremely good archer at the time. I wanted to compete, but of course, it wasn't allowed. My father told me no women were allowed to compete, especially not the princess, for I could get hurt and so on and so forth."

Jaide looked up from his plate and met her eyes.

"Naturally, I was angry," Amara continued. "I wanted to

compete!" She grinned. "So, I came up with a very clever disguise. I stole one of the Royal Guard uniforms and convinced the captain to help me with my deception. Passed myself off as a new recruit. Got myself through the preliminaries and straight into the competition." She laughed at the memory. "I took out every single man in the archery contest. I beat them all." She laughed harder at the way Jaide arched a skeptical eyebrow. "When they pronounced me the winner, I pulled off the helmet and shook my hair out. Everyone was stunned and shocked. My father especially, considering he'd thought I'd been in my room sulking." She shook her head. "To say the least, I earned the respect of all the members of the Royal Guard that day."

"Were you punished?" he questioned.

She gave a quizzical frown.

"For your disobedience. Did your father punish you?"

She smiled and shrugged. "He scolded me and gave me a lecture, but I know he was proud. We laugh about it now..." Her words trailed off as a wave of grief washed over her. She looked down and set her plate aside, her appetite vanishing. "Anyway, that was a long time ago," she murmured. "I was better at archery then than I am now. If I'd been as skilled now, that man wouldn't have gotten away." She stood, feeling disgusted with herself, and went to scrape the remains of her dinner into the fire.

"You did nothing wrong," Jaide said.

She looked over at him and frowned.

He shook his head. "In fact, you did much more than you rightly should have... You are very skilled."

She was shocked at the fact that the compliment left his lips, and the way he averted his gaze let her know he was as well. She said nothing, knowing he would not appreciate her making a big deal about it, but a small smile touched her lips and a bit of warmth chased away some of the cold she'd been feeling. "I need to make you a sling," she stated, setting her plate aside.

"I can manage without one."

"I'm sure you can." She grabbed what was left of the shirt she'd destroyed and went over to him. There was enough material left to make a sling out of, and he would heal faster if his arm movement was restricted.

He didn't object, which also surprised her, but she kept it to herself as she crafted the device. When she had finished, she draped the horse blanket over his bare shoulders and came around to take his plate from him. She flashed him a smile and went back to the fire. She stoked it, cleaned off his plate, and set the dishes off to the side. When she turned back, her breath caught in her throat.

Fireflies danced around Jaide like enchanted sparkles, and the light from the fire shadowed and highlighted his dark form in the most beautiful, mesmerizing way. To say he was handsome would be to label him with a weak word. He was magnificent. Intimidating, fear-inspiring, but magnificent.

He glanced up at her and frowned, catching her staring. "What are you looking at?" he muttered.

Something so much more than what he seems... She wanted to say those words, but she held back. They would put him on guard, and that was the last thing she wanted to do. "A man," she murmured.

His frown deepened. "You mean a fiend?"

She shook her head. "A warrior... A survivor." He fell silent for a long while, his eyes riveted to her face, searing her right where she stood. His expression was contemplative and it made a warm flush touch her cheeks and neck. She cleared her throat and averted her eyes for a few seconds before returning her gaze to him. "What are *you* looking at?" she asked, for lack of anything better.

His eyes narrowed and he was quiet for two heartbeats before he replied, "The same."

Amara's breath hitched and she looked away, her cheeks burning. Her lips curled into a smile and warmth stole throughout her entire body at his words. Up to this point, he had never said much in the way of niceness to her, but that statement... She grinned. Coming from someone like him, it meant absolutely everything.

"You should get some rest, Jaide," she whispered.

He said nothing more. He simply nodded and curled onto his side, falling asleep almost instantly. It took Amara awhile longer to sleep, for a hundred different thoughts plagued her mind, most of which centered around a certain surly and complex assassin.

Chapter Twelve

The field of flowers seemed to go on forever. Boundless and beautiful, all red perfection. Jaide's heart felt at peace as he walked through them. He heard laughter in the distance and turned toward it to see Amara. She was running with abandon through the field, the sun glinting off of her curling, golden aura of hair. She wore a white dress made of light material that seemed to dance around her. She turned to him and grinned, her face full of mischief and joy. She held her hand out to him and he wanted to take it. He wanted to take it with every fiber of his being. Could he? Could he touch her and allow her to pull him even the slightest bit into her world? Would he be allowed in the place she came from?

He hesitated. No, he was not of Amara's world. He was from a darker place. The black of his soul should never come in contact with the light of hers. He moved to turn away from her, but she called out to him, extending her hand further. His heart twisted as he looked up into her sparkling gray eyes. He was torn. For the first time in his life. He wanted to take her hand. Desperately. Could he? What would happen if he did? If he let her touch him?

Slowly, he extended his fingers toward hers.

He jumped back as a dark figure appeared behind Amara and grabbed her around the neck. She screamed and reached out to him. He retreated in horror as he realized the figure was himself. His eyes were full of malice and hatred, hatred for every living thing in the world. They reflected the same thing he'd seen in the commander's eyes. He cruelly twisted Amara's neck until it broke and her limp body fell to the ground, her light and beauty squelched for all time. He didn't even flinch, didn't bat an eye. He stepped over Amara's body and came to stand face to face with himself, sneering.

"You're a childish fool," the dark version of himself said. "To find joy in a laugh and a smile. You are not meant for joy. Don't forget what you are." He pointed down at Jaide's hands.

Jaide looked at them. They were covered in blood.

"You are the one responsible. You are the one who will kill her."

Jaide's eyes came open and he sucked in his breath as his heart beat out a peculiar rhythm. It almost felt like...fear.

He forced his breathing to slow as he stared off across the misty forest floor. It was early morning. Dawn was just breaking. The disturbing vestiges of his dream dissolved, but the troubling feeling within him did not. His eyes traveled over to Amara, who slept close by him, his sword gripped within her hand once again. As if she'd gone to sleep with the thought of protecting him against harm.

No one had ever wanted to protect him. He didn't need protecting. He had been alone his whole life. He lived solitary. He was all the protection he needed... Still, something about knowing that she cared enough to want to...

He sighed and sat up, letting his eyes rest upon the woman who caused such chaotic tumult within him. He would be responsible for her death. He would be the one to bring her to her end. The only creature in the world who had shown him an ounce of compassion. Was he really so soulless? Had he truly become everything he'd abhorred? Would a bag of useless gold be worth knowing that he had been the one behind the death of her laughter and her tender gray eyes? She had saved his life. Was she to be rewarded for that by paying with her own?

It had taken three men, two women, and one child to rid him of his conscience, or so he'd thought. Now he wondered if it had ever really died, or if it had merely been hibernating deep inside of him. Since leaving the Rezzegard, he hadn't thought twice about any job he'd been commissioned to do. It was his occupation. It was what it was. He'd never felt remorse... Or maybe he had, but was too cold and hardened to know it. Maybe he'd been tricking himself this entire time.

His eyes traveled over Amara, taking in the elegant, gentle curves of her body and the flowing mane that was her hair. Moved by a compulsion he couldn't resist, he reached out his fingers toward the silken strands then stopped, his hand hovering in mid-air. Caught halfway between what he wanted and what he feared more than all things. He wanted to touch her, wanted to sample a bit of softness, if just for a moment. He wanted to believe that he was capable of it. But what if he did? If he touched her, would his venom taint her unfathomable beauty? Her golden heart? What would become of her if he allowed himself to reach out and taste what had always been forbidden to him? More importantly, what would become of him? He had been hewn from violence and darkness, from the cold blade of cruelty. It was all he had ever known. It was the only constant he had ever had. If he allowed himself to trust, even in its smallest measurement, what would become of the world that was so familiar to him? Something deep within told him that allowing Amara to wriggle her way into his life anymore than she already had would be absolutely detrimental to everything he was. His life, his world, his very being, would never be the same. Dare he take that risk? Abolish years of discipline and cold acceptance for one moment of something warm and pure? Was it worth it?

His hand made the decision that his mind could not. It descended, and his fingers buried themselves within her golden tresses. He closed his eyes for the complete softness almost undid him. It was perfection. Just like her namesake. It was as resplendent as the immortal flower she had been named after.

It was the greatest tragedy to kill an amaranth.

She stirred, and he pulled his hand from her hair immediately. Her eyes fluttered open and fell on him. She frowned, then sat up with a start, breathing his name in concern. He held his hand up to quiet her and shook his head. "I'm fine, Amara." His voice was strangely husky and his throat felt tight.

She eased and let her eyes travel over him for a moment before they fell on his. Her smile was sweet and gentle. "Did you sleep well?"

"Well enough," was his only reply.

"Are you in pain?" She moved to his side to inspect his wound.

"I will survive," he stated.

She pulled back and gazed up into his eyes with more

kindness than he could readily bear. "I know you will."

Her hair was a wild tangle around her face and something foreign and bold came to life within him, making him burn and smolder. It was an intrusion that was unwelcome, yet he relished it at the same time. He loved the wild. He loved the untamed. Amara, for all the fact that she was a princess, looked and acted wild and untamed, completely free even as she was his captive. "Tell me something," he found himself saying. She looked at him in curiosity. "How do you smile when any other in your place would despair? How do you care when any other would have left me to die?"

She studied him for a long while, saying nothing. Her soft eyes bore into his in a way that made him feel exposed and vulnerable. Everything within him rebelled against the feeling. He was not vulnerable. He hadn't been for many, many years. How her eyes managed to strip away every defense he had and make him feel completely naked was a mystery to him. A mystery and a horror. He could handle the torture he had endured at the barracks. He could even handle the hellish nightmares. But Raglan Marden had handed him over to the worst torture imaginable when he had given him this assignment. It was one thing to fight against a cruel man with a weapon. It was another thing entirely when the cruel man with the weapon was your own self.

"We are all mortals," Amara's voice finally responded. "No one knows how long or short their life might be. We would all like to think that we will live a long life, but for some, it is not meant to happen that way. None of us know the future. I want to know that my life was full of joy. Even in dark times there is light. Sometimes you just have to look harder to find it. Like a tiny crack in a completely black room. A pinhole that only lets in the smallest point of light. It's almost nonexistent, but it's there. And if you find it, and hold onto it, not all is lost."

He stared at her, his ridiculous heart tripping over itself at her words. Had there ever been any light in his life? Even a tiny pinpoint? Had he overlooked it? Or was she just completely naïve? Had there been another path for him? A different way he could have gone? He didn't see how there could have been. In the end, if he hadn't conformed, he would have been killed...

Did that make him a survivor? Or did that make him a coward?

Amara knew he was transporting her to her death, yet she stared that fact boldly in the face. She stood her ground with dignity and poise. He had sold his soul for his measly existence. He had turned his back on everything he was.

He became aware of her tending to his wound again and he closed his eyes, allowing her to remove the bandages.

"I have to wash these," she stated. "I have used all that I have. And I've used almost all of the drinking water as well." She pushed a strand of wayward hair off of her forehead and looked up at him. "There must be a stream or something close by. I can hear the water running in the distance. I will find it and bring back more water so that I can boil some for washing. We'll leave your wound uncovered for now. The air will do it good. I'll put some more of the paste on it and start a fire. You sit quietly and wait for me."

He said nothing and watched her go about her routine. She was very efficient and smarter than he ever would have given her credit for. When the fire had been started, she slung the quiver of arrows over her shoulder and grabbed up the bow as well as the water skins. "I will return soon," she said.

Again, he said nothing. She looked so strong, so capable and confident. He'd done his best to break her, yet she still stood tall. He watched as she disappeared into the trees, and a strange tight feeling settled into his chest. He swallowed hard. She was free. Free to go and do as she pleased. She had been since she'd broken loose of her restraints. She was an idiot for staying with him this long. If she knew what was good for her, she would escape while she had the chance.

"Run," he whispered to himself. "Please run. Make the choice that I cannot." If she ran, he could still stay what he was, who he was. He would not have to betray himself. He would not have to stray into a territory that was dangerous and terrifying. He would just give Marden the gold back and tell him he had failed. Then he would move on, to another place and another client. He would forget Amaranth of Cat!aan had ever existed.

But if the fool woman did not run, he would be forced to stare himself straight in the face as he had in his dream. He would be forced to confront his darkest self, and he could not promise that the black half would not win. It was dominant. It was familiar. It was safe.

He did not want to make the choice. He didn't even want to venture down that path. She had to run...

* * * *

Amara hummed softly to herself as she made her way through the forest. The morning was warming up quickly and the sounds of the birds in the trees made her joyous. She followed the sound of the water and found the stream with little trouble, then set to filling up the water skins. It wasn't until she was on her way back that the realization hit her.

She was free.

She had been free this entire time.

She was all alone in the middle of the forest and Jaide was back at camp too wounded to stop her if she tried to escape. What was she doing? Was she out of her mind? Jaide was alive. She had done her duty. Why was she still lingering with a man who meant death when she had her opportunity to return home? He would never even know she'd gone. When he realized it, she would already be far away.

Without any further hesitation, she bolted off through the trees, running with a speed that caused her chest to burn. She didn't care. She had to get as far away from him as possible. She had to get home.

A vision of her father and Catlaan flashed through her mind, making her grin and spurring her onward. Trees zipped past her as she ran; leaves and branches crunched under her feet. She felt a laugh bubble up inside of her chest, but just as quickly as the happiness surged within her, it slammed back out as a vision of Jaide replaced the one of her father and home. Her breath left her in a rush and she stumbled to a stop, grief and guilt washing over her like icy waves.

She bent over, bracing her hands on her knees and laboring for air while his visage continued to taunt her. His harsh, beautiful face and mystical green eyes. Eyes that had revealed so much to her the night before. Usually kept so guarded and distant, she had glimpsed his pain and the sorrow he carried as he'd spoken of his past. Jaide had never known warmth or care. No one had ever given him a gentle touch or a reassuring word. He had been abandoned by his parents and kept in solitude his entire life. Could she abandon him too? Could she take off into the forest, leave him like everyone else had left him, to fend for himself and survive instead of live? Could she run home and forget she'd ever seen him? She knew she couldn't. For reasons she couldn't explain, she couldn't. She would never be able to forgive herself. She would never be able to banish his searing eyes from her memory or her soul.

He's going to take you to Lord Marden! Her mind screamed at her. *He's going to escort you straight to your death! Keep running! Who cares if he's alone? He has survived all this time without your help. He will continue to do so long after you are gone. You mean nothing to him.*

No, her heart argued. *I cannot abandon him. I cannot leave him to his demons and his suffering. He is not a bad man. He is lost. He is wild. It is my duty to take care of the wild things. It has always been my way.*

Even if that ridiculous philosophy gets you killed?

Yes. Tears welled in her eyes and spilled down her cheeks. Her heart had always held dominance over her mind. It was a foolish decision and she knew it even as her body turned back in the direction she had come. Why she couldn't leave him, she did not know. Why she cared the way she did, she did not know.

Her tears ran hot tracks down her cheeks and she cried softly as she made slow progress back toward the camp. Her vision was blurred from the tears she didn't bother to wipe, and her legs felt heavy, as if protesting her choice as much as her mind. But her heart moved her forward. It kept her stumbling through the dense foliage along the stream until she took one careless step.

The stream widened out and branched off into several narrow and pointless tributaries that only succeeded in forming a marshy bog. She had seen it, but in her meandering thoughts, had not been paying attention to her footing. Instead of remaining on the firm ground and skirting the marsh, she had wandered directly into the middle of it. She tramped through the mud, paying next to no attention, until one foot sank deep into the sediment and sent her sprawling forward to land in the muck. Jaide's bow immersed itself, still tightly clenched in her grip, and the quiver of arrows whacked her in the back of the head as she went down. She flailed around, trying to free herself as quickly as possible, but it wasn't much use. The mud and sludge clung to her clothes, face, and hair in a reeking disaster. She made a face and tried to wipe some of it off of her skirt as she stood, but she only succeeded in putting more on.

Feeling completely defeated, helpless, and confused, she gave way to sobs. She wanted to go home. More than anything she wanted to go home, but she couldn't. Why? Because she was stupid. That was why. She was stupid and cared so much more than she should for a man who thought nothing of her. She'd always considered herself an intelligent woman. Now, she questioned that.

Her heart ached worse than it ever had, and her shoulders felt like the world's weight rested upon them. Not knowing what else to do, she continued on her way back to camp.

* * * *

Jaide was quietly enjoying the warmth of the fire when Amara came tramping back into the clearing. He raised an eyebrow as she appeared, for she was covered head to toe in mud and filth, and she was crying like a lost child. She flung his bow, which was also covered in mud, aside. The quiver and water skins followed.

She plopped down onto a fallen log and sobbed, her slender shoulders shaking with the force of them. He blinked, taken aback by this sudden display, and frowned. He rose and went over to her. "Amara, what on earth?"

She shook her head and drew in a gasping breath. "I fell in the marsh," she mumbled. She put her hands over her face and continued to cry.

Jaide stared at her, completely at a loss as to what to do. He was not one to offer comfort. It was not his way, or his strong suit, but seeing her so dejected tugged at his heart in the most profound and unusual way. It annoyed him and he hated it so his first instinct was to squelch it as quickly as possible. "You look ridiculous," he declared. "And I will be lucky if my bow ever shoots properly again."

She sobbed louder and hunched her shoulders, curling as

much into a ball as possible given her position.

He heaved a sigh and knelt down in front of her. "For goodness sake," he muttered. "Stop crying." He reached up and, none too gently, pushed the hair away from her face. It was gnarled and tangled and caked with mud. Her face was covered in the same substance and he spotted a leech eating lunch on her jugular. "You have a leech on you," he stated.

She let out a very girlish wail, a noise he had never heard come from her, and she blindly clawed at her hair and clothing. "Get it off!" she cried.

He scowled and tried to stop her flailing hands. "Hold still," he demanded as he reached for the leech. "You don't bat an eye at a corpse, but a leech is going to be your undoing?"

"Corpses don't suck your blood!" she exclaimed.

He cracked a small smile and touched his fingers to her neck. "Come on now. Hold still." His voice sounded much softer than he would have liked it to, but he didn't dwell on it. Instead, he gently pried the leech from her skin and flung it off into the trees. "There." He looked up into her face. Her alabaster skin was mottled with mud and her tears had run tracks through it. She looked completely pathetic and he didn't know if he should laugh or feel sorry for her. He made his mind up when she hung her head and continued to cry softly. Something had greatly upset her and he had a feeling that it had nothing to do with the marsh she had tumbled into. His heart twisted, and he silently cursed her for not running when she had the chance. Both of their lives would have been much better if she had.

With another heavy sigh, he grabbed one of the water skins and poured the contents of it over her head. She gasped in surprise as the cold water cascaded over her, but said nothing. He knelt in front of her again and wiped the water off of her face, clearing the mud from her skin as he did so. She would have to wash the rest off of her clothing and out of her hair, but at least her face would be clean. He continued to concentrate on the task at hand until he realized that she had stopped crying. He glanced up at her and froze as his eyes met hers. She was staring at him in a way that made his entire body suddenly feel like it had caught fire. Her eyes were full of surprise, confusion, and a deep kind of tender warmth that he would never deserve as long as he lived.

His blood turned hot in his veins and made him feel feral and dangerous. It was a feeling he associated with being out of control, for there was no other category to put it in. It terrified him. He abhorred it. He wanted to kill it immediately.

It surged through him like a raging wave. It was the most amazing thing he had ever experienced. It felt like life.

Amara drew in a shaky breath and his gaze traveled across the flawless planes of her face to the perfect curve of her mouth. It continued lower down the pale column of her throat, then returned to her soul-probing eyes.

She moved too quickly for him to react soon enough. It was a whisper of air and nothing more, then her lips were suddenly upon his. Warm and supple. Sweet, tender...wrong.

Wrong!

He sucked his breath in like a hiss and jerked backwards as fire hotter than an inferno raged through him. He shook his head to clear his mind and turned his eyes to her, knowing the look in them was predatory, feeling the fierceness in his gaze.

Amara put her hand over her mouth as if she couldn't believe what she had done, and they stared at one another for several seconds of silence. She shook her head and extended a hand out to him, but he jumped back and lunged into a standing position with a sinister snarl. He held his finger up and shook his head slowly as walls went up, and locks and bars snapped back into place. The fire was doused and the comforting feeling of cold numbness returned to Jaide, calming him, soothing him. It was familiar. It was right. It was him. "No," he snarled, his voice sounding more menacing to his own ears than he had ever heard it.

"Jaide," she whispered, tears returning to her large gray eyes. "Jaide, I'm sorry."

"Don't ever," he growled. *"Never."* She was not allowed that close to him. No one was allowed that close to him. The fact that she had gotten that close in the first place was a mistake on his part, and not one he meant to duplicate. He may have let his guard slip because she had saved his life and had been caring for him while he was wounded, but no more. Wounded or not, *no one* was allowed to do what she had just done. Especially her.

Never her.

"We leave tomorrow," he said curtly, striding over to where the supplies were.

"Tomorrow?" Amara cried. "What? We can't! You're hurt!"

"I'll live." He grabbed up the chain and went back over to her, taking her wrist and slipping the shackle around it once again. "We've tarried here too long." What was he doing? Dwelling in the forest, star-gazing and telling her about his life as if he trusted her. Was he completely daft?

She stared at the shackle, then up at him in confusion as he staked the chain into the ground. "But Jaide, I—"

"I have a journey to finish!" he snapped. "I am not going to remain in the forest listening to your stupid stories and waiting for a Rezzegard mercenary to come back and kill me in my sleep! We leave in the morning. Lyanel is only a half a day away."

She looked up at him and her bottom lip trembled. Fear and pain reflected in her eyes. For a split second, his heart twinged with guilt, but the feeling was quickly banished by satisfaction. Fear and pain was what he should be seeing in her eyes when she looked at him. Not that tender nonsense she had gazed at him with a second ago.

"Jaide," she whispered. "I'm sorry."

He stared at her, cold, unfeeling. "You should be," he said flatly. "And you will be." He returned to the supplies and found a shirt. He pulled it on, ignoring the pain that tore through his chest and back in protest of his careless movement. "I'll take you down to the stream to wash yourself," he said. "Then do not speak to me for the rest of the day. I have no wish to hear your voice." He heard her sniffles and knew she'd started to cry again. He delighted in it.

For the moment, his tumultuous and out of character emotions were at bay. He was himself again. Jaide. The assassin. It was well-known and safe, feeling nothing.

Don't forget who you are.

How could he? It was the only thing he knew how to be.

Chapter Thirteen

He sat by the fire in brooding silence, the light from the flames playing over his face and body. He still looked magnificent. Even in his brutality.

Amara cursed herself for her own stupidity. She'd spent days and days trying to earn some semblance of Jaide's trust and she had ruined everything with one impulsive move that she didn't even understand. Why had she done what she had? What had compelled her to want to kiss him? She'd never kissed a man before, and even when she'd wanted to, she'd never been bold enough to make the first move. What had she hoped to accomplish by doing that? It made no sense. All she knew was that watching him wash her face, care for her in that very small way, and feeling his fingers on her skin, gentle instead of harsh, had brought something to life inside of her. Something she hadn't been able to control. In that moment all she'd wanted to do was offer him warmth and care, something soft and lovely in a world where he had only ever known pain and suffering. She had wanted to show him that beauty did exist, that he was not spoiled beyond repair. He could still know the lovely things that the world could offer.

There was still light in his dismal world.

But however pure her intentions might have been, the fact remained that what she had done was incredibly stupid. Jaide was made of iron and stone. It had taken her this long just to chisel enough away to get him to hold a civilized conversation with her. What had she expected, really? That he would suddenly transform into a golden paragon of chivalry and return her home, after kissing her breathless and vowing to protect her for all time? Was she delusional? Was she a complete child?

She didn't fault him for his reaction and she didn't fault him for shackling her again. It was her own fault. She accepted this. If she hadn't been so emotional, if she had carefully thought about what she was doing instead of just launching into an impulsive move, he might not have done what he had. He might have let them remain in the forest a little longer. He might have told her more about his past. He might have realized that there was more to life than what he had. He might have given up his campaign altogether and returned her home, or at least let her go free. She had done this to herself. In more ways than one. She had chosen to return for reasons she didn't even understand. She could have been rid of him and this situation completely. But, instead, she had chosen to return to him... And then kiss him.

She deserved everything he had to give her. She had ruined everything.

And still, she marveled over his dark beauty, and strangely, her heart felt peaceful. She lay there, shackled and imprisoned, and her heart felt peaceful because she was gazing upon him. It made no kind of sense, but it was true all the same.

"Jaide," she whispered. He slid his gaze to hers in a threatening fashion that sent chills along her spine. She swallowed. "You should let me dress your wound."

"I can manage," he spat. "I am not a child. I have tended my own wounds in the past."

She bit her bottom lip and felt tears threaten again. "But you can't reach your back. At least let me—"

He let out a low, rumbling growl in warning. "No."

She tensed and went silent, knowing she was pushing it. For a long while all that could be heard was the crackling of the fire, the distant running water, and the sounds of the forest. Then, Amara took a deep breath and blurted out what she needed to say, the consequences be damned. "Jaide," she murmured. "I know you don't want me to speak and that's fine. After I say this I will go silent for the rest of the night and you will have no more trouble from me. I just need you to know, what happened earlier—"

"Forget what happened earlier," he snapped.

She frowned and sat up to face him. "I can't forget what happened earlier! What happened earlier was insane! Do you know, I fell into the marsh because I was running. I was running from you! I was taking the opportunity to return home, leave you and this behind me once and for all! I was running through the forest, thinking of my father and my home, relishing in being free. Then, suddenly, I just couldn't." He frowned fiercely and she shook her head. "I don't know why! I hate myself for it! But I couldn't just abandon you! Tell me what that means! It's sick! I despise you and I despise myself, yet there it is."

He stared at her long and hard, her confession hanging heavy in the air between them. Then, he stood and paced for several agitated seconds before striding over to her and grabbing her arm, yanking her up to stand in front of him. "You defy any kind of logic!" he shouted, his face close to hers, his eyes flashing vehement fire.

She swallowed. "I know," she murmured.

"What you did was out of line!"

Tears stung her eyes. "I know."

"You are a supreme fool!"

"I know..." She met his eyes bravely, not fearing his temper as she should have.

His fingers tightened painfully around her upper arm and he drew her closer so that she felt his hot breath on her face. "Do not forget what I am," he growled, his voice low and threatening.

She didn't flinch, didn't back down. She met his gaze with defiance. "I never did," she said. "Did you?" She heard him suck his breath in and an unknown emotion flashed through his eyes before he crushed it. He took a step back and shot her a deadly glower. She shot him one of her own and felt her strength grow while her submissiveness faded. She took a step toward him to make up for the one he'd taken in retreat and she stabbed her finger at him. "You glare at me all you want," she hissed. "Snarl and growl and bite. Shackle me, starve me, feed me to the wolves. I don't care. Do whatever you have to do to convince yourself that you're as abominable as you think you are. If you really want to be the person they forced you to become, so be it. If you really did kill every bit of good in your soul, fine. But I won't play the stupid game of cat and mouse that you like to play with yourself. Either be the heartless assassin you claim you are, or be the slightly less heartless assassin that I have seen in the past twenty-four hours. Stop alternating between the two out of your own fear." He made a hissing noise and stood toe to toe with her, tall and powerful, exquisite in his sheer strength. She stayed solid, did not shrink back, and they stood so close together she could feel the angry heat emanating off of his body. "I said I was sorry for what I did," she continued, meeting his gaze with ferocity. "But I changed my mind. I'm not sorry. You have had a terrible life, I know this, and in order to survive, you have convinced yourself that anything human means pain. That every person in this world is full of nothing but malicious intent. You rationalize killing because you think life holds no value. One person is just as awful as the next so what does it matter?" She snorted. "Well, fine. Live that way if you must. But know this, there is nothing you can do to me that will merit me hurting you or hating you. I don't hate you, Jaide, even though you try your hardest to make me. I feel sorry for you." Her eyes narrowed. "You tell yourself I'm no one. You tell yourself I'm just a job you have to do, a contract you have to honor. But you forget, I know what lurks in your dreams, and because of that, I know what lurks in your heart." She put the point of her finger to his chest. "You made a mistake, great assassin. You opened the door just enough to let me get through. I am inside of you now. And I will spend the rest of my time with you showing you that not all human beings are out for blood and pain. Maybe it will matter. Maybe it won't, but I'll do it even if the only reason I have is just to spite you."

They stood there, shooting angry fire at each other with their eyes for a long, agonizing moment before Jaide made a growling snort, turned on his heel, and disappeared into the dark of the forest.

* * * *

"I know what lurks in your dreams, and because of that, I know what lurks in your heart. You made a mistake, great assassin. You opened the door just enough to let me get through. I am inside of you now."

Jaide glanced over at Amara as he finished packing up the last of his supplies. She was standing beside his horse, tall and statuesque. The morning sun glinted off of her hair, making her appear to have a halo. It was sickeningly ironic.

She hadn't spoken more than a sentence to him since their altercation the night before. She'd been asleep, or at least pretending to be asleep, when he'd returned from the forest. Then, to his surprise, when he'd awakened, she already had the horse packed and the camp stripped. Everything was ready to go save the bedroll he slept on. When he'd looked at her in question, she'd merely met his gaze with a level stare, arms crossed over her chest, proud and defiant. "What?" she'd muttered. "You said we were leaving this morning. No sense in dillydallying. You have a schedule to keep, remember? And I desperately don't want to be late for my date with death."

Her snide sarcasm was a surprise, as was her steely composure. He wasn't sure what to do with either one. And those words she had challenged him with the night before...they had taunted him for many hours in the dark of the forest and even the wild of nature could not save him from them. They continued to ring in his head now, reminding him of the conclusion he had come to the night before. He should have found the words infuriating, and he had. He should have found them terrifying, and he did. But what he hadn't expected was for them to ignite erotic fire deep within him that smoldered every time his mind touched on the thought of Amara living within him. To know that another person could know what he was, who he was, so completely that he could consider them a part of himself... He'd never even thought that a possibility before because doing so would mean he'd have to trust. He'd have to let his guard down. That was something he couldn't do.

But he already had, hadn't he? Just enough for Amara to squeeze her way in. She was cunning. And she was painfully astute. And quite possibly the strongest person he'd ever known. She was the only human being who'd ever stood up to him. Ever since his leaving the Rezzegard he'd ruled people through intimidation and fear. Even men larger than him had cowered before him. Not Amara. For as long as he lived, he would never forget the way her eyes had blazed with passion the night before. She'd threatened him with kindness. Who did that? Only her. Stabbed her finger at him and told him that, even if her only reason was to spite him, she would show him that kindness existed. She would punish him with goodness. It was the worst possible consequence, but her fire was intoxicating.

That was what she had left behind.

Right before he had banished her from seeing any more of his soul, she had left her fire within him. It threatened to consume him, devour him alive, and for the first time in his whole life, he was filled with wicked thoughts. Wicked thoughts that had nothing to do with killing or hurting. They were thoughts that made his body ache every time he looked at Amara, and made unsavory visions dance before his eyes. He wondered what her pale skin would look like naked in the moonlight, her golden hair fanning out all around her. He knew she would look like a work of art. He wondered what her body would feel like beneath his hands. He had never wanted to touch a woman, to share his body or any other part of himself with another. He still didn't, but the temptation was there. The temptation to let it all go, his composure, his fear, his discipline, and lose himself within the fire. What would it feel like to hand control of himself over to someone like Amara? Would it feel like death? Or would it feel like life? He wasn't sure which outcome he would prefer. He wasn't sure of much anymore.

Just one thing.

The thing he had decided the night before in the dark of the woods.

He would not be swayed from his purpose. He would not be swayed from the choice he had made.

It was the only decision he'd ever felt good about. And his heart felt a small measure of peace.

Neither he nor Amara said anything as he packed up the last of his things. He pried the stake attached to Amara's shackle from the ground and secured the chain to his belt, then pulled himself onto his horse, his wound protesting the movement. He looked down at Amara once he was in the saddle, and he held his right hand out to her.

She gave him a perplexed expression and stared at his outstretched hand. He said nothing, merely waited. Slowly, she reached out and slid her fingers into his. He grasped her hand and pulled her up onto the horse in front of him. He took the reins and urged the horse into a trot.

Amara's body jostled against his and she leaned back slightly before sucking in her breath and sitting up straight. "Oh, I'm sorry." She whispered it so softly he barely heard her.

He frowned. "What?"

"I didn't mean to lean against you..." She looked up at him over her shoulder. "Your wound. I don't want to hurt you."

He cocked an eyebrow, marveling over how she could still be so thoughtful even in her irritation. "It's fine, you didn't hurt me," he stated. "Just lean against the other side."

She blinked at him in bewilderment. "You mean you don't mind me leaning against you?" She snorted. "I thought my touch melted your flesh or something."

She had no idea. He let out a weary sigh. "Do or do not. It is not my concern."

She gave him a flat expression, but ended up leaning back against him anyway. They rode for a good portion of the day in silence, which he found strangely disconcerting. Since kidnapping Amara, he'd been subjected to her never-ending flow of babble. He'd had to get used to it in order to maintain his sanity. Now, he found the sudden silence odd. He didn't know what to do with that any more than he knew what to do with the other bizarre things he was feeling. He had never been a talkative person, and more than likely, he never would be, but he hadn't realized how completely bleak his solitary existence had been. Amara's presence in his world had altered his way of life despite how hard he'd tried to keep it the same. Over the past weeks, she had slowly and patiently been chipping away at the wall of unbending stone he placed around himself. She had spoken truth the night before when she'd said what she had. She was inside of him. He hated it and he wanted to find a way to obliterate the feeling, but he was not immature enough to lie to himself. He'd never been shown kindness a day in his life. How was he supposed to not react when someone who, by all rights, should wish nothing but harm upon him, showered him with goodness and light? How could he maintain his carefully crafted way of ice and iron when Amara's fire melted what was frozen and tempered the steel?

They traveled over the border into Lyanel just as dark clouds began to form over the horizon, and it was overcast and dismal when they finally made their way into the city of Toberton.

Jaide heard Amara draw in a sharp breath as he guided his horse down the cobbled streets, and he didn't blame her. There was only one place he hated more than Dother, and that was Toberton. There was no such thing as law enforcement and anarchy dominated the streets. It was every man for himself, and to not walk the streets without looking over your shoulder was a death wish.

Tavern upon tavern lined the streets and open drunken debauchery was everywhere you looked. He felt Amara curl closer to his body and he wondered if she knew she did it.

"I have to go to the courier," he said. "There is a message I must send. After that, we are going to an inn and you are to remain in the room for the rest of the evening. Do you understand?" She didn't even argue. She just gave an emphatic nod as she watched two men duel in the middle of the street not far away.

He pulled his horse to a stop in the front of the courier's office and dismounted. "Stay on the horse," he ordered, unhooking her chain from his belt. He met her eyes with force. "Do not try and escape here, Amara. It is not safe. Regardless of what you think of me or how much you want to go home, make your escape attempt someplace else. Stay on the horse. Understand?"

She nodded again, her eyes wide. "I won't move. I promise."

He knew she meant the words. He could see the fear in her gaze. He nodded. "I will return shortly."

"Who are you sending a message to?" she questioned.

He shot her a scowl. "My business is my own." He turned and entered the office with a sigh. A bell rang on the door and Jaide peered into the dimly lit room to see a man behind a counter. He arched an eyebrow as a pigeon flew over his head. There were birds everywhere, running amok. No cages. No order.

"Can I help you?" the man queried.

Jaide stepped forward. "I need to send a message," he stated. "It's urgent and very important."

The man nodded and pulled a piece of paper from somewhere underneath the counter he stood at. He took the pencil out from behind his ear and readied it. "Would you like a messenger boy or a pigeon?"

He thought for a moment, then decided that the bird would probably be faster. "Pigeon," he stated. He needed his message to arrive at its destination as soon as possible.

* * * *

Amara didn't need to be convinced to stay put. This place was terrifying and she had no desire to take off and try to escape. Besides, she'd tried that once already when conditions were ideal and hadn't been able to go through with it. Even if she wanted to run, what made her think this time would be any different? Something strange and unknown was insistent on binding her to Jaide, and she was powerless to stop it.

She glanced off to her right as she heard a ruckus coming up the street. She cringed as a slave trader led a procession of bound and shackled men and women into the town square, close to where Jaide's horse was standing. All of them were in nothing more than rags, and half of them looked sickly. She shivered and her stomach twisted at the thought of people being treated so cruelly.

"Slaves!" the trader began to shout. "Slaves for sale! We'll start the bidding with this one!" He pulled an emaciated young boy up to him. He trembled silently. "Good for work! Start the bidding at five gold pieces!"

She turned her attention away and tried not to listen as the auction went on, but the trader's voice was loud and the crowd around him grew to enormous proportions as everyone inspected the lot to see if any of the unfortunate captives were something they wanted to pay their gold for.

"Hey, what about that one?" a man exclaimed suddenly. "Why is she sitting all alone on that horse up there? For show? Come on, give us the quality slaves instead of these pitiful ones! They look they have one foot in the grave!"

Amara frowned and glanced back over to the crowd, wondering who the man was talking about. It wasn't until the slave trader leered at her that she realized all eyes were up-

on her. She looked down at her shackle, and the chain that
hung from it, and a ripple of unease went through her. She
raised her frightened eyes to the trader and shook her head,
but the idea had already planted in him. She screamed as he
grabbed her chain and yanked her down off the horse. She
barely had time to get her leg over the side and she fell to
the ground in a heap, landing hard on her right arm.

"This is a pretty one!" the trader shouted, hauling her up
by the back of her dress and shoving her out in front of the
crowd. "Healthy, sturdy, good for what ails ya!"

Amara tried to turn and run, her heart picking up speed
at the way all of the men started to make lewd remarks. "No,
I'm not a slave!" she cried.

The trader shoved her back toward the crowd. "That's
what they all say," he snarled. "Ten gold pieces!"

Amara's breath came in ragged gasps as numbers began
to fly from the mouths of the men who'd been jeering at her.
She glanced around frantically, but there was no way out.
Onlookers and bidders had her penned in at every turn, and
the lecherous men who were arguing over her were pressing
in closer. "No, I'm not a slave!" she shouted. "Please!" She
looked back over at the courier's. "Jaide!" she cried. "Jaide,
help!"

"One hundred gold pieces!"

"One fifty!"

"One seventy-five!"

"Four hundred!"

A hush fell over the crowd and Amara felt the hair on the
back of her neck prickle. Her eyes returned to the crowd and
she swallowed hard as she spotted a large, menacing man
with a beard and a potbelly standing in the forefront of the
crowd. A grotesque smile twisted his lips as he looked at her.

"Sold!" the trader announced. He placed his hand firmly
on Amara's back and sent her tumbling toward the man.

He smelled of horse and body odor mixed with a fair
amount of liquor. It turned her stomach and she tried to
push away, but he yanked her back to him, taking one of her
breasts in his large hand and giving a cruel squeeze.

"You'll be a lovely distraction," he said with a menacing
chuckle.

Amara gasped and struggled against him. "Let me go!

I'm not a slave! There's been a mistake!" He started to haul her away and back through the crowd. "Jaide!" she cried desperately over her shoulder as terrified tears slipped down her cheeks. "Jaide, please! Help!"

* * * *

Jaide frowned and turned away from where the courier was preparing his message. He strode to the window, swearing he'd heard Amara's voice. He saw a crowd huddled around what looked like a slave auction. His frown deepened and his eyes went to his horse. They widened upon seeing that Amara was no longer seated upon it.

He strode to the door. "Be sure that's sent immediately!" he ordered back at the courier as he made his way outside. He scanned the crowd for signs of Amara and his heart made a strange jolt in his chest as he heard her frightened cry. His eyes followed her voice over to the far side of the street, where a rotund man was dragging a struggling Amara by her chain. His lip curled and a strange, foreign rage welled up within him, especially when the man stopped with a fierce scowl and gave her chain a mighty tug, sending her tripping and falling to the ground. He pulled her back up by her hair, then forced his lips down on hers.

With a guttural growl, Jaide strode through the crowd, shoving people out of his way as he cut a path to Amara. He pulled his sword free of its baldric and, in one, fluid movement, held it at the throat of the man who had captured her. "Unhand her," he snarled.

The man seemed relatively unabashed at Jaide's weapon. He snorted in mockery and pulled Amara up close to his body. "I don't have to do a bloody thing. This wench is bought and paid for. I'm sure there's others. Go find your own."

Jaide met Amara's eyes. They were large, tear-filled, and full of fright. He scowled. "This woman is not a slave."

The man snorted again. "Well, the trader said otherwise when I paid four hundred gold pieces for her. Now leave me in peace. I want to explore my new prize in private." He gave Amara a suggestive, lascivious smile.

Jaide sheathed his blade and glowered. "You will take this woman nowhere, and I am going nowhere. She belongs to me."

He frowned. "Yeah? And who is she to you?"

"She's my wife!" The words flew out of Jaide's mouth of their own volition and Amara stared at him in shock. Well, it was true, and this man might be more willing to cooperate if he knew that piece of information.

The man stared at Jaide for a minute, then opened his mouth to let out a hearty laugh. "You keep your wife shackled?"

Jaide heaved a sigh and wondered if he should just slit the man's throat where he stood. That would be easier than haggling with the idiot.

He shook his head as he tried to contain his laughter. "You know what, mister? Fine. Take her if you want her that badly. But you're going to have to give me double what I paid for her."

Jaide's eyes narrowed and he turned the idea of murdering him there in cold blood over in his mind for several seconds before he decided against it. He was an assassin, not a murderer. He was a businessman. No sense in killing someone if they weren't going to pay him for it. On his belt he carried the pouch of gold that Marden had given him as a down payment for kidnapping Amara. There was easily over one thousand gold pieces in it. He yanked it off and flung it at the man's chest. "I'm sure you will find that more than satisfactory," he muttered.

The man blinked, opened up the pouch, and his eyes widened. He snorted. "Take the wench," he spat. "I can find better at a tavern anyway."

He shoved Amara toward Jaide and she crashed into his body. Her arms immediately went around his waist and she buried her face against his chest. He slipped one arm around her shoulders to keep her upright and he watched to make sure the man left, trying not to think about his lost gold. He frowned and reached down to remove the shackle around Amara's wrist. He threw it and the chain to the ground. "Obviously, this is not a good idea to have on you here," he muttered.

Her body shuddered and he tried to move away, but her arms tightened and she pressed closer to him, giving way to hard, body-wracking sobs. He blinked in bewilderment and stood still for a moment, feeling confused and at a loss as to what to do. His first instinct was to push her away, and he placed his hands on her shoulders, intent on doing just that, when something stopped him. He didn't know what. The same something that kept stopping him when he would rather move away from her. All he knew was that, suddenly, the sound of her tears was unbearable.

He heaved a weary, defeated sigh and his arms slowly crept around her. Her fingers gripped his shirt and she sobbed against his chest as if her heart had finally broken. After everything he had put her through, she had finally reached a moment when her great strength eluded her.

He knew he shouldn't feel sorry for her. He shouldn't feel anything for her at all, but he was tired of fighting with himself. He was tired of reminding himself of what he should feel. The truth of the matter was, he hadn't actually felt anything at all in over a decade. Not until now. Not until Amara had left her burning scorch upon his soul.

He pulled Amara over to an alleyway and eased her down so that they were both sitting. She was shaking so hard he was afraid her legs were going to give out on her. Forcing all of his stubborn, disciplined, stone-cold thoughts out of his mind, he closed his eyes and focused on the way she felt in his arms. Soft, warm, vulnerable. She sought his strength. The man who had taken so much from her. She sought his protection, his comfort. Comfort from a man who had no idea how to offer it. It was the first time he'd ever held anything, the first time anyone had ever taken refuge within his embrace. It was awkward and strange.

It was heaven.

The simple knowledge that she thought him worthy enough to keep her safe made him feel more powerful than he ever had while taking a life.

He tightened his arms around her and lowered his cheek to rest on the top of her head. Her hair was soft like strands of silk. "Shhhh," he whispered, so quietly it sounded like a breath on the wind. "Shhh." Slowly, her sobbing abated and her trembling decreased. She raised her head and looked up at him with tear-stained cheeks and red, sorrow-filled eyes. She looked lost and alone, and the image twisted his heart in an excruciating way.

He frowned and shook his head, reaching his fingers up to caress away her tears. He did it on instinct, without any kind of forethought, and the simple touch sent jolts throughout him. So did the way she drew in a soft, shuddering breath. "Are you hurt?" he queried.

She shook her head, her eyes searching his. "You came for me," she murmured, her voice carrying a note of surprise.

His frown remained. It was the only thing that felt familiar. "Of course I did," he stated. He marveled at the sound of his own voice. Low, husky, not the short, clipped and matter-of-fact way he was used to hearing himself sound.

A small amount of mirth came to life in her eyes. "Of course you did," she repeated. "You have a contract to honor... And now it's more important than ever considering you just tossed a bag of gold out the window."

He arched an eyebrow and his lips twitched at the corners. He saw her strength returning, her moment of weakness fading with her humor. He should have let her go at that moment, should have moved away from her. She had no more need of his comfort... But he didn't. "Exactly," he said. His eyes scanned over her porcelain face and across her neck. He stared at the bruises marring her skin where he had attacked her and a wave of blackness passed over him. What was he doing holding her the way he was? It was not his place. It was so far from his place it was sick. He was taint and rot and everything foul. Even if he allowed himself one moment of something good and soft, it was wrong. Her beauty was far too great, and he was far too toxic.

He made to pull away, but her delicate fingers stopped him as they reached up and threaded through his hair. Delightful tingles rippled along his skin and he closed his eyes. His mind reprimanded him and forcefully told him to push her away, but his body and heart relished the touch and overrode his logic. The same feeling washed over him as when he used to lie in the field of amaranths. Her touch banished all the darkness and replaced it with soft, soothing peace. It was strange and ironic that he would have been put in her path, the one woman named after the only thing he had ever loved. And to have her embody the flower he adored so completely...he wasn't sure if it was wondrous or twisted. Maybe both.

Her fingers descended down the side of his face and traced along the line of his jaw. He leaned into her touch, allowing himself to bask in the glory of such beauty for a small moment. He granted her permission to touch him, something he had never done before with anyone, and he relished it all the way into the very core of his being. Touch. Something he hated. Something that had always meant hurt. He'd never had any idea it could be so resplendent.

The shock of her soft lips on his rocked his body and he immediately pulled back, sucking his breath in like a hiss. Too close. She was not allowed that close. He scowled and looked away, trying to force his wall of iron back into place, but it seemed heavier than usual. And his mind, usually so clear and resolute, was muddled and confused.

His arms remained around her while his heart hammered out a peculiar rhythm, and though everything within him told him to tear himself away, he remained where he was, his lips burning from her touch.

She reached her hand up to cradle his jaw once again, and with force, she guided his mouth back to hers. Shock-waves jolted through him, and for one glorious second, he let her do what she would. It was out of sheer weakness that he did so. He was bewildered. He wasn't thinking clearly... And he was under her spell in a way he had never experienced. Her touch was intoxicating on the highest level.

Her lips moved over his with gentle urging, coaxing him to respond to her, but it was something he couldn't do. His mind was suddenly barraged by visions of every person he'd ever killed, of every horrid and sordid thing he'd been forced to do at the Rezzegard and elsewhere. He saw so much blood dripping from his hands. His hands should never touch something as pure as her.

He pulled away, averting his gaze as self-loathing threatened to consume him. Why would she touch him? Why would she kiss him? Her captor? The man who had ripped her from her home and told her that, because of him, she would be killed? How could anyone sane want to be close to the kind of complete beast that he knew himself to be?

"Jaide..."

He squeezed his eyes shut, finding her voice painful. He held his hand up between them, silencing her, and shook his head. "Amara," he rasped. He took a deep breath and forced some kind of calm to return to himself. He met her eyes, full of question and concern. Concern...for him. Why? Why did she have to look at him like that? Why did she have to do anything she did? Why did she have to be so perfectly beautiful?

A strange, foreign lump constricted his throat and made it difficult for him to breathe. "You must never..." He shook his head again and his eyes fell on her full lips. The only lips that had ever dared kiss him. The only lips he would ever allow so close. He raised his fingers to them and traced their perfection, etching their softness into his memory. "Amara, my poison, my taint, must never touch such perfect lips as yours..." He swallowed hard and met her gaze, feeling raw and as vulnerable as he had the first day he'd been taken to the Rezzegard. His chest felt tight and his heart ached. He hated it tremendously, but strangely, the pain of it was better than his usual numbness. It was the first remnant of emotion he had felt in over a decade. It let him know that, somewhere underneath all of his structure, the heart of a man still beat. The Rezzegard had not abolished him completely. Part of him, however small, did not belong to them.

His fingers came up to lightly touch one of her golden curls. He wished he was someone else, anyone else. Someone who could be worthy of her touch. Someone who could touch her and not feel sick to his stomach with abhorrence for his own character. He admired Amara more than anyone he had ever known. For her strength, for her goodness, for the bravery with which she faced all situations. He had seen and known many stern, stoic, trained men in his life. Not one of them had been as completely indomitable as her. "Do you understand me?" he murmured.

Her eyes searched his and grew sad. She looked away. "I'm sorry," she whispered.

He shook his head and dropped his hand. "No, don't apologize. I'm not angry with you. Just..." He swallowed again, but was unsuccessful at banishing the lump that had lodged itself in his throat. "Just say that you understand."

She focused her eyes on the ground and nodded. "I understand."

He drew in a deep breath and expelled it with power, then succeeded in forcing some control back into his person.

He bade goodbye to the fleeting moment of humanity Amara had given him, thanked her for it silently, and returned to the dark place within himself that was safe and familiar. However amazing it was to feel something, it was no longer his way. It hadn't been for a very long time, and the enormity in which she made him feel was frightening in a way that was ten times worse than anything he had experienced at the Rezzegard. Maybe he was nothing more than a selfish coward. So be it. He could only be what he was. It was too late for him to be anything more than that.

He pushed her away from him—gently—and stood, closing his eyes and banishing his troubling feelings and thoughts. "Come on," he said. "We need to get to an inn and stay there. It is not safe out here in the streets. It is not safe anywhere in this town. It is best if we just remain inside until our departure."

She stood with a nod and began to follow him out of the alley and back across the street to where his horse was. "Jaide," she called softly.

He relished the way he felt the coldness seeping back into his body like a slow-moving poison. He didn't know how to handle the things Amara made him feel. He at least knew what to do with the cold and the black. Those were his elements. He had no place for light and goodness. "What?" he muttered.

"I said I understand and I do," she said. "But for what it's worth, if it's worth anything at all, you're not tainted...and you are far from poisonous."

The breath slammed out of his lungs and he closed his eyes, forcing himself to continue on his path and pretend to be apathetic when everything that had slowly been growing cold within him incinerated and turned molten hot.

Chapter Fourteen

It was the thunder that woke her up. A loud crash of it that jolted adrenaline through her body and tore her from her dreams.

The storm had moved in close to sunset when she and Jaide had been eating supper. It had started as a gentle rain and quickly turned into a maelstrom that rattled the windows and split the skies with vicious lightning and cacophonous thunder. She and Jaide had ignored it mostly and had spent the better part of the evening sitting silently in the room they had gotten at the inn. Amara had done some washing, both of their clothing and of her person, and Jaide had remained stoic and silent. It wasn't unusual, and she had grown accustomed to his demeanor.

Although, her mind couldn't help but replay the earlier events of the day. The way he had held her as she cried...gentle, kind. He had soothed her with compassion and had cradled her close to his body as if he cared, as if his heart was somehow involved. He hadn't gotten angry at her for her forwardness, even though she had immediately wanted to kick herself for her bold display. She hadn't been able to help herself. The things he had done, the way he had wiped her tears, had spurred her into action before she could think it through. All she'd known was that she wanted to feel his lips on hers. She wanted to show him something beautiful, and had desperately wanted to sample some of the wildness that resided within him. She craved it still. Slowly, and rather stealthily, Jaide had managed to wrap himself around her heart in a way she couldn't even comprehend much less explain. She could sense that, deep within him, unbridled passion resided, waiting for the right person to unleash it.

She desperately wanted to be that person. She ached to know what Jaiden, the man who lurked beneath the callous assassin, was like. What he would have been like if given the chance to fly free.

She drew in a soft breath as another clap of thunder sounded and a flash of lightning illuminated his unyielding frame against the large window in the room. He stood staring out into the chaotic storm, his hands on his hips. His body was a black shadow against the bright flash of light, a stark contrast that seemed to reflect everything he saw himself to be. A spot of blackness, a shrouded shadow, a tainted, poisonous darkness. It wasn't what she saw when she looked upon him, even though it was what he tried to make her believe.

She saw strength. She saw survival. She saw elegance and grace. She saw a raw and primal sensuality in every line of his body that she could not pretend to ignore. It called to the deepest part of her.

Strange chills worked through her body and settled in her stomach, making her feel uneasy. The hair prickled on the back of her neck and she wrapped her arms around herself, sitting up in bed. She glanced at Jaide again, unmoving and unflappable. Another unsettling wave passed over her and she swung her legs out of bed, quietly making her way over to where he stood. She glanced up at his cruel profile, all hard lines and dramatic planes. His eyes remained staring ahead, and she wondered what had him so deep in thought.

"You were dreaming," he stated.

She swallowed. "Was I?" She thought it had only been the thunder that had roused her from sleep.

He nodded. "You were muttering under your breath, but I couldn't understand you."

She passed a hand through her hair and sighed. "I don't remember."

He glanced down and his voice grew quiet. "It seems you and I are vulnerable in our subconscious when we are otherwise in life."

She looked up at him, knowing he was referring to his delusions. She gave him a gentle smile. "That's because in life we pretend to be invincible, but in our dreams, our hearts speak to us."

He slid his gaze over to meet hers. "You believe that?"

She nodded and glanced out the window. In the street below some sort of brawl was occurring, resulting in one man slitting the throat of another while a toothless woman cackled nearby. Amara shuddered and hugged herself tighter. "I don't like this place," she whispered. "It feels wrong here."

He looked back down at her and studied her for a quiet moment. "You are safe, Amara."

The soft tone of his voice made everything within her come alive. Her lips quirked and she gave him a playful smirk. "Are you going to protect me?" She meant it as light teasing, wanting to draw a smile from him.

He didn't smile. He just kept his eyes focused ahead, and his sinful voice murmured, "Yes."

Her heart faltered, tripping over itself in a way that made her place her hand to her chest. She knew he only meant he would protect her from the things in the city. He wasn't saying he'd had a dramatic change of heart and would protect her from Lord Marden, or himself, but it didn't matter. Knowing that he wanted to protect her in any fashion created a feeling within her that was new and exhilarating. To be protected by a man who protected no one but himself was a privilege and an honor. It pulled her toward him even more than she was already drawn.

Without speaking, she reached her hand down and caressed his fingers, wondering if he would grant her access to touch him, or if he had shielded himself from her again. To her surprise, he moved his hand away from his hip and took her fingers in his, twining them in a gesture that seemed so much more intimate than it was. It caused her breath to hitch and tears to collect in her eyes. She gazed up at him; his face remained impassive.

That wave of unease washed over her again, more intense than the first, and she put her free hand over her stomach. Her heartbeat accelerated and she bit her bottom lip. "Jaide, something is wrong," she whispered.

He frowned down at her.

She shook her head. "Something doesn't feel right... I don't mean the anarchy of the city. It's...something else." She couldn't put her finger on it, but it was the same foreboding feeling she'd had right before the mercenaries had attacked Jaide in the forest.

His eyes scanned her face for a minute. "You think a threat is near?"

She nodded as tingles worked throughout her body. Her mind went to the one mercenary who had escaped. Was it possible that he was already on their trail again? Even after being so severely wounded? Remembering the torture Jaide had endured, she knew it was. Pain would be nothing to these men, just as it was nothing to Jaide. They had been taught to feel nothing physically or emotionally. She knew the mercenary would have resumed his mission as soon as he was able, just as Jaide had done.

She thought of Jaide and his hideous wound. While he was healing nicely and quickly due to her compresses, he would still have the disadvantage in a battle. Her fingers tightened over his. "I think we should go."

"You mean now? In the middle of the night? In a thunderstorm?"

She nodded emphatically. "I sensed the Rezzegard mercenaries before they attacked you. This feeling...it's the same. Please, I don't want you to get hurt again."

Something deep within his eyes softened, and he heaved a sigh. "All right. Help me gather the supplies."

She was surprised that he relented so quickly, but she didn't dwell on it. She made fast work out of getting their things together, and soon they were out of the inn and riding through the pouring rain. They were soaked through by the time they reached a deep section of forest with thick tree cover that minimized the effects of the rain. It was only then that Jaide slowed the horse. He dismounted with a frustrated-sounding snort and shook the water off his arms. "This is ridiculous!" he spat. "Have I taken leave of my senses? More importantly, woman, have you?" He turned on her with an annoyed expression and stabbed his finger up at her.

She remained seated on the horse and raised an eyebrow at him in confusion.

He huffed and ran his hands through his dripping hair. "I let you drag me out of a perfectly warm room into a torrential downpour because you had a feeling? I must be losing my mind." He paced a few agitated lines before he turned to face her again. "It's the middle of the bloody night! Where do you suggest we sleep? In the mud like the pigs?"

She smiled and dismounted. The thunder and lightning had abated, but the rain had not. It didn't bother her the way it did Jaide. She loved the rain. It was refreshing and beautiful, even in its intensity. "We're fine under this tree cover for now," she replied. "We can look for adequate shelter when the rain lets up."

"It'll be dawn by then," he muttered.

"Well, then it won't matter much, will it?" She shot a smile at him over her shoulder as she tethered the horse to the trunk of a tree. She giggled under her breath. He looked absolutely disgruntled.

She finished with the horse, then went back over to Jaide, a playful idea niggling in her mind. She walked past him and into a break in the heavy tree cover. She let the rain wash over her and she turned her face up to the sky, relishing the water as it washed over her skin. It felt like freedom.

"Have you gone completely mad?" Jaide called, although his voice didn't hold much conviction. Instead, it held a tiny note of wonder.

She grinned and held her arms out to her sides, then spun in a slow circle.

Jaide watched her, a pale, ethereal goddess in the middle of the dark forest. The rain cascaded down her slender body, molding her dress to her form and turning her hair into dripping tendrils. The euphoria on her face was amazing, and he remembered a similar time when he had stood in the rain, letting the drops fall on his face in the same manner, trying to banish the effects of Amara from his body, mind, and soul. He knew now that such a thing was impossible. She had invaded his very blood and bone. She had burned her presence into the very core of him.

He no longer felt the cold of the night. In fact, he was almost sure that the raindrops evaporated on contact with his skin because of the fire that burned through his veins. His body was tight. It ached. It was strange for him. He'd never desired anyone before, had never longed for anyone's touch. Now, he stood there watching Amara embrace the chaos of the storm with arms wide open, and he wanted to possess her so completely he trembled with the force of it. He wanted her light and her goodness, her bravery. He wanted it all over him, within him, living inside of him. He wanted her golden hair tangled in his hands and brushing over his skin. He wanted her body caressing his. He wanted to give himself over to her, let her consume him, and die in the rapture he knew it would bring him. It was wrong. It was forbidden. It was sickening to think that he would want to infect her with his darkness, but she was the one who kept pursuing him.

He tried to distance himself, tried to remain aloof and controlled. Her touches were persistent. Her kindness was never-ending. He was just a man, after all. And he couldn't remain ice forever. Not with her. She reached straight into him and found the last shard of humanity left, a shard he hadn't even known he possessed until meeting her. She grasped onto it with a relentless grip and pulled it past every other thing he knew. Past his training, past his discipline, past the locked and barred door of iron and stone. She yanked it into the forefront and held it there where she could play with it at will. She dissembled him while she brought air back into his lungs. It made him dangerous and ferocious in a way he had never known. If she knew what was good for her, she would turn and run very far away from him, leaving all of this behind her once and for all.

But she didn't. Instead, she turned and faced him. And grinned. The fire inside of him raged and roared.

She cocked her head to the side in a devious, playful manner. "Do you think you could find me if I ran away into the night? In the forest, in the rain?"

He slowly sauntered up to her, forcing his hands to remain at his sides and not reach out and claim every inch of her body. He stared down into her eyes, ignoring the rain that cascaded down his back and shoulders. "I can find you any-where." He didn't recognize his own voice. It was primal and raw in its deepness. It should have frightened her. It didn't.

She put her palms on his chest, leaning into his body. She brought her mouth up to his ear and he swore the heat between them turned the raindrops to steam. "Find me then," she whispered. Then, just like that, she took off run-ning into the trees, casting a look over her shoulder at him and grinning.

Jaide watched her go, took a second to get himself under control, and chided himself for even indulging her in such a silly game. He shook his head. It didn't matter. Maybe it was

silly. Who cared? He'd never played anything in his life except a few bad hands of cards. This would be a much more
fulfilling game...

And the prize would be extremely rewarding.

With a grin that he knew was sinister, he darted into the
darkness he knew so well. She could never elude him. Not
when she lived inside of him the way she did. He would be
able to find her anywhere, any time, any place.

For all time...

All he had to do was follow the burn. And the beat of his
heart.

* * * *

Amara smiled as she took refuge behind a large, sturdy
tree. She was out of breath, but felt exhilarated. The rain
was refreshing, as was the ridiculous game she sought to
play with Jaide. It felt good to be ridiculous. It felt good to
play. It felt good to be running free, knowing that her resilient captor had let his guard drop enough to indulge her in
silliness. For the first time, she didn't feel like his captive.
She felt like his companion, maybe even his friend.

She bit her bottom lip and giggled under her breath as
she peered around the tree into the darkness. There was no
sign of him anywhere and she delighted in the possibility that
she may have eluded him. She knew he would catch up to
her sooner or later, but for a short moment, maybe she had
actually won.

She sighed in satisfaction and turned back around to lean
against the tree and wait for his approach. She would rest for
a second. She choked on a scream as she turned, her heart
slamming against her rib cage in a violent attempt to escape
as she came face to face with Jaide standing silently behind
her. His eyes shielded any emotion from her, but his lips held
a small sneer mixed somewhere between malevolence and
triumph. "Jaide!" she exclaimed breathlessly, placing her
hand over her racing heart. "You scared me half to death!"

Her heartbeat should have calmed as her shock abated,
but it didn't. He stepped closer to her, backing her against
the tree and pinning her there with his unyielding body. She
drew in a soft, shuddering breath and placed her hands light-

ly on his chest, realizing that her fingers shook. He looked deadly and dangerous. His eyes came to life with a kind of dark passion she had never before seen in him, and she got the feeling that she was about to become prey to the powerful predator before her. The thought made her skin tingle and her body burn even as it trembled.

"Did you really think you could escape from me?" he murmured, his voice like a growling purr that reverberated throughout her entire being. He pressed his hips against her, making her gasp. The fire in his eyes blazed and a slow, sensual, yet demonic, smile curved his lips. "Amateur," he whispered. "You cannot escape me. Not now. Not ever."

She knew that better than anyone. Even when she'd had the chance, she hadn't been able to do it. Somewhere along their sordid journey, her heart had bound itself to him. Out of pity. Out of compassion. Out of a blind, all-consuming need to know him. Out of an animalistic attraction that she could not deny.

She closed her eyes as he reached up to trap one bedraggled piece of her hair with his fingers. He wrapped the strand around his hand and cupped her cheek in his palm, tracing the contours of her lips with his thumb. "Nothing has changed between us," he stated.

She smiled as she basked in his touch, knowing he was trying to convince himself. He fought to remain in what he knew even as he lost his control. "Everything has changed," she countered.

He brought his face closer to hers and his breath caressed her lips, filling her with erotic anticipation.

"I am still taking you to Dother," he said.

Her smile widened and she trailed her fingers up his chest and neck. "I expect nothing less." His lips descended onto hers with ferocious dominance and she bunched her fingers in the wet material of his shirt as she clutched at him. He tilted her head sideways and his tongue invaded her mouth, causing an infernal heat to sweep throughout her body. His savage kiss claimed her, marauded her, and took possession of her. She brought her fingers up to tangle in his dark hair and he pulled away just long enough to allow her to gasp in a breath of air.

He pressed his body even closer to hers, making escape

impossible. He filled every single one of her senses with his raw power and complete, starved passion, and she almost couldn't tell where he ended and she began.

"You taste sweet," he rasped, drawing his fingers down the column of her throat in a possessive caress that bordered on fierce.

She tilted her head back, allowing him access, and grinned, relishing every ounce of whatever he had to give her. "You taste wild." She heard the joy in her own voice just as she felt it come to life within her. The wild called to her; it always had. His untamed nature freed her soul in a way she had never before experienced. She knotted her fingers in his hair and crushed her lips back on his. One of his arms wedged itself between her lower back and the tree she was leaning against, successfully pinning her against him in an unrelenting hold. In a moment of passion-induced boldness, she braced herself against him and lifted both of her legs to wrap them around his waist. The fabric of her skirt caught on her boot and tore, but she didn't care. The only thing that mattered to her was the low growl that came from his throat and the way his towering frame shuddered against her. One hand continued to cradle her face while the other one traveled a brazen path down her body.

Amara trembled against him, not out of fear, but out of an intense longing for more of him, for all of him. His hand lifted her skirt and slipped underneath, tracing the length of one of her legs. He stopped his path at her hip and went very still for a moment before he tore his lips from hers and turned his head. She opened her eyes in confusion, and her heart twisted as she felt his entire body grow rigid. He squeezed his eyes shut and she could see the muscle in his jaw clenching. She was losing him. The dark prison he lived in was threatening to pull him back. She could see it in every troubled line of his face.

Slowly, she eased her legs back down, and he yanked his hand away from her body. His chest labored with the force of his breath and she grasped his hand before he could pull away completely. She didn't want him to retreat back into what was familiar, then shackle her, yell at her, not speak to her for another day and a half, and pretend like none of this had ever happened between them. Whatever it was they shared, it was real. The attraction was real. The chemistry was real. The aching longing in her heart was real...

"Jaide," she murmured.

He frowned furiously at the mention of his name and he tried to retreat further. She shackled his wrist with her fingers, not that it would do much good if he decided he really wanted to get away from her. "Jaide," she called again, her voice firmer than before. She felt the heat that had passed between the abating, leaving only cold, dismal loneliness in its wake. She didn't want that. She wanted him claiming her body and her heart. If nothing else, she wanted him to stay close to her, to let her remain in the inner sanctum of his soul that even he rarely ventured into. She didn't want to be banished into the cold and dark again.

A thought flashed through her mind and she acted on the impulse it created, knowing it was better than doing nothing, and knowing she had nothing to lose. "Jaiden!" Her voice snapped like one of the lightning whips from the storm that had gone from tempest to quiet rainfall.

He sucked his breath in sharply, held it for a heartbeat, then let it out in a shaky rush of air. His face contorted and she felt the agonizing turmoil within him as if it was her own. "Say it again," he finally rasped.

She frowned and reached her hand up to rest on his shoulder. "What?"

"My name," he whispered. He swallowed and pain flashed across his features. "The name of the man...instead of the monster."

If there had been reservations in her heart, they dissolved at that moment. That statement, that simple string of words, held more vulnerability than any dramatic display ever would, and she knew that, at that moment, she was in a place no one had ever been granted access to. She was standing in the very inner core of a man who had taken great precautions to make sure no living person would ever reach the part of him that still felt. He had even kept himself out of it. She had done what she'd thought was impossible. She had done more than she'd ever set out to accomplish. Somewhere along her path to try and coerce him to trust her in order to escape, she had broken down an impenetrable fortress.

No. She hadn't broken it down. She had just managed to chip a hole large enough for herself to fit into. And for some reason she couldn't even understand, the guardian at the gate had let her enter.

She let out a soft sigh and trailed her fingers around to the nape of his neck, entwining them in his hair again, and she moved to place her mouth against his ear. She closed her eyes and, in the most tender and sensuous tone she had ever heard issue forth from her, whispered, "Jaiden."

He let out a long, slow breath and the tense muscles of his body slowly uncoiled. He opened his eyes as the troubled lines of his face relaxed. He remained silent, staring into the dark of the trees for a long while. "You see him, don't you?" he finally murmured. He turned his gaze to meet hers, his amazing eyes sad and serene all at the same time.

"I always have," she replied.

Unknown emotion turned his eyes dark, and he studied her for several breaths before he reached up and took her face in both of his hands. With deliberate slowness, he placed the warmest, gentlest kiss to her lips. It was the kind of kiss that rocked the very ground she stood on. It made her go weak and pliant against him. There was more unspoken feeling generated in that one simple kiss than any words could ever express.

When he pulled away, he buried his face against her neck and her arms went around his shoulders in an embrace. She felt his mouth attach onto the flesh of her throat and she sucked her breath in, delighting in the sensation. She closed her eyes and held him there, smiling as one of his hands entwined in her hair and tugged her head back slightly. Seconds later, he raised his head and inspected her neck, then smiled a devil's smile and ran his fingers over where he must have left his mark on her.

He stood straight and his eyes met hers, flashing with devious mirth before they returned to their usual shadowed depths. She grinned, and would have reached up to touch his face, but he pushed himself away from her body and turned, heading back to where they had left the horse and their supplies.

Amara's happiness vanished and cold disappointment filled her. Tears stung her eyes as she watched his retreating form, but just as she was about to give into them, he stopped. He stood still and didn't turn, but he held his arm out and extended his hand back to her. He waited.

Hope and joy surged to life again within Amara and she stumbled through the mud toward him, catching his hand in hers and holding on tight. She glanced up at him and saw him smirk right before he began to lead her back through the forest.

Chapter Fifteen

He was not unaccustomed to the beauty of nature and the splendor of that which did not come in a human form, but this morning...this time...was more spectacular than anything he had ever witnessed.

Jaide sat on his horse, Amara asleep nestled against his chest, and he watched with wonderment as the sun rose over the sea, glinting like sparkling jewels on the water and turning the sky a bright crimson hue. The thunderous sound of the waves against the shore filled him with a serenity he had never before experienced, and he watched in silent contemplation for a long while.

Slowly, he turned his gaze down to Amara. The ocean breeze tugged ever so slightly on her hair, and the sun made it look like spun gold. They had ridden through the night and through the storm. She had fallen asleep curled against him as much as she could manage without falling off the saddle, and she remained there with a trust he did not understand.

He should never have kissed her the way he had the night before. He should never have given into his base desires. Strangely, though, he didn't really care. Any other time he would have felt foolish and weak for giving in to something as pointless and stupid as sexual want, but something that lived deep within him whispered that sex had played next to no part in his desire. He had never, not once in his life, looked the way of a beautiful woman. Sexual impulse was not something he'd ever had trouble with. No, the desire he felt for Amara came from a different source, and everything else fell into place like an ignited wildfire.

Her kisses, her reckless abandon, and her response to him had been more than he ever would have expected, and more than he knew how to deal with. All he knew, and the only thing that filled his mind now, was that he wanted more of it. All of it. All of her.

With a heavy sigh, he nudged her awake. He was tired and was going to make camp on the beach. Neither he, nor his horse, was in the frame of mind to ride any longer, and it would only be another day before they reached the Lyanel port and could start off across the sea toward Dother.

His stomach clenched at the thought of Lord Marden, and his thoughts grew dark. He had much to come to grips with, and much to confront.

Amara stirred slightly, but it was only to frown and to snuggle closer to him. She buried her face against his chest and tingles worked throughout his body. She baffled him in ways he would never be able to comprehend. How such a pristine woman saw any kind of good in him was something he'd never understand. She saw the deepest part of his inner self, a part he had buried for years under layers of pain and suffering and hatred. She saw it and was able to bring it forward, at the same time enduring and leashing the snapping, venomous demons that sought to destroy her. Not only did she endure them, but she laid her hands on them boldly and soothed them until they calmed.

"You smell good," she whispered suddenly.

He blinked, bewildered, and not knowing how to react to that one simple statement. He frowned because it was easy. "You need to wake up, Amara," he stated. "I have to get off the horse before my backside attaches to the saddle. I'm going to make camp here. We can rest for the day."

She frowned and her eyes fluttered open. She glanced up at him, looking disoriented, but she must have heard the waves because her attention snapped to the ocean and she sat up with a gasp. "Oh my goodness!" she murmured. A slow, broad grin split her lips. "It's so beautiful!" She scrambled down off the horse and stood facing the majestic sea. She looked enthralled and overjoyed and it brought a small smirk to his lips as he dismounted and began to remove the supplies.

"I love the sea," she stated with rapture. She smiled back at him. "Want to go in?"

He arched an eyebrow. "Are you out of your mind?"

Her grin grew and took on a mischievous gleam. She said nothing, but unlaced her bodice and slipped her dress off, then stepped out of it in only her undergarments. "Come on," she urged.

He snorted. "Absolutely not. I've spent enough time being wet in the last twenty-four hours." He thought maybe she was only trying to bait him, but he should have known better. With a shrug, she took off running toward the shore, her hair flowing down her back in shimmering waves. She splashed through the waves without apprehension, and drove straight down into the water. She emerged moments later, laughing.

He felt an appreciative smile curve his lips, and a small sigh escaped him. The woman was an enigma. She lived every single day like it was a precious gift. She took nothing for granted. It was strange and beautiful and made him ache to possess her in every possible way. The feelings were odd and not like himself, but he was no longer afraid of them. They were what they were. He desired Amara above all others. She was the only one who had ever touched him. She was the only one who had ever seen. Jaiden emerged in her presence when Jaide thought he'd been eradicated from his very being. He only lived around her. And in those moments, he wasn't the weak, frightened youth he had once been. He was strong. He was competent and capable and, quite possibly, much more dangerous than the shell of Jaide, the assassin. Nothing fueled the assassin but survival. Jaiden was powered by repressed emotion. Twelve years' worth of it. He was angry at being locked away for so long, full of vengeance and power. And he ached.

He ached for Amara and her touch. Her wild soul and her indomitable spirit. He yearned for it all, everything he had been denied.

He dismissed his thoughts and tore his gaze away from the woman who had turned his entire existence inside out. He set up camp and started a fire using driftwood he found along the beach. When he finished, he took off his shirt, which was still damp from the storm, and set it out to dry on a large rock. By this time, Amara had tired of playing in the waves and she ran back up to him, dripping, smiling, and with her arms hugging herself.

"I'm cold," she announced as she approached.

He glanced up at her and tried not to notice how her wet undergarments had turned practically transparent. "And you're surprised?" he muttered.

She grinned and stepped closer to him. She cocked her

head to the side. "Will you put your arms around me?"

His heart lurched at the thought and his body ignited, but he frowned. "Absolutely not. I just dried off."

She held his gaze and chewed on her bottom lip in a coy gesture that converted his blood to magma. "Please?"

"No," he stated emphatically.

Her eyes narrowed and she boldly walked around to the front of him, placing one leg on either side of him and settling himself down on his lap. He heaved an exasperated sigh, but allowed her to do as she would, much to his chagrin. "Woman, you possess no common sense," he grumbled.

She gazed at him with warm tenderness in her eyes. "Please?" she murmured. "I'm cold."

His heartbeat quickened, but he held firm. "No," he challenged. "You're the one who decided to leap into the sea. Now you must reap the consequences." She rolled her eyes and shook her head, but did not seem annoyed with him. He got the strange feeling that she delighted in his prickly demeanor. That fact was probably more unnerving than some of her other qualities.

She gave up the argument, but didn't move off of his lap. Instead, she settled herself comfortably across his hips, uncaring of what her presence nestled against that portion of his body did to him, and let her fingers idly trail across the burn from where she had cauterized his wound. "You're healing nicely."

He nodded. It was sore still, but she had done an excellent job in treating it.

"It'll leave a scar."

He gave her a twisted smile. "Just one of many."

She didn't seem to find humor in his words. Instead, her eyes grew sad and she absently drew her fingers along his collarbone, dipping them down to caress along the scar he hand in the middle of his chest. "Do you still hate touch?" she murmured.

He gave a short chuckle. "I apparently don't seem to hate yours," he admitted. There was no point in denying what was blatantly obvious.

She smiled and looked up at him. "Do you trust me?"

He stared into her eyes for a long moment then studied the elegant contours of her face. His cold, unfeeling barrier moved back slightly. Jaiden wanted out. Jaide didn't feel like fighting with him.

He reached for her exploring fingers and placed her hand back over the burn. "With my life." His voice was raw when he said it, raw with the feelings that lurked beneath the surface. He meant the words. She had saved his life. She had cared for him when everyone else would have left him to die. She had stayed with him when everyone else would have fled. She had seen a man when everyone else would have only seen a ruthless killer. She was unlike any other, and he could say in all truth that she was the only living person that he really did trust.

She smiled and she reached one of her hands up to comb her fingers through his hair. "Will you tell me about the amaranth?"

He frowned in question.

"Tell me why you're so enthralled by them."

A wave of cold washed over him and he looked away. That was why she had asked if he trusted her. She sought to know if she was granted permission to ask him the most personal question she could voice. It was more personal than asking him about what had happened to him at the Rezzegard because the amaranth was the one thing he had held sacred, the one thing he'd allowed himself to remain attached to. It was, quite possibly, the one and only thing that had kept him from becoming completely numb and cold. That small, perfect flower had kept him sane, and deep beneath the layers of stone, had kept him human. By asking if he trusted her, she had been asking him to let her all the way in, share the very core of him with her.

Surprisingly, it wasn't as difficult as he would have imagined. Her fingers continued their trails through his hair and she waited patiently for his response. He took a deep breath and closed his eyes for a moment, concentrating on the soothing rhythm of her touch. She calmed him every bit as much as the flower she'd been named after. It was ironic. It was fitting.

"The amaranth is something that never loses its beauty, never fades, never dies. As long as it is allowed to remain rooted in the ground, it stays resilient and unwavering in its gorgeous complexity. It looks so delicate, and yet is so very strong..." His words trailed off as he realized that the woman before him was similar to the flower in more ways than just her calming effect on his spirit. If anything, she was the complete embodiment of it.

An overwhelming wave of unfamiliar emotion flooded him and he squeezed his eyes shut against the onslaught, having no idea how to deal with such a foreign and unexpected thing. In that moment, she became more to him that just a woman who had managed to work her way inside of him. More than just a woman who bore the name of the only thing he'd ever cherished. More than a captive, or a contract, or a person at all. She was life. She was breath. She was the driving force that kept him in existence. She was the flower he adored in human form.

It wasn't until she frowned and looked at him in concern that he realized he had been staring at her in something close to shocked horror. He averted his eyes and tried to breathe normally, but his chest hurt to the point of agony.

"Jaide?" she whispered.

He let out a shuddering breath, closed his eyes, then gathered her in his arms and rolled her onto her back, pressing her into the soft sand. She let out a gasp and looked up at him in surprise. He lowered his lips to hers, delved his tongue into her mouth and caught her shocked breath, taking it into himself. He took her arms and stretched them above her head, pinning her wrists with his hands and leaving her vulnerable. "The amaranth is life," he whispered in her ear. "It is immortal beauty that never fades. It is the last shred of delicate hope in an ugly, ugly world." He released her wrists and moved his hand in a slow descent down the line of her body, examining the texture of every soft curve he encountered along the way. She trembled, and he smiled when her fingers returned to his hair, tugging slightly. He glanced up and met her wide eyes. "The amaranth is everything," he finished.

Her gray eyes turned soft and her fingers came down to trace along every angle of his face. "How can a man who claims to be so toxic and defiled have so much affection for one small, insignificant flower?"

He shook his head. "It is my one weakness."

She propped herself up on her elbow and cupped his jaw. "No, it is your deepest strength," she countered. "It has kept the man in you alive. Your love for that flower is a love for something when the Rezzegard would have abolished all remnants of the emotion from you. Don't you see? It's what makes you different from them." She touched the scar on the middle of his chest again. "They marked your body. They tortured your soul." She moved her palm to the left side of his chest, careful of his still tender burn. "But they do not own your heart."

Her words created shudders deep inside of him, and he closed his eyes against the intolerable emotion that would not leave him in peace. It geysered forth from where he had kept it dammed and all he could do was bury his face against her neck and breathe in the salty smell of the sea that clung to her skin. She eased back down to the ground, taking him with her, and he lay there beside her. He listened to her breathe and matched it to the rhythm of the waves. She stroked his hair in quiet comfort and he allowed his body to relax against her. It was the first moment of real peace he had known in longer than he could remember.

* * * *

When Jaide awoke, he felt cold and bereft. It turned his stomach for it felt much too familiar. What had once been a comforting defense now felt sickening. Instead of relishing the cold, it made him ache. Amara's soothing presence was no longer beside him, and for the first time in over twelve years, he felt extremely lonely.

He scowled and blinked the sleep out of his eyes, then sat up, scanning the area for Amara. He frowned as he noticed the fire smoldering, and a bolt of unease rippled through him. There was no sign of her anywhere, and her dress was still lying discarded on the sand.

Jaide stood, coming fully awake and alert. He scanned the beach with his eyes once more, then his heart slammed against his chest as they fell on a deliberate message written in the sand. Time to come home, brother. Bile rose in his throat as one clear, horrifying vision assaulted his mind. He saw Amara laughing, dancing in the waves and in the rain, running her delicate fingers through his hair and caressing his face. In one short second, those images were replaced with ones of her being tied up and beaten, hurt, touched and fondled where no man should ever have the audacity to touch her. Rezzegard men finding delight in her screams and cries...

Gruesome, black panic welled up inside of him like poisonous death, and for several agonizing moments that he had absolutely no control over, he was terrified. He had no grip on anything and all he felt was a cauldron of seething rage and disgusting despair. He knotted his fingers in his hair and squeezed his eyes shut, trying desperately to force his control back into place. He was a fool, a stupid idiot who had let his guard down and let himself be lulled into a false sense of security. Had he forgotten who he was, everything he had been through in his life, because of one sweet kiss and several moments of stolen serenity? He was a trained assassin. He was a hunted man. How could he have forgotten that?

Amara had known. She had felt the lurking danger in Toberton. Why hadn't he paid more attention to that? He had thrown years of discipline out the window for one gentle touch.

He took a deep breath, forcing the air into his lungs, and let his tumultuous emotions flow through him and run their course. He forced his self doubt to a halt. This was what they wanted. It had been their plan. They wanted him to feel responsible for her disappearance. Guilt, coupled with rage, made a man irrational. They were banking on him to react out of emotion. He had to remember what he had trained himself to be. Perhaps he could let the harshness soften just slightly when he was with Amara, but he was not a gentle man. He never would be. He was a killer. He was a solider of life. He was someone that these men never should have made an enemy out of.

Slowly, he stood tall as the cold, calculated calm returned to him. He let his breath out in a long, slow exhale and cracked his neck on one side, then the other. They thought they would bait him by taking Amara. They thought they would get him to react out of rage and fear. They underestimated him and they underestimated his skill.

They also had forgotten to factor in one very important thing: They had taken something that belonged to him, and that was a crime punishable by death.

Chapter Sixteen

Amara had been afraid when she'd awakened in the cave after Jaide had abducted her. She had been afraid when she'd attempted to escape and he'd caught up to her. She'd been afraid probably a hundred times since crossing paths with the fearless assassin she traveled with. But none of those times were anything compared to the terror she now felt.

She'd awakened before Jaide, and had wiggled out from beneath him in order to stoke the fire. When she'd stood, someone had grabbed her from behind like a phantom shadow. She hadn't heard their approach and hadn't suspected anything out of the ordinary. She had gotten the fire going, and had turned back to study Jaide as he slept, admiring his beauty and marveling over the things he had revealed to her earlier. The hand over her mouth had caught her by complete surprise, and she'd been rendered unconscious before she could even formulate a thought. She'd been awakened by someone dousing her body in freezing water and then ripping off all of her clothing. She'd been confused and disoriented, but knew two things. She was terrified beyond comprehension, and she recognized one of the men. He stood by while several other men taunted her, a sadistic and dark smile twisting his lips. It was the mercenary she had failed to kill.

He allowed his cohorts to manhandle her for a few moments then ordered her to be taken to a room that was no more than a prison cell, where another woman and a small girl were also huddled together in fright. Amara was slung none too gently inside and the two men handling her locked her in while shooting crude remarks back at her and degrading promises of what they would soon do with her.

Amara scrambled to a sitting position and pulled her knees

up to her chest, shivering with both terror and cold. She pushed herself back against a wall and closed her eyes, trying to calm herself and use her brain. She knew she had to be in some faction of the Rezzegard, some kind of holding cell for prisoners or something else. She knew she was being used as bait to get to Jaide, and that realization made a different kind of fear take over her heart. An all-encompassing fear for his wellbeing. She knew he guarded himself before he guarded anyone else and she hoped he would not be foolish enough to fall into their trap. If he was smart, he would move on and forget he'd ever seen her. He would be safe that way. She could get out of this. She just had to calm down enough to think. This wasn't the same situation as when she had failed to run from Jaide. This was something altogether different.

Taking a deep breath, she glanced over to the other woman in the cell clutching the child to her desperately. They were both dirty and skinny and resembled frightened deer. Amara did her best to give them a gentle smile. "What is your name?" she questioned.

The woman looked confused for a second, then swallowed and replied, "My name is Lana. This is my daughter Emile." Her voice was no more than a whisper of sound.

Amara tried to smile wider. "My name is Amara... What is this place?"

Lana shook her head. "I don't know. We were taken from the marketplace in Toberton. I don't know who these men are or what they want with us. We have been here for three days."

Amara's frown deepened as she tried to apply the information she knew about the Rezzegard to what Lana was telling her. Why would they abduct perfect strangers from a marketplace? And what would they want with a little girl?

Her stomach revolted in sudden awareness, and her heart thudded sickeningly in her chest. Jaide's recollection of his training, of what the Rezzegard commander had forced him to do, came rushing back to her. In order to lose his conscience, he had been forced to do terrible things. She saw the six perfect lines on his back. Three men, two women.

One child...

They were in the holding cell for the victims of the Rezzegard soldiers.

She looked over at the frightened girl clinging to her mother and Amara felt ill in every possible way. She was so tiny and frail. She had her whole life ahead of her.

Steely determination filled Amara and she forced her own fear and apprehension away. She had to get them out of there. She had to keep that innocent little girl from suffering the twisted fate Jaide had described. Immediately, she started to look around the room for any kind of way to escape.

She wasn't able to look for long. The door burst open again and that mercenary and his lackeys returned. They paid little to no attention to Lana and Emile and went straight for Amara. She shrieked and tried to get away, but they grabbed her before she could move a muscle. They pinned her limbs to keep her from flailing and one man bound her wrists, then hoisted her up and secured her arms high above her head in a pair of metal shackles on the wall. The other man secured her ankles in much the same fashion. When they stepped away, Amara squeezed her eyes shut and trembled against the wall, feeling vulnerable and exposed in a way that frightened her beyond anything else she had ever known.

"Well now, that will be a pretty sight for Jaiden to see when he comes for you," the mercenary muttered arrogantly.

Amara drew in a shaky breath and tried to find her inner strength. She tried not to think about the fact that she was naked, or the fact that she knew these men would ultimately kill her after doing who knew what to her. She focused on Jaide's eyes, remembered what they looked like when he was being stoic and invincible. He would never show fear. He would never give them the satisfaction. His green eyes would be cold and devoid of emotion.

A small amount of solid courage grew inside of her and she opened her eyes to meet the mercenary's in defiance. "He isn't going to come for me," she stated.

The mercenary cocked an eyebrow. "Oh no?"

She shook her head. "What use does he have for me? I'm only a contract to him. He won't risk his life to find me."

The mercenary gave a sinister chuckle that sent ripples of fear along Amara's spine. "You didn't look like only a contract to me when I watched you kissing and cuddling on the beach." He rolled his eyes. "It was enough to make me gag."

Amara swallowed hard and tried to quell her shaking as

the mercenary took several steps closer to her and let his black, dead eyes travel the length of her body in a slow, nauseating caress. She felt like serpents were crawling across her skin.

"I can't say I blame him, really. He's been alone for such a long time. His ridiculous pride must not make for a very warm companion at night." He lifted one hand and slowly, one finger at a time, removed his black glove. His bare hand descended to Amara's shoulder and worked its way down her body, touching all it came in contact with in lascivious, sordid torment. "I must admit, you are very inviting. When we catch him, I'm not going to kill him right away." He shook his head and turned his black eyes up to her. "I'll bring him in here, make him watch me take you. I want both of you to suffer before you die. Especially you." A sneer crossed his lips. "You shoot me full of arrows while protecting that swine?" He spat to the side and then moved away. He stared at her for several more agonizing moments, then turned and snapped his fingers at the other two men. All three of them disappeared out the door.

Amara let out a shuddering breath and slumped against her restraints, tears spilling down her cheeks and her body shivered uncontrollably. She looked over at Lana and Emile and realized that the men had bound their hands behind their backs, keeping them from being able to help Amara. She was on her own, and she had to find a way out. She had to.

She shook her head and forced panic away, keeping the vision of Jaide's fearless eyes in her mind. It was a focal point, and something she could draw strength from. He had survived Rezzegard torture. So could she.

She studied the feel of the shackles around her wrists, then looked over at Lana. "Lana," she murmured, "what kind of contraption do they have me in?"

Lana looked up at her with large, terrified eyes. "Your wrists are bound with rope and secured by a metal shackle."

"Does the shackle lock?"

Lana shook her head. "No, it looks more like a latch of some kind. It has a crossbar between the two wrists."

Amara tried to twist her wrists, but there was nowhere near enough room for her to get the knots out. She abandoned the thought of freeing her wrists and glanced down at her ankle shackle. It had a latch also. She grinned and looked back to Lana. "Come over here," she demanded. Lana looked horrified and Amara sighed. "Listen to me, I can get you out of here. I have an idea, but I need your help. Please, trust me. They're going to kill you and Emile both if you don't get out of here."

Emile huddled closer to her mother and started to cry. Lana looked panicked for a moment, but to the woman's credit, she got a hold of herself and swallowed hard, meeting Amara's gaze. "What do you need me to do?"

"Come over here and sit in front of the shackle around my ankle. See if you can't position yourself to be able to undo the latch with your hands from behind. They bound your wrists, not your fingers. You should be able to get the shackle off."

Lana was quick to obey, but looked perplexed. "But your ankles are still going to be bound by the rope."

Amara smirked. "Not for long."

"What do you plan to do? You can't free your hands."

She watched Lana slide the latch free from the shackle and smiled. "If I can manage it right, I won't need my hands."

* * * *

Blood ran freely across the stone floor by the time Jaide had made his way to the cells where the prisoners were kept. Blood dripped from his blade. It was a sadistic satisfaction that ran through his veins, knowing that he had rid the world of so many of the fiends the Rezzegard produced. They had underestimated him. They had made a grave error. They had sought to break him by taking his amaranth. They'd miscalculated.

The amaranth wasn't his weakness as they'd guessed. It was his greatest strength. It unleashed the man he'd held imprisoned for so long. The man was not a disadvantage. On the contrary, when the emotion deprived Jaiden mixed with the heartless, calculating Jaide, he realized he was not a mere assassin. He was not a soldier acting on duty. He was not a shell acting on selfish pursuit. He was a man with a purpose, and a drive, and skill that made him unstoppable.

He was lethal.

And he was hell bent on revenge.

No one would touch his amaranth and live.

He raised his sword in his hand and gripped it with intent as he stepped methodically toward the prison. For the first time in his life, he did not feel stone where his heart should be. He felt fire. The white-hot, all-consuming fire of rage.

Don't forget who you are.

Look what you've done!

The voices echoed in his mind and he glanced at his hands. The glove that gripped his sword was covered in blood. He knew who he was. Someone no one should ever cross. And he knew very well what he had done and what he would do. He was making the world a slightly safer place for everyone by ridding it of as many Rezzegard mercenaries as he could, and he was going to get his immortal flower back.

No one would touch his amaranth and live.

Chapter Seventeen

Amara didn't know how long she waited, freezing, for someone to return to the cell. It seemed like forever. When someone finally did come, it was no one for her. It was another Rezzegard mercenary, and he had brutally ripped Emile away from her mother and toted the screaming child out of the room to somewhere Amara didn't even want to think about. Lana had spent a good deal of time wailing until Amara thought she wouldn't be able to take the pain and sorrow any longer. She was quiet now, unnaturally so, and Amara's heart ached for her in the most profound way.

Without warning, the door opened and Amara stiffened as the dark man with the wicked eyes sauntered in. This time, he was not flanked by his guards. She swallowed hard and stayed very still, not wanting to belie that her ankles were free. Before the guards had come to take Emile, Lana had made sure that the ropes still looked as if they were around Amara's ankles, even though she'd been able to free herself from them. Now, she just needed to bide her time and pay close attention. She needed to find the exact right moment to strike.

The mercenary spent a great deal of time staring at her with that sadistic smirk on his lips. It made her skin crawl, but she remained firm.

His eyes narrowed. "You have a quiet determination in you," he finally stated, folding his arms across his chest. "Something that tells me you would be very difficult to break under pressure. It's the same as him..."

She swallowed and her chin went up a notch. Jaide was the strongest person she had ever known. Being compared to him in that respect was a great honor.

He shook his head. "It's a shame really, that people with such potential hold onto such pitiful and useless ideals." He gave a careless shrug. "It will, however, make breaking you all the more satisfying in the long run."

His grin was pure evil, and Amara's stomach churned.

He took a step closer. "Do you know what place this is?"

"A part of the Rezzegard," she replied.

He raised an eyebrow. "So he has told you about his past. Very odd...and intriguing." He tapped his finger to his chin. "A mere woman like yourself found a way past the cold stone that is Jaiden Sideth? It's almost a pity I have to kill you. I would love to explore your unusual personality in more detail."

"Know what I'd like to do?" she stated boldly. "Have a second chance to launch a couple more arrows into you."

His eyes narrowed threateningly and he made to advance toward her, but a loud noise sounded from somewhere close by and he turned his attention to the door. Amara snatched the opportunity.

With strength she didn't even know she had, she braced her hands against the crossbar of the wrist shackle and lifted her legs up straight, wrapping them around his neck and pulling him back against her, squeezing as hard as she could with her knees. He gasped and clawed at her legs, but she only squeezed that much harder. It was an awkward position, but it was the only weapon she had. Her wrists and shoulders protested the uneven distribution of her weight, but she ignored the pain.

She saw the mercenary reach down to his belt, grasping for his sword, and she closed her eyes tight, preparing herself for any slashing blow he might land. To her surprise, however, she heard Lana let out a vicious, wrathful scream, and she opened her eyes just in time to see the woman land a kick to the man's groin. His body slumped, causing Amara's hold around his neck to pull even tighter. Lana kicked him again, and he thrashed and wheezed fruitlessly for a few more moments before he went limp.

Lana stumbled backward and sat down, sobbing. Amara uncoiled her legs and let the body of the mercenary fall to the ground, her chest laboring with her exertion. Tears fill her eyes and she had no idea why. She shook her head and tried to focus on what to do next. She had to find some way to get her wrists free.

Suddenly, with a dissonant crash, the door to the prison cell burst open with a force that made Amara jump and Lana shriek. A scream lodged itself in Amara's throat as the very figure of death stepped into the room. He was cloaked, swathed in black from head to toe, and she could see nothing save the trail of blood his sword was leaving in its wake.

Emile suddenly ran into the room behind the shadow, and she fell against her shocked mother, sobbing and clutching at her. Amara frowned in confusion and her eyes riveted to the foreboding figure as he turned toward her. With one black-gloved hand, he reached up to pull the hood of his cloak down.

Amara's heart tripped over itself and she started to quake as the most perfect pair of jade green eyes met and held hers. Relief rushed over her in heady waves, followed by the release of all the panic she had been holding at bay. "Jaide?" she whispered feebly, her voice wavering like that of a tiny child.

His stone-faced expression dissolved, and he let his sword fall to the ground with a clamor. He strode forward and made quick work out of freeing her wrists from their bindings. "Amara," he murmured. He whipped his cloak off and wrapped it around her naked body, pulling it closed. He tugged off his black gloves and flung them aside, then reached up to smooth her hair and trail his fingers across her cheek. "Are you hurt?"

She shook her head as she trembled, and tears cascaded down her cheeks. He was the most beautiful thing she had ever seen. He was power and grace and rough-hewn protection. She glanced down at the body of the mercenary on the floor and overwhelming emotion rose up within her. Emotion she couldn't even put a finger or a name on. Her bottom lip quivered as she met Jaide's eyes again. "I really killed him this time," she whimpered.

His eyes softened and he cradled her face in his hands. "You are very brave," he commended.

Those four words unleashed a torrent she could not contain. She threw her arms around his waist and clung to him with ferocity. His arms came around her as well, and he held her close. The solid warmth of him, his unyielding strength, and his spicy scent mixed together to create a haven unlike anything she had ever known. She sobbed like her heart was breaking, and maybe it finally was. Maybe she had finally been pushed past her limit. Or maybe she just didn't know how to handle hearing such warm words from a man who had been nothing but ice. Whatever the reason, she cried until she was hiccupping and her chest hurt.

He held onto her the entire time. Not once did he try to push her away. Not once did his embrace loosen. He held her tight and close, and slowly, strength eased back into her body. She relaxed her grip on him and curled herself into his towering frame, finding refuge in the man who had so often been the object of her fear.

"You came for me," she murmured, awestruck that he had risked his own life just to find her.

His fingers tangled in her hair. "Of course I came for you, you stupid woman."

She smiled, for his voice held no bite to it, nor any note of real insult.

He placed his hands on her shoulders and pushed her away slightly so that he could look down at her. "Did they do anything to you?" he questioned.

She shook her head. "Just humiliated me."

He cupped her cheek in his palm and his scowling frown returned. "No one from this facility will be humiliating anyone ever again," he ground out.

She raised an eyebrow, not sure whether to be terrified at the fact that he had methodically done away with all the Rezzegard men, or awestruck at his sheer power. "This is not the main barracks, though," she assumed.

He shook his head and a shadow passed over his features. "This is an outpost. A place where the prisoners were kept until they were needed at the main barracks." He spat the words out as if they were bitter on his tongue. He glanced over to Lana and Emile. The girl had untied her mother and the two were standing together, holding onto one another and shooting Jaide skeptical glances. "You two are free now," he stated.

Lana blinked in bewilderment, but Emile tore away from her mother and walked up to Jaide. She stared at him with large blue eyes, then reached out and tugged on his hand. He frowned, but knelt down in front of her with an impassive expression.

Emile chewed on her bottom lip for a moment before she reached her tiny hand out and touched Jaide's cheek. "Are you an angel?" she whispered.

Jaide made a noise that fell somewhere between a snort and a cough and his frown grew deeper. "Far from it," he muttered.

A beautiful grin blossomed across Emile's face. "You saved us."

"Yes, thank you, whoever you are," Lana spoke up. "We are in your debt. We owe you everything. If you had not come here, my daughter would have been killed. Thanks to you, we can return to Toberton and continue our lives."

Jaide made a displeased face. "Toberton? You are raising a child in Toberton?"

Lana blinked. "It is the only place we can afford, sir."

Amara watched in shocked fascination as Jaide turned his attention back to the little girl for several seconds, then heaved a sigh and stood. He reached for the coin purse on his belt and grasped Lana's arm, dumping most of the contents into her hand. "Take your daughter somewhere safe," he demanded.

Lana stared the gold coins in astonishment, and she slowly turned her attention back to Jaide. "You *are* an angel," she whispered.

Jaide scowled furiously and made a disgruntled growling noise deep in his throat. "Off with the both of you," he said. "In a few seconds this building is going to be burning. Get clear of it."

Lana nodded and grasped her daughter by the hand, pulling her out of the cell and away.

Jaide gazed down into his coin purse and sighed. "I am impoverished," he grumbled.

A small smile touched Amara's lips as she pulled his cloak closer around her, inhaling the delicious smell of the man who wore it. Her heart softened and felt warm at what she had just witnessed. As a trained assassin, Jaide's only motivation had been money. He had tossed an entire bag of gold out the window to retrieve her from the man who'd taken her at the slave auction, and now he had given most of the rest of his coin to a woman and child in order for them to have a better life. Amara almost didn't know who she was looking at.

But then she remembered as she watched him notice the body of the fallen mercenary, go over to it, and yank off his coin purse. She bit back a grin.

"Never mind," he stated as he attached the bag to his belt.

Amara met his eyes and shook her head.

"What? He's not going to need it anymore."

She giggled. "You are incorrigible."

The grin he gave her was out of character and wolfish. It was the sexiest thing she had ever seen and it lit her blood on fire.

He cleaned the blood from his blade and arched an eyebrow at her. "Amara, out of sheer, morbid curiosity, how did you kill that mercenary when you were shackled to a wall?"

She blinked then gave a small shrug. "I choked him."

He frowned. "With what?"

She swallowed, feeling silly. "My legs?"

His eyes widened with surprise and he sheathed his sword. "You killed a man with your *legs*?" He shook his head, grumbled something she couldn't make out, then turned and held his hand out to her. She took it with a smile and he led her out of the cell and down a long corridor. As they went, he took the torches lining the wall down and flung them into locations that would quickly catch fire. The entire facility was smoldering by the time they broke into the open air.

Amara stayed close to Jaide and observed his expression as he pulled himself up into the saddle and then moved to hoist her up as well. He looked stern, emotionless, blank. It was the expression he usually wore, but she knew better. She knew that just below the surface, his rage boiled. He was burning a part of his past, a terrible part that he wanted to eradicate from the world and his memory. It had to have been strangely difficult for him, facing part of the Rezzegard, and now effacing it from the land. In order to do any of it, he had been forced to stand toe-to-toe with his own history. She couldn't imagine that had been easy.

She watched the black smoke curl into the sky as he turned his horse away and started to gallop off in a southeasterly direction. She turned her attention up to his dark face and remembered how he had burst into the cell, looking like a demon, avenging like an angel. He had come for her. He had confronted the most horrific part of his life just to find her.

Closing her eyes, Amara snuggled close to him, resting her head against his chest and listening to the thunderous rhythm of his heart. One of his hands came up to tangle in her hair, and she sighed in contentment. Her heart skipped a beat at the words she heard leave his lips.

"No one will touch my amaranth and live."

They were spoken quietly, and she was almost positive that he had not intended for her to hear them, but she had. Tears welled in her eyes at him laying claim to her, vowing to protect her. It was the last thing she had ever expected. It was a turning point within herself, and she knew that no man would ever be able to touch her life and her heart the way Jaide had. She had not seen it coming. She had never thought she would come to care so much for her captor, but she saw something no one else did. She could reach a part of him that no one else could. And, in turn, he could reach a part of her that no one else had ever even come close to.

It should have been frightening, but it wasn't. It should have alarmed her, and she knew if she was smart, she would shut off the blossoming emotion she felt, but she already knew she was not as smart as she should be. Not when it came to Jaide. So she let the emotion unfold, like the petals of a blooming flower. It washed over her and took firm root in her heart, and she knew deep within what it was.

Against all odds, and against everything sane and rational, she was in love with him.

Chapter Eighteen

Amara sighed as she combed her hair out in front of the small, oval bathroom mirror at the inn they had checked into. She had taken a hot bath, scrubbing all traces of dirt, grime, and Rezzegard filth from her body. Her reflection looked different than she remembered. It seemed like a lifetime since that night she'd sat in her bedchamber, combing her hair in much the same fashion.

She'd been so disillusioned by the world before that night. Her entire existence had been her father and the castle and playing with the children in the fields and the forest. Then, swift and unrelenting, a shadow had entered her life and turned everything she'd ever known inside out.

Jaide.

She smiled as she recalled all of their adventures together. For, despite the terror he had caused her and the horrible things she'd had to encounter and face while she'd been under his captivity, she could not deny that what they had been through was, in fact, an adventure. She'd feared and loathed him so much in the beginning. Now...

She sighed softly. Now he had become something precious to her, something beautiful to her soul. No one else would ever see it. No one else would understand it. It didn't matter. She had always loved the wild, and Jaide was the wildest of all things.

A knock sounded quietly on the closed door and then opened a crack. "Amara," Jaide's voice came, softer than usual. "I purchased you some things since the Rezzegard men disposed of your clothing. I'll leave them outside the door."

"Are they as hideous as the last dress you bought me?" she teased.

A deep, rumbling chuckle warmed her blood. "Probably."

He pulled the door closed with a click.

Amara smiled and stood, going over to open the door and retrieving the packages he'd left. There was one practical blue dress that was rather plain, and another set of undergarments. There was also a new pair of boots and a black cloak of her own. She made to don the undergarments, but there was one last parcel that she turned to with curiosity. She unwrapped it, and her breath caught in a small gasp.

The fabric was shimmering and soft, made of a light, elegant material that she knew to be imported from one of the countries of the far north. She pulled the garment free and could only stare in shock. It was a long, form-fitting gown of the deepest shade of red. It was not made for everyday use and it was not meant for travel. It was not something that would be considered useful at all. It was a luxury, an extravagance, a gift. Jaide had actually bought her a gift.

She couldn't help but notice that the color of the gown was the exact shade of the flower he so adored, the flower that she had been named after. She knew the symbolism was what had driven his decision to purchase such an expensive and useless gift.

She grinned and stood, pulling the gown over her head and letting the soft fabric slide over her skin in a sensual kind of caress. It felt sinful and perfect, and as she glanced back at her reflection, she felt richer than she ever had living in the palace with servants and fine clothing. The dress hugged her slender form in all the right places, and the sleeves were long but split all the way up the arm, causing them to fall in two slits of material and baring her pale shoulders. The vibrant color contrasted with her porcelain skin and light hair. Her heart skipped a beat as she studied herself. Knowing Jaide had gone out of his way to buy her such a meaningful thing caused the last piece of a complex puzzle to slip into place. She smoothed the fabric and closed her eyes for a moment, wondering what his hands would feel like if they were to caress the garment as she was doing.

The images that invaded her mind brought a warm flush to her cheeks and neck and she bit her bottom lip. To say she desired him would be an understatement, and the brazen boldness of her realization should have mortified her, but it didn't. Instead, the fantasy she created in her mind of the wild assassin claiming her stoked the fire that was already smoldering.

With a soft sigh, she smiled at her own reflection for no reason at all before turning and making her way out of the room. She opened the door and her gaze fell on Jaide's spectacular form, sitting shirtless before the hearth. They were staying in a coastal town, and the fog and ocean air made the otherwise summer night chilly. The firelight sent shapes dancing across the dark room and bathed him in amber light, softening certain hard lines of his body and magnifying others. Her eyes traveled across the powerful muscles of his back and shoulders, lingering for a moment on the six scars and all of the lash marks that marred his perfect beauty. A twinge went through her heart.

"Jaide," she all but whispered.

He turned his head to look at her over his shoulder and he froze. His eyes widened ever so slightly before they traveled the length of her body. She saw his throat move as he swallowed. She smiled and walked over to him slowly. His eyes remained on her the entire time. "It suits you," he said, his voice low with a strange rasp.

"It's beautiful," she said as she came to stand before him. "Thank you."

He averted his eyes and his frown returned. He shook his head. "It was a foolish expense." His voice had a bite to it, but he wasn't able to maintain it for long. He heaved a sigh and met her eyes again. "I just...I had to."

She gave him a warm smile and went around behind him. She sat down and placed her hands on his shoulders, tracing the lines of muscle and memorizing the feel of his skin. He sighed again and she felt some of the rigid tension slip from his body. She ran her hands up and around to his chest, resting her cheek against one shoulder and embracing him from behind. He said nothing and they remained like that for a quiet moment as she watched the flames dance in the hearth and relished the solid warmth of his body.

"What are you thinking about?" she finally asked.

"That man you killed," he stated.

She frowned. "What about him?"

He shrugged. "I don't know. Just..."

Amara's eyebrows shot up as an uncharacteristic laugh

was torn from his throat. She raised her head and craned her neck around his shoulder to look at him.

He shook his head. "Humiliating death for a Rezzegard mercenary," he continued. "Strangled by a woman's legs...what a way to go."

She smiled, her heart soaring within her at the sound of his laughter.

He glanced over to meet her eyes and raised an eyebrow. "What kind of princess are you anyway?"

She giggled. "An unusual one."

He rolled his eyes. "That is an understatement."

She moved around in front of him and sat on her knees, reaching her fingers up to thread through his dark hair. He closed his eyes and leaned into her touch. She smiled and let one of her hands come down to trace the line of his jaw. Her fingers descended to his lips, moving over their fullness and exploring the softness that contrasted with everything else about him. She continued on to his throat, where she felt his pulse hammering. She moved close and pressed her lips to the hollow, drawing a shuddering breath from him as his hands slowly ran up her back.

His intoxicating scent invaded her senses, making her head reel and her body come to life. She trailed unhurried kisses up his neck and over to his chin before seizing his lips with hers. Fire tore through her as his mouth opened and his tongue swept into her mouth. She could taste his hunger, the passion she desperately wanted for her own. His arms tightened around her, pulling her up so that she was sitting in his lap, pressed against him.

She returned her fingers to his hair, letting the silky strands play against her hands before she gave them a gentle tug. A low, growling sound came from Jaide's throat and he bit down slightly on her bottom lip before he pulled it into his mouth and sucked. She sighed and allowed him dominance for a moment before she took his face in her hands and plundered his mouth in the same aggressive way he had done to hers. She knew she caught him off guard and she delighted in that fact.

She let her arms wrap around him and traced the contours of his back, trailing down the line of his spine and back up to his shoulders. She dug her nails in just slightly and made him catch his breath. His fingers came up to touch her face with tremendous tenderness before he buried them in her hair.

Amara pressed as close to him as she could manage, wanting the heat of his body and the dangerous fire of his soul. She half expected him to match her passion, as he had done that night in the rain, but she should have known better. His solid, domineering discipline had stopped him that night, and it surfaced again. He moved away from the kiss, not unkindly, but with a definite purpose. He trailed his fingers along the line of her jaw and sighed, then rested his forehead against hers and closed his eyes.

She remained still and quiet for a few moments, in spite of the fact that her body ached and her heart was beating with ferocity. Jaide only knew one way, and he had existed that way for a very long time. She could not expect him to change what had kept him alive through so much. He survived by keeping himself in check, keeping his emotions at bay. How could she expect him to throw it all aside because of her own selfish desire to know him intimately? She should leave him alone, not push him, and definitely not bring the subject up. If he wanted her, she had no doubt he would go after what he wanted. She should not press her luck. All that usually got her was yelled at and shackled.

But could she honestly believe he would do that to her now? After everything they had been through? Her instincts told her to tread carefully, and she knew that was true. Jaide was more animal than he was man. She would never want to startle a cautious animal. All the more reason to just leave things as they were between her and Jaide. What would be would be.

She closed her eyes and her heart fluttered as his fingers came up to thread through her hair once again. He slowly dragged them the length of her golden tresses, then pressed the sweetest of kisses to either side of her mouth. It sent shivers all along her spine, followed by waves of warmth. The action reflected innocence, which was something she never thought she would experience from a man like Jaide, and it brought tears to her eyes.

She wrapped her arms around his neck and held him close. He smelled divine and he felt perfect. It made her head swim with desire and longing.

Drawing in a shaky breath, Amara threw all of her previous rationale out the window and placed her lips to his ear. "Jaide," she whispered, "make love to me."

She felt the coiled steel that was his muscles tense, and he jerked his head back to stare at her in shock and confusion. "What?" he rasped.

She swallowed hard and hoped she hadn't made a mistake in her boldness. Her heart would ache if he pushed her away and returned to scowling, brooding silence. She met his eyes, which were still wide with bafflement, and she brought her palms up to rest on his chest. "I want to know you," she murmured. "I want to know all of you." She saw the emotion in his green eyes. She knew it was there, and she hoped with all of her heart that he didn't push it away. She cradled his stern jaw in her palm. "Please, let me know you." At his silence, she sought to ease the tension of the situation. "You are my husband, after all."

He frowned. "Amara, that was a business transaction."

She shrugged. "Maybe so, but it's true all the same."

He stared at her long and hard with a mixed look of confusion and panic. It was the first time since meeting him that she had seen him look flustered and lost. He shivered visibly and his breath reflected the shudder that tore through him. He averted his eyes and shook his head. "Amara..." He swallowed and shook his head again, trying to push away and distance himself from her. "I...you don't know what you're saying."

She grasped onto his hands and squeezed. "I do know what I'm saying, Jaide. Look at me." She surprised herself with the command her voice held, and it seemed to surprise him too because he obeyed. She sighed, knowing the thoughts that went through his mind to cause him such apprehension. "You are not poisonous," she stated.

His brow furrowed and he looked down at his lap. "There is blackness in me."

"I know that. I have always known that."

"I don't want to tarnish your goodness."

His voice was so soft and so weak that she barely heard it. It tugged at her heart to hear all of his demanding power diminished. "Jaiden Sideth," she murmured, reaching up to brush her fingers through his hair. "You compare me with the flower you love, but do not mistake me for it. That flower is the thing that epitomizes supreme goodness to you. Flowers full of goodness don't stab people, shoot arrows into them, or strangle men with their legs while being bound naked to a wall." A small smile twitched at the corners of his mouth and she grinned. She scooted closer to him and trailed her fingers along the back of his neck. "Do not forget that I thrive on the untamed. Your blackness is not going to tarnish me, Jaide. I want to experience the passion I know you keep so carefully harnessed. For one moment in time, I want you to do the impossible."

He looked up to meet her eyes in question.

She smiled softly. "I want you to trust me."

He swallowed. "I do trust you," he muttered. "You know that."

She shook her head. "Trust me *completely*."

He held her gaze for a long moment before letting out a slow breath. "I have never been with anyone before," he admitted quietly.

She gave him a look that she knew reflected the warmth she felt. "Neither have I."

"I...I don't want to hurt you."

Her heart somersaulted in her chest at that soft admission. Tears stung her eyes. His words were heartfelt and full of tender emotion. She felt herself sitting within the inner sanctum of his soul, the place where no one was allowed, and she felt honored at having been granted such a rare privilege. She reached up and took his face in her hands, staring into his eyes. "You won't," she stated with assurance. "I trust you."

He flinched at her words, as if they had been unexpected, and emotion filled his eyes before he looked away. He drew in another shaky breath and she noticed his hands trembling as he clenched and unclenched them, no doubt in an attempt to make that very trembling stop. He still seemed uncertain and reluctant, and her heart broke just a little. She bit her bottom lip and averted her gaze. "Don't...don't you want me?" she whispered, fearing his answer, fearing his rejection, fearing she had made a grave mistake.

His eyes snapped up to hers and she gasped softly for

the uncertainty was gone and replaced by a dark, smoldering hunger that made her tingle with something that was akin to fear, even though she knew that's not what the emotion was.

"Amara," he said, all traces of self doubt gone from his voice, "I desire you when I have never desired another in my entire life." His smoldering gaze traveled over her body, leaving fire in its wake. "My lips never kissed another's before yours. My hands never caressed another. It has only ever been you that makes me burn inside, makes me feel anything other than ice. I look at you, I touch you, and my desire is so strong I fear I will never be able to escape it." He pushed her gently off of his lap and stood, graceful power radiating from every motion of his body. He held his hand out to her and she slid her fingers into his, uncertain of his intention. She gasped when he pulled her up and swept her into his arms, carrying her over to the bed and laying her gently down on top of it.

He leaned over her, his eyes traveling the length of her body before coming to rest on hers. "I have done many things wrong in my life, Amara," he whispered. "I have never been a good man and my hands are permanently stained with blood, but if this is what you truly want..." He framed her face with one hand and caressed his thumb across her cheek. "This will be the one thing I promise to do right."

Her heart thumped hard and erratic and her eyelids fluttered closed at his touch. She reached for his hand and took it in her own, watching as their fingers entwined. "I don't see any blood on your hands, Jaide," she breathed. "Only the calluses of the strongest warrior." She caught sight of the inferno that blazed to life in his eyes right before his lips descended onto hers and he swept her away in a kiss that went beyond everything she had ever experienced and shattered any boundary that had existed between them. She knew they had crossed the point of no return, and she buried her fingers in his hair as her heart came alive with his nearness and her body ached with anticipation and want.

To her surprise, the intensity of his kiss diminished, but when she would have protested, he pulled back and covered her lips with his fingers, shushing her quietly. He drew his hand down her chin and throat, tracing along her collarbone and down the side of her body until he reached the bottom of her gown. He delved his hand beneath it, tracing the line of her leg back up the way he had come. Amara shivered at the feel of his hand on her skin, and she drew in a soft breath as he pulled the gown over her head in a quick, fluid movement. The cool air hit her bare skin and she heard him make a low growl in his throat. She glanced over to see him taking in all of her pale skin as if mesmerized.

Slowly, he raised his eyes to hers. "Did you plan this, Amara?" he questioned.

She frowned.

He cocked an eyebrow. "There is a mysterious lack of undergarments on your body."

She giggled and felt her face flush. "Not planned," she murmured. "Just hoped for."

A rare smile graced his lips and she sucked her breath in as he pressed a hot kiss low on her stomach, low enough to cause her heartbeat to falter and her body to blaze to life. He raised his eyes to hers with a wicked glance before he stood and shed the rest of his clothing.

Amara trembled as he approached her, but not out of fear. He looked like a panther as he moved, the firelight reflecting off of every elegant line. Her eyes boldly assessed his body and she bit her bottom lip as he sat beside her. She thought he would come to lie next to her, but he didn't. He maintained careful distance even as his hands came up to trace the curves of her body that no one had even dared look upon, let alone touch. She closed her eyes in bliss as she surrendered to his ministrations, but the gentle, almost timid touch of his fingers was out of character and not what she had expected. She had sampled Jaide's passion, she had tasted the wild abandon when he'd let his control slip for just a moment. That was how she wanted him. Not disciplined and methodical. This was not a task he needed to accomplish. This was the ultimate sharing of himself with another. She knew he was apprehensive, but she would not allow him to shut his heart off from her even as he offered her his body.

She moved away and sat up with a suddenness that startled him, and she stabbed her finger at him. "Stand up," she commanded with authority. She would have smiled any other time at the swiftness of his compliance, but she had other items on her agenda. She rose up onto her knees and placed her hands on his chest. She felt his heart racing and she smiled softly as she looked up into his eyes. She pulled his head down so she could kiss him, and as he returned it, she maneuvered herself so that she could slip her legs around his waist.

Jaide sucked his breath in harshly and pulled his lips off of hers as her body aligned itself with his in the most intimate of positions. His arms came up to support her and he closed his eyes, shuddering so hard it was almost a convulsion. Amara's own body trembled at the feel of being pressed so close to him, and she tangled her fingers in his hair as he drew in ragged, harsh breaths.

"I'm not a flower," she whispered into his ear. "Don't treat me like one." She nipped on his earlobe, and his arms tightened around her just slightly. "You may be the assassin," she continued to whisper, "but these are my greatest weapons." She tightened her legs and squeezed a little, causing him to shiver again and lower his forehead to her shoulder. "You could be my next victim."

A breathy chuckle left him and he buried his lips against her throat. "I could think of worse ways to die," he rasped.

She grinned and closed her eyes as his fingers came up to twine through her hair and he tugged her head back gently, exposing her neck. His teeth descended to the soft part of her throat in a bite that stung, but that he instantly soothed with a velvet stroke of his tongue. A soft moan was torn from her mouth, and before she knew what was happening, he had laid her back on the bed, blanketing her body with his and consuming all of her senses with his powerful presence.

"I was going to be gentle," he murmured, nibbling along her jaw line.

She smiled and wrapped her arms around his shoulders, holding him close. "I don't want gentle," she said. "I want you." She felt his lips smile against her skin and his hands started a soft assault on her body, followed by his mouth, seeking out every soft curve and secret place. She gasped and writhed as he explored her body with unhurried diligence and skill that contrasted with his inexperience.

Jaide gave into the passion he felt, and the desire that burned through his veins. He'd be lying if he said it didn't frighten the hell out of him, because it did. Losing control in any way had always been out of the question, not an option, but to hand control over to anyone else was taboo. Amara had complete dominance over him in this moment, and he was powerless to do anything but comply with her every wish. The second his eyes had gazed upon her perfect body, he had been hypnotized. The second her long legs had wrapped around him, he had been imprisoned. And the second she had spoken the words that she wanted *him*, unskilled, rough and with all of his imperfections, he had been lost. She was the only creature who had ever accepted him the way he was. Blindly, completely, without apprehension. She had begun a quest to the center of his soul, and against all odds, she had managed to find it. And damned if he could keep her out now. She held the one and only key to the lock that held Jaiden at bay. Somewhere amidst their strange journey, he had become her captive.

He had never been intimate with a woman. He had never desired to be that close with someone. To him, lust was just another factor that could blur your thinking. Giving into it was losing control. It was not allowed. Part of him was shocked at himself for giving into Amara, but the other part was not. She was the most amazing and beautiful thing he had ever laid eyes on, and she accepted him in ways he could never even begin to understand. His occupation did not disgust her. His past did not revolt her. His roughness did not deter her. She remained steadfast, by his side, even when he had not wanted her there.

For the first time in his solitary existence, he did not feel cold. He did not feel empty.

He pressed his lips to her low belly, then dragged his teeth over to nibble at her hip bone. He drew his fingers down, starting at her throat and gliding over all of her soft skin. His hand, always so sure and so certain, so unwavering, trembled like a frightened child's as he slid his fingers into the warmth of her body. She gasped and arched upwards, her fists gripping the cover on the bed while a sultry groan left her mouth. His name left her lips in a whispered breath and he shivered. He moved up to claim her lips again, thrusting his tongue into her mouth, wanting to drink the sweet decadence that made up her extraordinary character.

Her fingers twined in his hair and she returned his kiss hungrily. He moved his fingers deeper, and she shuddered in his arms, pressing close to him and whimpering. A twinge of apprehension went through him and he pulled back to look at her. "Did I hurt you?" he whispered.

Her eyes were warm and full of tenderness. "No," she murmured, shaking her head. "No, far from it. Don't stop." She touched his face and pulled his lips back to hers, kissing him deeply while he explored her body, stoking an untamed fire within her that was slowly threatening to devour everything in its path.

He continued his erotic assault for a long while, building an inferno with his fingers while his mouth paid sweet attention to the rest of her. He slowly unraveled every ounce of her self control until she found herself clutching at him and begging for him to claim her body with his.

His devil's smile was upon his lips as he aligned his body with hers, and he brushed her hair away from her face, gazing down into her eyes. "I'll go slow," he whispered. "I don't want to hurt you."

She smiled at his continued concern and kissed him, more than ready for whatever it was he had to offer. A moment of pain didn't matter to her. She was no fragile being. Her heart thundered in her chest as he moved into position and she waited, every single nerve in her body tingling with anticipation.

The first wave of dread washed over her when she heard him suck in a sharp breath and he went completely still. The second wave came when she opened her eyes and saw his closed and his brow furrowed. "Jaide," she said. It sounded like a warning, which she supposed it was. He retreated from her just slightly, and alarm bells went off in her head. He could not do this to her now. She wouldn't have him thinking he was going to taint her, then tear away and leave her all alone in the cold. It wasn't going to happen. Not this time.

Taking control of the situation, she took his face in her hands and forced his lips down on hers, then managed to overturn him and roll him beneath her on the bed. She came up on top of him, and in one swift movement, took him into herself. She gasped at the sharp pain the invasion caused, and a hoarse cry was torn from his throat, followed by a shuddering breath that racked his entire body. She stayed still for a long moment, giving her body time to adjust to him while her heart wrapped itself around the fact that they were joined as one, the way a husband and wife were meant to be. That thought made heat rush throughout her body, and she smiled at the thought of being Jaide's wife. What did it matter that they had been married for legal purposes only? It was still valid and still true.

She ran her palms up his torso and chest, studying all of his sculpted muscle while she shifted against him slightly, moving her hips in a way that tore a guttural groan from him. She smiled and leaned forward to press kisses across his chest. "You feel incredible," she whispered, nibbling at his neck. "How do I feel?"

His hands came up to fist in her hair and tugged slightly so she looked up at him. She met his eyes, which were almost luminescent with their intensity, and a tremor went along her spine. One of deep longing and desire. "You feel..." He drew in a breath and closed his eyes for a moment, no doubt in order to gain some kind of control over himself. He calmed visibly, but he could not banish the emotion from his voice. "You feel like you're made of velvet fire," he whispered. "Like Ulyxes faced and slew Ulfarr then found Elendria...and the sky exploded into stars."

She stared at him for a long moment, awestruck at his poetic words and at the gentle way in which he kept touching her face, as if she was precious, as if she was cherished. By him. The man who loved nothing. He looked beautiful in the firelight, allowing her dominance over him for one small moment, the lines of his face reflecting passion, the depth of his eyes revealing emotion he would never be able to voice, but she heard the message just the same.

She drew in a soft, startled breath as he took control once again and rolled her back beneath him. His mouth came up against her ear and she closed her eyes, holding him to her.

"Amaranth of Catlaan," he whispered. "The greatest weapon I could not conquer. My destruction and salvation." He drew in a shaky breath. "The only thing that has ever brought me peace and joy."

Tears stung her eyes at his words, and she clung to him fiercely as he began to move against her. She cried out as pleasure tore through her, and again as it intensified.

Jaide fused his lips with hers, making love to her mouth as he made love to her body. She was wild in his arms, holding nothing back from him, not afraid to show him the passion she felt. She was as untamed as he was, and she made him feel the most amazing freedom. He had always been a slave to something. The orphanage, the Rezzegard, his own stubborn discipline. He couldn't even remember a time when he had felt free. Amara made him feel that. It was the greatest gift she ever could have given him.

He reached for one of her long, slender legs, running his hand along the length of it before pulling it up to wrap around his waist. A very desirable noise came from her throat and he smiled as he moved his lips to her neck. He loved feeling her legs around him. They were power and grace all at once.

He took his time with her, wanting the ecstasy to last beyond a stolen moment. He went slow, then fast, only to go slow again. He found that doing that created many more desirable noises and caused her to dig her fingers into his shoulders in a desperate, frenzied expression of passion.

He'd never felt like he'd been missing anything when he'd decided that celibacy was his best course of action. He still held to that decision. He knew no other woman would ever stir his blood the way his Amaranth could. He would never even want to look for one. This right belonged to her and her alone.

"Jaide, please," she whimpered, "I feel like I'm burning up."

"So do I." He took her hands in his and linked their fingers, pulling her arms up over her head. She arched her body against him and tossed her head to the side. He smiled and brought his lips to hover over hers. "Just let it happen, Amara," he whispered. "I'll let go when you do." He'd never thought that he could get such joy out of bringing another person pleasure, but watching Amara react to him was one of the most gratifying feelings of his life.

The release of her passion came upon her suddenly and she threw her head back, screaming his name in a way that made shivering tingles run along his spine. He caught her mouth with his and gave into his own passion as wave upon wave of overwhelming, all-consuming feeling crashed over him. A noise left his throat caught somewhere between a groan and a growl and he trembled like a boy as all of his strength left him and he collapsed against her, shivering and gasping for breath.

She clutched him close to her, her own breathing ragged. Her fingers came up to stroke through his hair, and he closed his eyes in bliss. If heaven existed, he had found it in that moment.

Slowly, Amara's heart rate returned to a steady, even pace and the sweat that had beaded on her skin cooled. Jaide moved off of her and came to lie beside her, pulling her up against him so that her head was resting on his shoulder. She closed her eyes and basked in the warmth of his body and the delicious tingles that worked through her in the aftermath of their lovemaking.

She glanced up at him and watched as he gazed into the fire for a long moment. He turned his attention to her slowly and looked down into her eyes for almost as long as he'd stared into the fire. He said nothing, but that was expected. She didn't mind. He'd said more than enough while wrapped in the throes of passion. Jaide wasn't a man of words. He never would be. She knew and accepted that. Besides, all she needed to know was reflected in the depths of his eyes.

She smiled as she watched a thousand different things flash through those eyes right before the frown returned to crease his brow. Her smile morphed into a grin and she reached up to smooth the wrinkle away. "Always so serious," she teased.

He smiled softly and closed his eyes, then pressed a gentle kiss to her lips. "Don't leave," he murmured. "Don't leave my arms tonight."

She shook her head as she nestled close to him. "There's no chance of that."

She reached one arm across his chest and absently trailed her fingers along his skin, tracing muscles, soothing old scars. He grasped her wrist and pulled her hand over to the left side of his chest, saying nothing, but pressing her palm over his heart. He caressed her arm and held her tight, falling into silence and deep into thought.

Amara kept her hand over his heart, feeling the beat as if it echoed through her own soul. She let the rhythm of it lull her into contented sleep.

Chapter Nineteen

She was humming. Humming because she was happy. Happier than she had been in a long time. She folded her red dress from the night before, then plaited her golden hair into a braid. She smiled as she thought of Jaide and their night together. She'd never imagined being with a man could be so incredible, and she'd never thought that sleeping within the embrace of an assassin could bring her such warm joy. But it had. And she would be lying to herself if she said she didn't want to experience that feeling over and over again. Jaide, in spite of all of his prickles, was addictive. His touch, his scent, his taste, and the look in his eyes when he let his barriers drop just for her, all of it combined created a powerful concoction that she loved and adored. She had started out fearing and despising him. Now, she couldn't even begin to imagine not having him with her. Life had a bizarre and twisted sense of humor.

She swaggered past his sleeping form to put something away, and as she walked back by, he snatched her wrist and pulled her down onto the bed. She let out a squeak of surprise as she fell on top of him, and she blinked at him in bewilderment.

Jaide kept his face expressionless, even though he couldn't keep the spark of amusement out of his eyes.

Amara shook her head. "You scared me half to death."

He reached up to tangle his fingers in her hair. "I'm good at that."

She snorted. "You've got that right." The tension eased out of her body and a soft smile curved her lips. "Good morning."

"Good morning." He wrapped one arm around her shoulders and rolled her onto her back, cradling her close and touching her face tenderly.

Amara's heart fluttered and she grinned, reaching up to tousle his already disheveled black hair. She marveled over his playfulness, even if it was minute. For Jaide, it was enormous. She studied his face, which was still placid, still difficult to read, even as his hands trailed lazy patterns along her skin. His touch revealed what his face could not.

She placed her hands on his chest and a naughty thought entered her mind. She bit her bottom lip and looked up at him coyly from under her lashes. "You should bathe," she stated.

He arched an eyebrow. "You trying to tell me something?"

She giggled and pressed closer to him. "I'm trying to tell you that I'd really like to see what you look like wet and naked."

His grin was warm and brilliant, and his chuckle heated her blood. "You already know what I look like wet and naked. With frogs in my hair, no less."

She laughed as she remembered that incident. It seemed like a lifetime ago, with a completely different man. She pushed herself into a sitting position and trailed her fingertips along his torso. "I was going to see if the innkeeper would let me make you breakfast." She grinned, delighting in the thought of doing something so simple for him. She had been cooking for him since all of this had begun. It shouldn't have mattered, but it did somehow. The small gesture made her feel like she was taking care of him. It was the first thing that had softened him toward her.

His sigh was heavy and he glanced to the window. His expression shifted, and some of the cold steel he cloaked himself with returned to his features. "There really isn't any time, Amara. Things are going to start happening very quickly." He gently pushed her away from him while he sat up and swung his legs out of bed, searching for his clothing.

She sat back on her knees and frowned. "What do you mean? What is going to start happening?" A strange twinge went through her stomach.

He glanced back at her over his shoulder. "I have a mission to finish. Loose ends need to be tied up."

Her frown deepened and her voice wavered when she spoke. Slow panic crept into her, chasing her jubilation away. "What are you talking about?"

He stood and pulled on his pants. "You know I have been sending messages." He met her eyes. "Well, those messages have been going somewhere." She noticed his eyes were distant, not as warm as she would have imagined them to be after their night together. The cold panic within her intensified. She watched him dress methodically, with purpose, as if he had a...

She swallowed hard.

As if he had a job to do.

"Jaide?" She sounded frightened even to herself.

Her tone caught his attention and he looked at her with confusion. He frowned and held his hand out to her. She took it immediately and went into his arms. The protection of his embrace chased away her fears momentarily, and his lips descended onto hers with soft, tender pressure. She felt the fire come to life within her and she melted against him.

"You don't need to be so worried," he whispered, nuzzling his nose against hers. "All of this will be over soon."

She moved away with a frown, her heart skipping a beat at his choice of words. "What do you mean? I don't understand."

He opened his mouth to answer her, but a tremendous pounding on the door caused her to jump and him to scowl.

"Sideth! Are you in there, you miserable scoundrel?"

Amara glanced up at Jaide in confusion and he heaved a sigh, running a hand through his hair. "Go downstairs!" he commanded. His voice sounded more than a little annoyed.

"You don't give me orders! You work for me, not the other way around! I paid you fine money to bring the girl to me and you make me traipse all the way across the sea to meet you here? I've had just about enough of your antics. Open the door and give me what I asked for!"

Amara felt the color drain from her face, and her heart plummeted in a way that almost made her throw up. She gasped and staggered away from Jaide, horrified at the voice at the other end of the door.

He was quick to grasp her by the wrist to keep her from retreating. "I made you traipse all the way over here because

I cannot stand one more second of this bloody job! I am an assassin, not a blasted nanny! This woman is trying my patience and I'm at the end of my rope. You take her off my hands here and give me my pay!"

"I'll gladly take her off your hands if you open the bloody door!"

Jaide let out something close to a snarl. "I said go downstairs, Marden! I will not be ordered around by the likes of you! Wait for me outside! Otherwise I will keep your money and dispatch her myself, then see to it that you rot in a shallow grave!"

Lord Marden grumbled something incoherent and his footsteps could be heard descending the stairs.

Amara shook her head, blind panic and sorrow welling up within her. She tried to yank her arm out of Jaide's grasp as tears spilled down her cheeks. "You betrayed me!" she cried. "You're going to have me killed anyway?" Her voice wavered, her words a question more than a statement. "You sent for him to meet you here?" She tugged on her arm again as she sobbed, but his hold was relentless.

"Amara," he snapped, "listen to me."

She looked up at him, but flinched, especially when she saw that he had the audacity to smile. What was he doing? Had this been his plan all along? To get her to cooperate? Had he outfoxed her, and she had been that stupid? That arrogant to believe...to believe he could...that she could actually mean something to him? Had her original quest to dupe him ended up in him duping her? That was all well and good except...she loved him. Was she the weak one after all?

"Sometimes, when you wander into a badger's lair, all the badger does is make noise," he murmured.

She stared at him for one long moment of silence, wondering if he'd completely lost his mind. "What?" she whimpered. "What are you talking about?" He chuckled and tried to pull her closer, but she shrieked and jerked away. "Are you insane?" She couldn't even align her mind with his to try and understand what he was saying. Badgers only made noise? Badgers be damned! Marden was waiting downstairs to kill her and destroy her father, as well as the people of Catlaan. She didn't give a flying fig about badgers! "Badgers don't just make noise! They bite you!" She managed to pull her arm free, and she slapped him hard across the cheek, the grief she felt at knowing he was going to turn her over to Marden threatening to strangle her and crush her heart. After everything they had shared. After they had made love...

Why?

She took several steps back and sobbed, wrapping her arms around herself. "A badger always bites!" she continued. "And you almost feel sorry for it because you know that the only reason it's attacking you is because it's afraid. And in the deepest part of your heart, you want to soothe it, and tell it you're not going to hurt it, but in the end, you know it'll never listen. It's a wild thing, and it's not in the nature of the beast to be anything other than savage." She drew in a shuddering breath while the tears continued to flow. "Sooner or later, no matter how badly you may want to hold it and keep it close to you, you have to *pry it loose*!"

He stared at her for a long moment, saying nothing, with the strangest look in his eyes. All it did was make her heart crumble just a little bit more and fuel her rage. Had she only been a game to him this entire time? Had she only been a curiosity, something for him to pass the time? While she had fallen in love with him, had he only been toying with her for his own sick sadism? Her entire body quaked with sorrow, rage, and fear. The man who was going to end her life was waiting for Jaide right outside of the inn. Her last moments were upon her.

He had brought her here.

He had orchestrated this.

Jaide.

The heartless assassin. That was who he was. That was all he would ever be.

With a horrible, heart-wrenching sob, she lashed out at him and let her fist fly. It made contact with his jaw and sent pain flaring up her arm, but she barely felt it. His head jerked to one side and his lip started to bleed, but he said nothing. He remained still and calm. She hated it. She hated when he was calm.

He drew in a deep breath, and with frightening speed, he latched onto her shoulders, staring down at her with dark, un-feeling eyes. "Amara," he said, his voice a command in itself. She screamed and tried to get out of his grip, but his fingers only tightened, and he gave her an almost violent shake. "Listen to me, woman!" he bellowed. "You're being a fool!"

"I am a fool!" she cried. "I am the biggest fool ever born for thinking you could be anything other than the hideous monster you are!"

His body stiffened and his face turned dark.

She went on, not caring what she said. It didn't matter now anyway. She just wanted to hurt him, hurt him the way he had hurt her. "You're no better than any of them! You're all the same, and you're the worst! You are black poison! Black poison that kills and kills again!"

He went rigid and something that looked like pain flashed through his eyes before she saw nothing. His eyes grew vacant and his face became devoid of all emotion. It was the exact same face she had looked into the night he'd abducted her on the terrace. She abhorred it, and yet it was still the most beautiful thing she had ever seen. Pain like she had never known lanced through her heart until she felt as if it lay in shards.

Hoof beats sounded outside, a clattering, thunderous noise that made her insides squirm with the thought of hundreds of Marden's soldiers, all waiting to escort her to her final resting place, wherever that might be.

Jaide stepped back, releasing her shoulders. He said nothing, but reached out and opened the door. She looked at him in confusion, not understanding his actions. He said nothing and stared straight ahead, showing no life in his eyes, no emotion in any line of his face.

She didn't understand, but she wasn't about to stand there and try to figure it out. She bolted out the door and down the stairs, wondering if there was a back door, or some way she might be able to escape Marden and his men. Had Jaide let her go as a last act of mercy? Had he been trying to give her one last chance to escape? Or was it all just part of his sick game?

Her mind still spinning, she tore through the inn and burst out the front door, prepared to dodge anything that might come her direction. She all but skidded to a stop, her heart thudding against her ribcage as utter confusion gripped onto her and wouldn't let go.

She blinked in bafflement, disoriented and shocked, as

her eyes fell upon the troop of soldiers in the distance. All of them were dressed in the colors of Catlaan. Several soldiers held Lord Marden and his few men at bay, and...

She swallowed hard and could barely find her breath. Striding toward her was the most amazing thing she had ever seen. New tears filled her eyes and she started to shake so hard she was afraid she wouldn't be able to stand. "Father?" she murmured. He was so tall and statuesque, so strong. He was everything in her entire world. "Father!" She shouted it in a tear-laden voice and ran to him, throwing herself into his arms and sobbing like a little child. He clutched her close and she held onto him with vehemence, burying her face against his chest and crying until it hurt.

"It's all right," he soothed. "You're safe now. You're safe..."

His voice was like music and she clung to him, trembling. "Wh-What are you doing here?" She pulled back just enough to look up at him and she saw that his attention diverted to the front door of the inn. Amara turned to see Jaide as he walked out.

"You!" Marden shouted. "You double-crossing bastard!"

Jaide glanced his direction, then shrugged nonchalantly. "You were never that great of a client anyway."

Amara frowned and glanced from her father back to Jaide.

"I take it you are the assassin who has been communicating with me?" her father said, stoic and calm.

Jaide dipped his head in a respectful gesture, as well as an affirmative reply. "I have done what I promised, Your Majesty."

Amara's frown deepened and she shook her head. "What? What you promised? Father, what's going on?" She looked back at Jaide and a different kind of sickening feeling took possession of her.

"This man has been sending me messages," her father replied. "He revealed Marden's plan, how he was paying him to bring you to him. He told me he couldn't fulfill his end of the bargain and he wanted me to bring a regiment of men and meet him here. He lured Marden here by himself, with only a few men as guards, knowing that he would never think he was being double-crossed. We intercepted."

"You were given your daughter, as well as your adversary," Jaide's smooth voice said. "I have done as I said."

Amara's father gave a curt nod. "It is done." His face grew deadly. "Now, leave my presence and hope I never see you near my daughter again. Your actions have bought you your life and your freedom, but not my compassion."

Amara blinked rapidly and shook her head, trying to process everything that had occurred. Jaide bowed deep before her father and nodded. "My shadow will never darken your path again." He turned and began to retreat.

"Wait!" Amara called. He had been planning to return her to her father the entire time? He had double-crossed Marden for her...because he cared for her? Because he couldn't go through with the job? She remembered him sending the message in Toberton. He had been planning this since then? Since the night she had told him what-for in the forest, after she had saved his life...

A life for a life.

Guilt washed over her for the things she had thought and said. Was she so quick to think he would hurt her in such a way? Did she really have such little faith in the man she loved? She loved him for a reason. She had grown to love him because he had shown her the man inside. How could she have been so quick to throw that aside?

She tried to go to him, but her father firmly clamped a hold of her arm. "Amara," he protested. "What are you doing?"

"Father, let me go," she insisted. His grip only tightened and he muttered something about keeping her away from the filthy assassin. She scowled and yanked her arm out of his hold. "I said, *let me go*!" Her voice snapped like a whip and held more command than she'd ever thought she was capable of. It was enough to make her father comply and she ran back over to Jaide, shouting his name.

He turned, and she flung her arms around him, crying all over again and clinging to him in much the same way she had done to her father. "Jaide, I'm so sorry. The things I said..." She buried her face against his shoulder and felt his fingers come up to stroke through her hair.

"It's all right," he murmured.

She shook her head and looked up at him. "No, it isn't. You were right. Sometimes badgers only make noise. I didn't understand. I was so scared. I didn't realize... I'm such an idiot." She reached up and feathered her fingers across his split lip. "I struck you. I'm so sorry."

A small smile graced his lips, and he took her face in his hands. "You've struck me before. It will heal. And, Amara, you were the one who was right."

She frowned.

"I was stupid to think this could last, that this could even happen." He sighed. "Our paths were never supposed to cross. My darkness never should have touched you."

She shook her head adamantly. "No, you're wrong. I didn't mean any of what I said. You're not black poison. You're not—"

"I know you didn't mean what you said, but it was true all the same," he said, his voice never raising above a soft, velvety cadence. "You gave me a moment of peace in a life-time of nothing but cold, aching pain. For that, I will always be grateful, but that is all it can ever be. A moment."

Her bottom lip trembled and she felt like her heart was breaking all over again, for a hundred different reasons. "But-but...we're married." She gasped, feeling as if she had the upper hand with that one little fact. "Father, we were married!"

"It was for legality only," Jaide replied calmly, glancing over to her father. "It is a technicality I am sure you can ab-solve as king."

"You can rest assured of that," her father growled.

The momentary stab of hope Amara had felt dissolved and she looked back at Jaide with tears hovering in her eyes. "Jaide, please," she whimpered. "Don't do this."

He shook his head and closed his eyes. "Hush now," he whispered, resting his forehead against hers. "You are not meant for the life I lead. You know this." One of his arms slipped around her waist and pulled her close to him.

She wrapped her arms tight around him, breathing deep-ly of his scent in an effort to etch it firmly into her memory. "Jaide," she whispered feebly. "Please, don't leave. You don't understand." Her grief gathered and clogged her throat. She forced in a breath. "Jaide, I lo—"

He pulled back and put his fingers to her lips. "No," he murmured, shaking his head. "Don't you ever say those words to me. They are words I do not deserve and will not accept. You are the one good thing that has ever entered my life, and this is the one good thing I have ever done. This is not duty, not obligation. This is right. Please, let me finish it." He cradled her face in his hand and sighed, trailing his thumb over her trembling bottom lip. "Go live your life, Amaranth of the Wild Things. Live well. Live long." A lovely smile graced his perfect lips and the warmth she adored returned to his eyes. "And know that, somewhere in the wilderness, an assassin is thinking of you fondly." He grasped her hand and pulled it to his lips, then stepped away. "Go on now."

Amara couldn't move. She couldn't speak. All she could do was stand there and tremble silently. She didn't want to see him walk away. She didn't want him to disappear from her life forever. He would return to his solitary life, alone, cold, isolated. He would be left to battle his demons all alone. The thought made her ache inside.

She reached out to him one more time, but he caught her shoulder and turned her around, shoving her forward with a well-placed hand on her back. "Go," he demanded, his voice betraying a strange, foreign rasp.

She looked over her shoulder, but he was already retreating, his magnificent form disappearing back into the darkness of the inn. She felt her heart splinter, but instead of the crushing pain she had expected, all she felt was a dull, throbbing ache. In some ways, that was much, much worse.

* * * *

Jaide watched from the window as the regiment of Catlaan men rode away, taking Marden, and Amara, with them. He hadn't felt pain in his heart since the day he'd resigned himself to the fact that he belonged to the Rezzegard. Not real pain. Maybe he'd had fleeting moments, but this... This was torture.

Her red dress still lay where she had left it, and he had trouble wrapping his mind around the fact that, just the previous evening, he had made love to her, had gone to sleep holding her in his arms. It had been the most peaceful moment of his life. He would never find one to equal it. He never wanted to.

He'd never expected her to react the way she had that

morning, but then again, he hadn't expected Marden to come bludgeon the door either. He had planned on explaining things to her before Marden showed up. He'd been eager to see the elation in her gray eyes when he'd told her that she would be seeing her father and going home. Instead, everything had been a disaster. She'd taken everything he'd said completely wrong and had thought he'd betrayed her. She'd hurled the cruelest words at him that he had ever heard.

And the severely painful part was, all of her words had been true. Even though she hadn't meant them, they'd been true. He was poison and he was darkness. He was a monster, and he never should have even entertained the fact of being able to keep her close to him. He knew better. They were from two completely different worlds. They both had their path to walk amongst the stars, and they would never cross. Much like Ulyxes and Elendria.

He sighed and sat down on the end of the bed, feeling empty and cold in a way that went beyond the norm. He closed his eyes and tried to remember her smell, the feel of her soft hair against his hands, the sound of her laugh and the touch of her lips.

Amaranth of Catlaan.

The greatest weapon.

His greatest downfall.

Chapter Twenty

Nothing was the same. Nothing would ever be the same again. Her life, which had at one time been simple and beautiful now seemed monotonous. The last thing she wanted to do was her studies, and even playing with the children did not give her the joy it used to.

All she did was think of Jaide. Even when she didn't want to. She closed her eyes at night and recalled what his hands felt like on her skin, what his lips felt like against her own, so sinful and full of dark magic. She replayed every moment of their time together, even the frightening and horrible ones. Remembering the unpleasant was better than remembering nothing at all, and she was terrified of having his memory leave her. She didn't want to return to life before Jaide. He'd been the most beautiful thing she had ever encountered, in his own twisted and unconventional way.

Her father had nullified their marriage almost instantly, which made her sick inside. Even though she'd been tricked into marrying him, in the end, it was a union she'd wanted to hold onto. She'd loved the idea of being his wife, sharing his bed and his heart. She wished he had wanted the same, but she knew how difficult it was for him to change, for him to see himself through her eyes. She didn't fault him for any of what had happened. If anything, it was her fault. Her fault for overreacting. Her fault for thinking so little of him. If she had taken a moment to listen to him, to let him explain instead of automatically assuming the worst, maybe things would have turned out differently.

She sat in her room now, wondering where he was, what he was doing. Had he been contracted by someone, given a job to accomplish, which he would do with no qualms and no remorse? Did he think of her? Or had he forgotten about her as soon as she'd left his sight? No, she didn't believe that. She knew Jaide cared, even if he had decided that being with her was not what he wanted.

It had been two weeks since they'd parted. Marden had been imprisoned. The threat to her father was gone. Life had returned to normal, at least for everyone else. For her, life would never be normal again. It would be empty and hollow, nothing more than a routine she was required to obey.

A soft knock sounded on her door and she glanced up, beckoning whoever it was to come in. Her father entered, giving her a gentle smile when he spotted her sitting on her bed, no doubt looking as dejected as she felt.

"Hello, darling," he greeted, coming to sit on the foot of the bed beside her.

She forced a smile. "Hello, Father."

Something softened in his eyes and he sighed, reaching over to pat her knee. "Did I ever tell you about my old royal advisor?"

She frowned and shook her head, wondering what in the world that had to do with anything.

He sighed. "Well, he was probably the most disgruntled man I have ever known. He hated children, couldn't stand the sight of them, and most of the time, they avoided him like the plague."

She glanced up at him and arched an eyebrow.

He grinned and ran his hand down the length of her hair with a chuckle. "You never seemed fazed by him, though. Whenever you were near him, you would follow him around, drool on the hem of his coat, try to play with his boot buckles. I know it bothered him on the highest level, but there wasn't much he could do about it. You were the princess so he had to let you do what you would. And I got great amusement out of watching him squirm, so I let you do what you would also."

She giggled in spite of herself.

"Anyway, you apparently decided after a while that you weren't getting enough of a reaction out of him so you started a new routine. Every time I would have a meeting with him, you would crawl up into his lap and start playing with his hair, babbling in baby talk."

She laughed and shook her head. "How old was I?"

"Around two, I think. I always had you with me. Your mother tried to keep you with her, but I couldn't bear to have you out of my sight."

Warmth and affection filled Amara's heart and she leaned over to rest her head on her father's shoulder. She closed her eyes as a small measure of comforting peace stole into her broken heart.

He slipped his arm around her and gave her a gentle embrace. "Anyway, it mortified my advisor, but there wasn't anything he could do about it. He just had to let you sit there. He took great precautions to avoid you at all costs, but somehow, you always found him. You were very persistent." He chuckled again. "Something about that sour man really drew your attention. I couldn't for the life of me figure out what, but then one day, it became very clear to me.

"You were supposed to be with your mother, but I suppose you had escaped again. I was heading to the main hall to have a discussion with some of the lords of the neighboring kingdoms and, as I walked in, I saw something so extraordinary that it baffles me to this day."

Amara sat up and looked at her father with interest, wondering where the story was headed.

He reached up and smoothed a few locks of her wayward hair. "I saw my advisor, that bitter, agitated man, holding you on his lap, bouncing you up and down on his knees, laughing like I had never seen him laugh before. You were squealing with delight and you flung your arms around him with laughter and squeezed the life out of him. He embraced you with the biggest grin. I saw his face light up for the first time since I'd appointed him to his position." He shook his head. "You two were inseparable after that. You were always playing with him. You were great friends until he resigned around the time you were five..." His sigh was large and sounded slightly defeated. "Amara, you saw something in that man, even at such a young age, that no one else ever would have been able to pick up on. Despite his less than charming disposition, you saw straight into his heart and knew what was inside. You were able to bring that to the fore with your patient diligence. You have always been able to do that, even with the worst of creatures."

Her heart tripped over itself and started to ache because his words made her think of Jaide.

"You had so many wild animals as your friends when you were a girl," he continued. "Injured things that everyone else would have been terrified of. You cared for them and they never once harmed you. It's like they could sense your goodness. They took refuge in you when everyone else caused them despair and angst."

Tears filled her eyes and she looked down at her lap.

"You have always known your path, my daughter." Her father's voice was soft and tender. "You have always been strong and capable and independent. You've never made a choice without having a perfectly sound reason for it. I may not be able to see in people what you do, but I trust your judgment."

She frowned and met his eyes, not understanding what he was getting at.

He sighed and took her chin in between his thumb and forefinger. "I have never seen you look so sad."

Her heart throbbed in her chest and two tears managed to escape her eyes and run tracks down her cheeks.

Her father wiped them with gentleness, but he frowned as he did it. "Did he touch you, Amara? The assassin?"

She sniffled and reached up to wipe at her eyes. She averted her attention and felt a flush creep into her cheeks at the straightforward question. Visions of her and Jaide making love filled her mind and made her ache with so much longing she thought she would die from the pain of it. "Not until I asked him to," she finally murmured, then forced a dry laugh. "And even then he was reluctant."

To her surprise, her father's sigh sounded more like playful exasperation. "You attacked the poor man, didn't you?"

She blinked up at him in shock at his teasing.

He shook his head. "Just like your mother. No wonder the man loves you."

She felt her cheeks go crimson, and she let out a breathy laugh. "Oh, no, he—"

He took her gently by the shoulders. "Amara, men like that do not have compassion. Men like that do not have mercy or conscience. For him to do what he did, betray his client, turn his back on the money he was being offered, and send a message to me to come and retrieve you... The only motive he could have had was love." Tears filled her eyes again and hovered on her lashes at the thought of Jaide feeling for her the way she did for him. Her father smiled and pressed a kiss to her forehead, then pulled a letter out of the folds of his doublet. "Go find your husband," he said, handing the letter to her.

She blinked in bewilderment and gave him a questioning frown.

"Read it," he urged.

She did so, and her heart began to beat with an urgent hope that threatened to take her breath. She threw her arms around her father and held on, elated and overjoyed.

He chuckled. "I will send you with several guards in a carriage. I have faith you can track him down."

She grinned and pulled back to look at him. "I think I can." A fleeting thought entered her mind and she frowned. "But, Father..." She bit her bottom lip and sighed. "There's something I must ask you. A favor... I'm not sure if you can do anything about it."

He pressed another kiss to her forehead and smoothed her hair again. "Tell me, sweetheart. If it is in my power, it will be done."

* * * *

Jaide had never been extremely fond of liquor. It was something that dulled the senses and impaired reflexes. It was detrimental to him doing his job correctly. Right now, however, the fiery liquid burning down his throat into his gut seemed to be doing just the job.

"Are you the one they call Jaide Sideth?" a silken, purring voice came suddenly from next to him at the bar.

He heaved a sigh and held his glass up to gaze through it, watching the light refract off of the amber liquid inside. "They call me Jaide Sideth because that is my name," he drawled, downing the contents. "Who's asking?"

The purring voice had an equally purring laugh. "Someone who can pay you very handsomely if you choose to take me up on my offer."

He slid a sidelong glance over to the owner of the voice.

Regal, slender, with the blackest hair and eyes he had ever seen. She was absolutely beautiful and it made him scowl. A beautiful death-dealer. A black widow at her best. "And what makes a woman like you interested in my services?" he asked without inflection, turning in his chair to look at her full on.

She crossed one leg over the other, showing off an abundant amount of skin considering the way her form-fitting black skirt was slit. She leaned nonchalantly against the bar, twirling her fingers idly through her hair. "Well, they say you're the best." Her eyes darkened. "And the best is what I need." Her grin was almost slimy. "I'm rumored to be the best at other things. Maybe we can trade off."

Her words made his stomach turn. He motioned to the bartender. He brought him another drink, which Jaide threw back without any qualms. "Who are you trying to off? Your husband?"

She laughed melodically and tossed her hair. "No, no one so trivial as that. This is a man who should be a sitting duck for you. He was imprisoned two weeks ago, but that's really not enough for me. You see, he not only made off with a significant amount of my money, but he tried to take my land as well."

Jaide frowned. "Where are you from?"

"Across the sea, just south of Dother. Lord Raglan Marden tried to ally himself with me as he did with the other three lords of the province, but took me for a fool and decided to rob me right before he attempted to lay siege on my castle." She snorted with disdain. "I would have done away with him myself, but shortly after that, he disappeared across the sea and got himself arrested by the king of Catlaan."

Jaide stared at her for a long moment, wondering what kind of sick luck he really had. Why could he not seem to get away from Raglan Marden? He sighed. "Is there no end to that man's idiocy?" he grumbled.

She arched an elegant eyebrow. "You know of Raglan Marden?"

He smiled ruefully. "You might say that." He set his glass down on the bar and sighed. "I am not interested in your proposition if he is your target. Find another assassin."

She frowned. "But why? Are you a friend of his? I thought men like you had no friends."

"I don't," he stated, "and he is certainly no such thing, but my dealings with Marden have brought me nothing but grief and headaches. If you want to off him, fine, but find another man for the job. I am not interested." He pushed himself away from the bar and stood, intending to make his way back to his room. Her hand on his arm both stopped him and annoyed him. He shot her a black scowl. "Unhand me, woman," he warned.

She was impertinent enough to tighten her grip. "Now you listen here, assassin. I traveled all this way to seek you out because you are rumored to be the best in the business and I don't want this job botched. I am willing to pay you more gold than you've probably ever laid eyes on so the least you can do is hear me out."

His lip curled into a snarl, and the growl that came from his throat made her eyes widen. "I owe you nothing. Unhand me and leave me in peace before I decide to target you for my own enjoyment." She was quick to obey and he moved swiftly away from her, ascending the staircase and seeking refuge in his room.

He sighed deeply as he closed the door behind him, but almost instantly felt uneasy tingles ripple along his spine. He was not alone. And that irritated him on the highest level. He just wanted some blasted peace. He unsheathed his sword with a swift movement and had the blade at the throat of the cloaked figure in his room before his heart could beat twice. "State your purpose," he snarled. "Are you with that woman downstairs?"

There was a long moment of silence before the strangest and most unexpected voice assaulted his ears. "Are you going to kill me, Jaide?"

His eyes widened and the air slammed out of his lungs. The hand of the cloaked figure gently pushed his sword aside and turned, pulling down the hood of the cloak to reveal the visage that had haunted his nightmares and wicked fantasies, that tortured him every waking moment. His heart tripped over itself. "Amara?" he rasped. She was radiant, dressed in a rich, shining light blue dress that made her ethereal beauty even greater and her gray eyes seem like soft clouds in the summer sky. His hand trembled and he quickly sheathed his weapon and fisted it to disguise that traitorous expression of how her presence affected him. "What are you doing here?"

She smirked and her eyes filled with tremendous warmth as they traveled across his face. She studied him for a long moment, but made no movement toward him. It was something he was more than grateful for. If she'd tried to touch him, tried to approach him, keeping his distance from her would have been impossible. "You said there was a woman downstairs. Did she get to you before I did?"

He frowned.

"Did she hire you?"

He snorted. "No, and if you can believe it, the man she wanted me to do away with was Marden."

She arched an eyebrow. "That is ironic."

"To say the least." He folded his arms across his chest, his heart still hammering at her very nearness. "What are you doing here? How did you find me?"

Her smile was like the sunrise. "With some difficulty, but I would not be dissuaded. I have a job for you."

He blinked, then frowned deeply. "You have a job for me?"

She shrugged one shoulder. "Actually, my father has a job for you." She pulled a folded paper from a pocket inside her cloak and handed it to him.

Jaide gave her a skeptical look, but took the paper anyway. He unfolded it and let his eyes scan over the bold script of the King of Catlaan. As he read, he felt the color drain from his face, and his stomach took on a strange, hollow feeling. The words he read were foreign and odd. "Your father..." He cleared his throat for his voice tried to fail him. "He wants me to be the Captain of his Royal Guard?"

She nodded. "Yes. I told him about how skilled you were and he wants you to train the new recruits... You would get a regular salary, which in the end, would amount to far greater riches than several freelance assassinations. He sent this with me to give to you as a down payment." She pulled a bag of gold from her pocket and plopped it into his hand.

Jaide stared at the gold in his one hand, a greater amount than anything he'd ever been paid, then he directed his attention to the letter in his other hand. His mind had difficulty wrapping around the information being handed to him. "I...I don't understand," he muttered, turning his eyes up to her. "Why would your father want me anywhere near you after what I did? I almost ended your life, Amara."

"Yes, but you didn't," she stated. "And my father is a smart man. He knows a good warrior when he sees one. Plus, there is the small fact that I am completely and hopelessly in love with you and he doesn't want to see me sad any longer."

Jaide felt like someone had delivered a harsh blow to his chest. The air left his lungs in such a way that he feared he would never be able to take in a full breath again. Those words... She had spoken them so matter-of-fact. The hand that held the letter began to tremble so badly he had to put it behind his back. His mind swirled as it tried to wrap around her statement. "What did you just say?" He couldn't have heard her right. It had to be just his own deluded fantasy. He was a monster and a dark stain. He would bring nothing but blackness to her beautiful life. She could never—

His eyes closed and he dropped both the letter and the bag of gold to the floor as she suddenly threw her calm composure to the wind and flung herself into his arms, pressing her lips to his with a fervor that threatened to rock the ground on which he stood. Fire exploded along every surface of his body and he clutched her to him, matching her with the starved passion of his own soul. Her scent assaulted him, intoxicated him, and her taste threatened to unravel everything that made him who he was. It had been roughly a month since he had bid farewell to his Amaranth. All of that time disappeared while everything else fell back into place.

"You're so stupid," she whispered as she pulled away from him and knotted her fingers in his hair. "Black poison and all of that nonsense." She shook her head. "Stop being such a baby."

He blinked down at her, at a loss for words. Amara always did have a knack for telling things the way they were. Her grin lit up his entire world.

She trailed her hands down his chest and reached for his hands, taking them in her own. "My father has also said that, as a gift for your acceptance of the position he's offering, he's prepared to give you my hand in marriage."

If it was possible, his heart started to beat even faster than it already was.

"That is..." She bit her bottom lip and looked down. "That

is, if you want me."

He opened his mouth to speak, but nothing came out. He couldn't find any words. So, instead, he frowned. If he wanted her? Was she daft? He had never wanted another living soul in his entire life. It had only ever been her. It would remain only her for the rest of his days. But as much as he wanted to express that to her, the words converged in his throat and stuck there, making it almost impossible to breathe, let alone speak. Her father was offering him something he couldn't even begin to comprehend. Something he would never deserve.

Amara looked up at him and smiled softly. "You don't have to tell me right now," she said. "I have to show you something first. Then you can make your decision. All right?"

He nodded, feeling like a fool, but it was all he could bring himself to do. His torrential emotions were attacking his inadequate mind and there was nothing he could say. He briefly wondered if he would ever be able to say what his heart felt in that moment.

It didn't matter much. Amara knew the words of his heart. She always had, and she did still. He could tell by the way she gently took his hand in hers and guided him toward the door.

* * * *

The sight that met his eyes made the boy that had once been taken from the orphanage and thrown to the Rezzegard, the boy who still lived deep within him, tremble with mottled emotions so powerful they could not be named.

The Rezzegard.

What had once been his home and his prison was now nothing more than charred and blackened ruins. His greatest nightmare had been destroyed...

He had no idea how to handle it. It had always been the black stain. It had always been the poison tainting him. As long as the Rezzegard existed, he had been a slave to it in some fashion.

Now...

He didn't know what freedom felt like. He had never really been free. If freedom was what he was currently feeling, it was the most terrifying feeling in the world. "What happened to it?" It was the only thing he could force out of his mouth.

"Turns out the Rezzegard operated on land that Marden bought out from underneath the ruling lord shortly after you kidnapped me. When my father imprisoned Marden, he seized control of his lands. Therefore, the Rezzegard became property of my father. All of the Rezzegard mercenaries were arrested and imprisoned for numerous heinous offenses."

"Someone burned it down."

"I did."

He blinked in surprise and glanced down at her. She stared ahead at the ruins with a stone cold expression, one of hatred. It filled his heart with the strangest kind of warmth because he knew the reason she hated it with such ferocity was because of what they had done to him.

He glanced back to the place that had haunted him for years with its demons and ghosts. They were gone now. They would no longer be coming after him. He was no longer hunted, and innocent children would no longer have to fall prey to the Rezzegard's sickness.

Amara...she had liberated him. In every single sense of the word.

The foreign emotion he could not name threatened to squeeze the life right out of him. It was unbearable. Unbearable because he didn't know what it was. He couldn't handle it. It was a hundred times worse than any kind of physical pain.

"Jaide."

He closed his eyes as he felt her soft hand twine her fingers with his. Her voice was like the sweetest music, anchoring him as it always did.

"Jaide, turn around."

He did so, slowly, and all of the breath within him evaporated, leaving him gasping painfully at the sight that met his eyes. It was like an explosion. An explosion of red, euphoric heaven.

Amaranths...

So many of them. The field that had once been his only solace had grown to enormous proportions.

The emotion he could not name erupted within him in a kind of painful, searing release, and he felt something hot

trail a wet track down his cheek. He paid it next to no attention because all he could do was stare. Stare at the gorgeous
splendor before him.

He didn't realize how tightly he was gripping onto Amara's hand until she turned her attention up to him. She drew
in a sharp breath and her face contorted with sympathy and
love as she reached up to touch the tear that had escaped.
She breathed his name like a promise and he closed his
eyes, relishing her touch in a way that went beyond what
was normal.

Love...

That was what she had looked at him with. It was what
had prompted her to do all of this. Her love for him, in spite
of what he was, in spite of all he had done, in spite of his
twisted past and his scarred person.

Love.

That was the name of the emotion he did not recognize.

Finally able to exhale a shaky breath, he placed his mouth
to her ear and let her warmth permeate his soul. He inhaled
her scent, and the fragrance seemed to calm him to the point
where his chest did not feel so agonizingly tight. His throat,
which had been feeling as if a hand of steel was squeezing it,
opened enough for him to be able to get out the most important thing he would ever say. His entire body trembled as
he took her in his arms. "I love you," he whispered.

Her intake of breath was sudden, and she pulled back to
stare up into his eyes. Shock was mirrored in hers.

He took her face in his hands and shook his head. "I have
never been a gentle man, Amara," he murmured. "I am not
good with emotions and I am not good with words. I am
harsh and cold and unfeeling most of the time. It has been
who I am for so long. It is ingrained in me. It is part of my
make up. But I swear to you, if you want me, if you'll have
me, if I really am the one you want to choose, despite all of
my flaws, I will love you to the best of my ability until my
dying breath."

Her answer was a kiss like velvet cloaked midnight. A sinful, decadent kiss that promised so many things and said so
much. "It was a wild thing that attacked me on my balcony,
and a wild thing I came to know. It is a wild thing I love, and
I have no wish to tame him."

He smiled and bent to kiss her again, but she darted out of his arms and away, running down to the field of amaranths. She tossed her cloak off and spun, laughing. "Come on, Jaide!" she urged.

It was like his dream. The one he'd had right after she'd saved his life. Only, this time, there was no lurking shadow waiting to bring her to her demise.

Don't forget who you are.

The voice still lived within him. He imagined it always would, but he didn't need to listen to it. He knew who he was. More so now than ever before.

Look what you've done!

He looked down at his hands. Hands that had caressed. Hands that had touched with reverence the most beautiful of all flowers. Yes, indeed, look at what he had done. The impossible. He had learned to love.

A grin blossomed across his lips as he watched Amara twirl around with her arms held high, then flop down onto her back amidst the flowers. He walked toward her and met her where she lay, coming to lie next to her and pulling her into his arms. He kissed her, and all voices were silent as he tangled his fingers in her golden hair and basked in the sweetness of her mouth.

"Jaide?" she whispered.

He pulled back to gaze down at her, tracing his fingers along the contours of her face.

She grinned. "Did you keep my red dress for me?"

With a soft chuckle, he nodded. As if he could have discarded it...

"Good. I thought I might wear it for my wedding."

He arched an eyebrow. "You want to wear red to your wedding?"

"Better than the dirty undergarments I wore to my first one."

He laughed out loud, the sound ripped from his throat with genuine jubilation. She threaded her fingers through his hair and sat up to press kisses all over his face and neck. He smiled, then eased himself down so that his head was pillowed in her lap.

He closed his eyes and took several deep breaths as the last of the constricting feelings loosened their grip. He

opened his eyes and gazed at the red flowers that surrounded him, immortal beauty that would never fade, that had
never abandoned him. He reached out to caress one of the
petals just as Amara stroked her fingers through his hair. His
eyes closed again in ultimate bliss.

Peace...

About the Author

If someone were to ask me what I am, it could be summed up in one, simple word: Dreamer. Ever since I was a small child my imagination has run wild. I have been telling stories for as long as I can remember, creating grand worlds in my head and going on adventures that were invisible to others around me. Am I eccentric? Yes. Am I proud of that? Absolutely.

I write about the things that inspire me, both in this world and in realms only seen with the imagination. My heroines are sassy and strong. My heroes are sometimes shy. I have an obsession with music (and musicians) and a fascination with wings. I believe true love does exist, and sometimes it is found in the strangest, most unexpected places. I also believe that family and close friends are the glue that hold people together.

Above all things, I believe in being true to yourself and seizing the day. Life is an amazing gift. Make your experience as beautiful as you possibly can.